NATURAL BORN
SINNERS

J.M. KEEP

Pathforgers Publishing
legal@pathforgers.com
www.pathforgers.com

This is a work of fiction. Names, characters, business, events and incidents are the products of the author's imagination. Any resemblance to actual persons, living or dead, or actual events is purely coincidental.
This book is intended for sale to Adult Audiences only. All sexually active characters in this work are over 18. All sexual activity is between non-blood related, consenting adults.

Cover Art & Character Design: R.A. Masters
Cover Design: Pathforgers Publishing
Marketing: Peachy Keen Author Services
Yataghan is a font by Daniel Midgley

To all the weirdos and tender goths out there,
Welcome home

Preface

Contains themes of violence, non-monogamy, immoral behaviour, and abuse. Full details available on the author's website at http://jmkeep.com

PROLOGUE

LAMB TO THE SLAUGHTER

> Train up a child in the way he should go; even when he is old he will not depart from it.
>
> — PROVERBS 22:6

"Hail Satan!" chirped six-year-old Valeska, her cherubic face beaming at the blonde boy at the iron gate.

Her raven black hair bounced on her shoulders as she skipped forward. She hadn't seen another child in so long she couldn't remember. Instead, she spent all her time in the shadow of giants, the adults of House Void Star.

It was actually strange that none of them were around just then, but the young girl saw it as a blessing. The guards weren't there to stop the boy from wandering into the estate!

"I'm Valeska, who are you?"

"Hey!" he said with such brightness and exuberance. "I'm not sure," he said, his shaggy blonde hair tousled by the breeze as he stuck out a boyish hand.

She grabbed it eagerly, easily, her grip so strong for such a tiny young thing. Her pale skin was covered in a black dress, the bottom of it puffed out over her scrawny legs.

The Magister had always told her not to let her guard down around strangers, but he looked about her age, and she'd never had a friend before. She barely knew of the concept. But seeing him, all she wanted was to learn everything about him. And he couldn't even offer her his name.

"Where are you from? Another House?"

"No," he said shaking his head. "We live in a little apartment. Or I think that's what they call it," he said. "I don't get out real often. They say it's dangerous out here."

"Only if you're a lamb," Valeska said with a bright smile, "and I'm a wolf! See my fangs?"

She opened her mouth, revealing that capped on top of her baby teeth was a set of silver fangs. She ran her tongue over one of them, feeling the pointed edge with a grin. They were brand new, and she was quite proud of them.

"The Magister says that when I grow up, I'll be able to slaughter all the lambs I want, but for now, I have to stay on the estate and train. Wanna see?" she asked, already beginning to tug him along.

The estate itself was a large, ostentatious thing, melding together old Victorian houses, gothic iron, and lined with hideous statuary that always seemed to be watching her. It seemed well suited to the cool chill of autumn that had begun to arrive on the ocean breeze.

"Today the Magister told me I have to learn how to jump really far, so I have to learn to jump over the pit."

She arrived at their destination, a deep pool of black water that was carved into a rectangle around three feet wide and six feet across. Neither of them could see the bottom of it, but she knew it had to go very far into the ground.

"Look, I can already go the short way!" she gushed, and her black mary-janes brought her to the edge of the pool. With one fluid motion, she leapt over it, gracefully landing on the other side with around a foot of extra space.

She bounced up and down, her raven black hair fluttering around her as she smiled back at her new, mysterious friend.

"Do you want to try?"

For Valeska, it was an easy task. She was six years old, but she had never been allowed a childhood. The path that was laid for her was one of combat precision, mental acuity, and intelligence gathering. Failure was not an option. House Void Star saw to that.

But for the blonde boy who lived in an apartment—whatever that was – it was a task beyond him. He was excited to try, but his limbs betrayed him. When he tried to make that leap, his footing failed, his fear gripped him, and in his last second decision to not jump, he damned himself.

He slid into that inky water, and floated down.

Valeska stared in shock and horror, looking around for an adult, but there was no one. No one to save him.

So, she jumped in.

The pool was so narrow that it was hard to not kick him as she went under, the black dress swirling around her delicate body. Her foot found him first, and it guided her hand to his arm. She wrapped her hand around his wrist, and tried tugging him up, but he felt so heavy. He thrashed, and she lost her grip on him, bobbing up to the surface for air.

That was when she saw him.

The Magister.

His long, white hair flowed around his stately shoulders; his pale skin covered with a fine, black robe. His ruby eyes were watching her from twenty feet away, his arms folded over his chest in a familiar way.

It was the same stance he always had when he was waiting for her to learn a lesson.

She didn't call out to him, not then. Instead, she bobbed back down, finding the boy's arm, and beginning to drag him up.

He was flailing in a panic, sending him in all directions as he struggled desperately to get to the surface, but his actions were only damning them both.

He was heavier than her, maybe a year or two older, and she was still just a child, but she refused to give up. Several more times, she bobbed to the surface for a gasp of air before diving back under, and finally, her arms went under his armpits, and she used the earthen side of the pit to get up upright.

When his head finally broke the tension of the water, the relief that flooded her was immense.

She had passed the test. She had saved the boy.

She turned to beam triumphantly at the Magister, only to find him looming above her with a disappointed scowl on his face.

Before she could make sense of it, his leather boot was on her shoulder, and both her and the boy were pressed back beneath the surface of the water.

Her confusion caused her to twist the wrong way, and she lost her grip on the boy, and as the Magister's boot pushed down further, she became disoriented. No longer could she see the brightness of the sun, the shadow of the man who was raising her. It was darkness all around.

Those brief breaths of air were not going to last long, but she had been trained to hold her breath, and that was what she focused on. She wouldn't allow herself to panic. She wouldn't fail the Magister's test.

She got her bearings once more, but couldn't find her companion, and after a minute of searching, she was forced to return to the surface. This time, the Magister didn't push her back down.

"Have you learned your lesson yet?"

She stared at him in shock, nodding her head, but the second she dove back down to rescue the boy, that boot pressed between her shoulders.

She couldn't get back to the surface. He wouldn't let her. He was trying to kill her!

Why? What had she ever done to disappoint him?

The tears in her eyes were whisked away by the water that had become so oppressively heavy atop her. It weighed her down just as much as the boot, and she knew that her companion didn't have much longer. She had to rescue him.

When her hand found his again, it was still. There was no more thrashing, no more fighting.

She was too late.

And still, her little hand wrapped around his wrist, and this time, she launched herself to the long side, away from the Magister. Her hand searched the side of the earth, and finally she found what she was looking for. A root.

She grabbed onto it as she dove beneath the boy, and bracing her body against the soil, her hand wrapped around the root, she began to push him upwards.

His head broke the surface, and she felt the weight begin to grow atop her. The Magister was pushing down on the boy, but she was in a defensive position for the assault. She kept him lifted there, her spritely body fighting against the much larger man's casual strength. Her limbs trembled, the oxygen in her body depleting, and she began to feel her mind grow dim.

She didn't know how long she stayed there, fighting a losing battle to keep the boy's head above water, but seconds passed, then minutes, and they might as well have been an eternity. Her lips parted, and she knew that it was time. This was how she was to die.

But just before she inhaled the water into her lungs, the pressure lessened.

She pushed frantically to the surface, swallowing the air the moment she broke free, and the tears streamed from her eyes.

She could still feel the Magister's presence, but her vision was foggy, the tears and the lack of oxygen both taking a toll on her.

And even then, she brought her hand to the boy's chest, slamming against it, sending that tepid water splashing over her face as it was ejected from his lungs. He began to vomit, but the relief that washed through her that she had saved him was immense.

Until the Magister's hand wrapped around the back of his neck, dragging him out of the water like a disobedient pup.

"Weakness, Valeska. That is what I see in you right now. Frail, pathetic weakness," the Magister scolded her, his ruby eyes boring into her like she was lower than dirt itself. "You almost died, and for what?" he said, the distaste oozing from his full lips. "To save some immature lamb? Foolish girl. Don't you know what lambs are for? They are for slaughter. And your efforts were in vain," he chastised so cruelly.

Valeska cried out, reaching for her friend, but it was too late. The adults of House Void Star had returned, as if they were all just waiting for her out of the peripherals of her vision. She scrambled from the pit of water, the hard ground beneath her knees as she trembled with impotent rage.

"He's not a lamb! He's my friend!" she cried out, and the Magister bent down to her level, squeezing her chin between his thumb and a finger.

"He was sent here to kill you. There are no friends for you in this world. The moment you trust someone is the moment you find a blade between your shoulders."

The Magister stood back up, and looked towards one of the women. She was a Lieutenant, dressed in dark leathers, and carrying a large gun. Valeska recognized her as one of the most ruthless of her guardians.

"Valeska needs to repeat last week's training. Don't let

her out of the basement until she understands the truth of the Chimera's ways"

"No! No! Please, Magister," she crawled towards him, reaching out for him. "Don't make me repeat that. I'll be better! I'll be stronger! I'll make you proud!"

But he pushed her off him into the dirt, and the officer claimed her, dragging her into the pit of shadows and pain.

CHAPTER 1

PEAK AESTHETIC

The first secret to winning the game is knowing you're playing one.

— HOUSE VOID STAR MOTTO

"I'm not a fucking pussy, Over-Lieutenant. With all due respect."

Videl—her second in command—couldn't even swear without sounding a little stuffy.

Valeska giggled as she leaned back on the hood of her black, military hummer. She tilted her head so that she could see him sitting in the cupola at the mounted machine-gun.

"Well, I'm just sayin'. You almost seemed hesitant to..." She lifted her fingers to her temple like a gun, squeezing the imaginary trigger and twitching as if she was dying.

Videl frowned at her, staring down at her youthful face.

She was only twenty, and he was in his thirties she figured, but he never disrespected her. Somehow, she'd managed to find a loyal follower on the Isle of Satanos, the place you couldn't trust anyone.

Six houses reigned over the lawless haven, and each vied for prestige and power. Those outside your house were considered potential enemies.

Those inside your House?

They were the ones that would tear you apart the second you stopped being useful.

"It wasn't the killing him I had an issue with. The venue..."

"What, you don't like an audience?" Valeska interrupted, her voice sweet enough to cover the poison beneath. She tugged at her fishnet stockings, readjusting them idly as she took a long drag of her cigarette. "It sends a message, Under-Lieutenant."

"I didn't think House Void Star liked to send such loud messages is all, Over-Lieutenant."

He was right, and she knew it. But at the time she'd simply gotten caught up in the thrill of it all. Her expression softened as she met his gaze, both of them wearing special contacts that made their eyes glow an eerie red.

"Fine, I won't bust your balls since you were trying to keep me out of trouble," she conceded, and there was a flicker of tenderness in his gaze that made her flinch like she was struck.

She averted her eyes, instead staring down at the new insignia her jacket bore of a silver, upside-down cross.

Her promotion to over-Lieutenant was still recent, and she

was at risk of letting it go to her head. Videl was probably one of the few who both respected her enough to give her a warning, and loyal enough to her that she wouldn't shank him for it.

"You're a Wolf, don't give me those sheep eyes," Valeska sighed. That was what the commoners thought of her type, in the military. Wolves.

And the Wolves thought of them as lambs in return. That was probably how it all started.

She grabbed one of the daggers on her hips, twirling it as she finished her smoke and flicked it aside, a ring of black lipstick around the tip. The leather of her black jacket groaned as it strained across her cleavage, her tall, black boots crossed at her heel.

Videl had taken less liberties to personalize his military officer's uniform than her, the black material looking darker than night. He was always so stern, and more serious than Valeska liked, but she had to admit that with his impressive height and lean strength, he always cut a sharp figure. Plus, the scar over his cheek and eye *did* make him look pretty badass.

He had served her since she got her position in the Island's militia, and he didn't ask for a lot. He was the brooding type, quiet and dependable, and when she asked for his opinion, he didn't bullshit her. Even better than that? His advice was solid.

He hadn't been born on the Isle, unlike her, so he could never rise up very high in the ranks.

That worked out just fine for Valeska. Gave him one less reason for him to stab her in the back.

She stared out at the dark ocean, hearing the water

churn against the cliffs below. The sea salt spray mingled with the acrid scent of the volcano behind them.

Despite it only being the two of them, a drone hovered nearby, recording everything. The Eyes, as they were called, were a constant presence on the island, and Valeska had never known a life that included the word 'privacy'. Not that it really mattered. Satanos was a sprawling volcanic island founded by people who embraced sin, and the rules were pretty fucking lax. Violence was a way of life, and every rule had an exception if you had enough power.

Especially if you were a military enforcer on duty, like she was.

"You know, most guys here would kill for me to bust their balls," Valeska said after a pause, looking back up at Videl, his pale skin nearly glowing in the silver moonlight.

"I'm not most guys, Over-Lieutenant."

"That's right," Valeska teased, her tongue running over the silver capped dental implants that looked like vampire fangs. It was a common body-mod, a weapon not easily removed. A last line of defence if someone tried to take something from her that wasn't on offer.

Besides, it was peak aesthetic.

"You're a special boy."

Videl glowered at her mocking him, and he was about to snark back when Valeska's smart watch vibrated, followed by his.

"Orders coming in. Oh shit, it's even official tonight! Might finally have some fun," Valeska said as she hopped off the hood of the hummer.

"Escaped convict, heading for the little port

village on the north-west shore. Execute with extreme prejudice."

"The spies always make for that place," Videl said with less enthusiasm than she had. "What are your commands, Over-Lieutenant?"

Official orders or not, she was the boss. She gathered her hair back into a glistening, black ponytail, tugging the collar of her leather jacket up to cover the pale skin on the back of her neck, then grabbed her dagger, holstering it on her hip.

"You feel like getting up close and personal or just spray-and-praying it tonight? You know me, I could go either way," she teased as she opened the driver side door, hopping into the cool, leather seats.

"If the convict has already gotten to the village, spray-and-pray could land us in hot water. So, it depends," Videl said, careful not to draw her ire by reminding her of the caution she had just promised him.

Valeska chuckled as she put the hummer in reverse, getting back on the road and heading down the familiar path. He was a smart man. If he'd been born in Satanos, he'd be a real threat. Since he wasn't, well... It was a manageable threat.

She drove alongside the volcano, towards the massive, carved statue of Baphomet. She'd always been fascinated with it ever since she was a child, and as awe inspiring as it was in the light of day, the ram-headed visage of a dark lord of the always seemed transformed at night. The eyes were otherworldly, as if the ruby were instead a void, able to draw attention to itself even apart from the natural darkness, and they always seemed to follow her.

It always filled her with comfort, instead of dread.

The interior of the hummer lit up, and Valeska looked towards the digital screen that had synced to her watch. The face of a rather handsome brown-haired young man stared forlornly ahead. He couldn't have been any older than Valeska, but of a completely different sort.

"He doesn't look like much anyhow," said her second.

"He looks cute," she said to Videl, unable to help herself from teasing him. "Death's gonna be the best thing to happen to him today. I doubt he'd last a week in the village. He's so... soft and innocent. Did you ever look like that, Under-Lieutenant? Back in the normie world?"

"I've never been that weak," he gruffly replied.

Valeska's heart skipped a beat, and some forgotten memory threatened to surface before she pushed it back down.

"I wouldn't have you under me if you were," she said, fighting to keep the vulnerable quiver out of her voice.

Videl was quiet for a moment, and she worried that he might have picked up on something. He was annoyingly intuitive at times. He used the flood lamp to search the dark evening field near the trees, keeping watch in that cupola, swivelling the machine-gun turret around. The village wasn't far from their location, and she could see the road leading down from the cliffs that would spiral towards the little enclave.

"If he's a spy, he might have means to bribe someone there for a way out in a shipping container or boat. Or there might be someone waiting to get him out," he replied as if nothing was amiss. But Valeska knew that didn't mean he didn't catch the change in her tone. Just that he was clever enough to pretend he didn't.

"He stands out like a sore thumb. No one would ever believe he was a resident. Hell, even a tourist wouldn't look so..."

"So pristine?"

"You could say that. He's just begging to be made into someone's sex toy. Literally the worst spy," Valeska said as her eyes went from the road ahead to the picture on the screen. He had a unique charm about him, his features youthful and boyish, yet distinctly masculine. She might be interested herself in seeing what delights he could offer her, but she had her orders.

"Unless he was sent to seduce someone with specific tastes, and then escape."

Valeska rolled her eyes at him, not as though he could see it. He was so serious. It was one of the things she valued about him, as much as it annoyed her. She always knew what he was thinking, where his head was.

But he wasn't much fun to joke around with.

"Or maybe he was just sent here as punishment by the outside world. Someone wanted him gone, but couldn't take matters into their own hands."

Valeska didn't know a lot about the world beyond their isolated island, but she knew that the laws out there were stifling. People had so little control over their own lives. The island had more than their fair share of thrill seekers looking to indulge in a life worth living before returning back to be endlessly controlled and scolded.

Valeska didn't have much respect for those who thought

of the Isle of Satanos as a vacation spot, however. A temporary reprieve from law and order before meekly returning to tell tale tales to their friends about what badasses they were when they likely never even left the brothel.

She was going to die on this soil and be grateful she had lived as humans were intended to live.

As they neared the outline of that cozy little village on the water, a second command came in.

This one was a private order.

Just for her.

She was fucked.

CHAPTER 2

DUMPSTER DIVING

Come and see my rose-coloured bath full of death!

— ROBERT W. CHAMBERS; THE KING
IN YELLOW

"**S**pare the convict. Bring him in alive to us. Damage not an issue, as long as he is still alive and will survive."

House Void Star was always a tricky house. They were always looking for ways to undermine others and grow, and they often operated in the realm of espionage and subterfuge. It wasn't unusual for them to send her a secretive order, but it was the first time they'd ever commanded her to outright defy an official order through the chain of command.

It sent a chill down her spine.

Refusal wasn't an option. The cost to her future, her

reputation, and her place in the House was always on the line. Every decision she made was carefully scrutinized for a shift in loyalty or obedience.

Nobody got anywhere without their house's blessing. She could impress her military superiors to Hell and back, but if her house didn't approve it... she'd never get another promotion again.

And House Void Star was not a particularly forgiving house.

Not that any were.

"Fuck," she cursed.

Videl was loyal, she knew that, and he was a part of the House. But she couldn't capture him without bringing Videl in on the change of plans, and everyone had the limits to their loyalty. She didn't want to have to push him, especially not over some machination she wasn't even privy to, let alone benefitting from.

The Isle had plenty of money, but offers, favours, refusals? Those were the real currency. And just because she obeyed the House didn't mean they viewed that as a favour, and the refusal of official orders would be hers to deal with.

"What is it, Over-Lieutenant?"

She looked at the drone as it hovered alongside the hummer, its dim, red light a constant companion. She was accruing a debt from the Isle, to avoid getting one from the House. Void Star would know her allegiance is to them, but the other Houses would punish her for disobeying official orders.

It was a shitty place to be put in, but it wasn't worth fighting against.

The Isle was good at teaching you what battles to pick.

"Don't open fire if you see him," she said to Videl, her voice dripping and malice. "We're taking him in. You see him, you let me know. I'll play the sweet rescuer; you stay invisible unless I need you. Got it?"

Videl instantly snapped to alert. He didn't know why her command had changed, but he instinctively understood things had just gotten more serious. Spies from some western nation out to crush their little rebel island were a somewhat frequent occurrence, to the point that their orders to eliminate the threat was almost mundane. Saving a criminal, disobeying official orders?

It was a first for both of them.

As she said that, she noticed a curious thing: the light on the drone that hovered by her side had gone out, indicating it was no longer recording.

Like any technology, malfunctions happened. But it was rare; this was top of the line stuff.

The only rational explanation was... her house had done her the kindness of sparing her culpability in disobeying orders.

She didn't even know that was possible, let alone that she'd be worthy of the gift of privacy. It was a show of trust and protection she'd never experienced before.

"Yes ma'am," Videl said, even though she could detect the shift in his demeanour. He wasn't one to disobey orders. But he'd always obeyed her over anyone, so her commands came first.

"I imagine this has something to do with why the Eyes are offline?"

"Yea, our people are looking out for us," she said, surprise and curiosity mingling in her voice. This must be something big. Or maybe it was just someone in the mood for a pretty boy for the night.

She'd been on the Isle her whole life, and she couldn't pretend to know all the secrets that surrounded her.

Videl turned off the spotlight as they pulled into the small village. It wasn't the party central that the main city was, but still there was music and lights coming from the biggest building, a tavern Valeska hadn't visited before.

"If I were a spy, and I looked like him, I would know that I'd stick out like a sore thumb in a place like this. But I'd probably be hungry and thirsty..." she said, more to herself than to Videl. "If I intend on escaping, I'd know that night is my friend, and staying in the shadows is safest. The alleys might let me get a feel for people, look for an opportunity. I'm going to start there," she said before opening the hummer door and planting her black, platform boots on the ground.

She was only five foot tall, but she was raised to be ruthless. She was one of the first generation of the island, and so a lot of people had a hand in bringing her up, molding her into the ideal Satanosite. She was a defender against the outsiders that sought to take her away and bring her into a world of crushing poverty and lawfulness, and a hedonistic worshiper of their faith.

That also meant that expectations of her were higher than most people. The older generation that had moved here and created their commune, the others who moved here to escape their oppressive world, they weren't given any slack. No one was.

But House Void Star saw her as the embodiment of their achievements and methods.

Failure was never an option.

"If anyone else seems to be looking for our guy, they can't find him first, got it?"

Videl climbed down from the hummer, and stood beside her. He was over a foot taller than her and then some, but he looked at the much shorter woman as if she were the far more fearsome intimidating force.

He took out his sword in hand, the obsidian hilt gilded with a few red rubies. It was one of the few flourishes his outfit had that marked it as his own. He still had a handgun at his hip, but he left the rifle in the vehicle. Among the forces, swords were often preferred. Only the military could possess guns, and some of the Island's only laws were reserved for when and how guns should be used.

In short, it was kind of a pain in the ass, and killing someone with a sword had less paperwork.

"Understood, Over-Lieutenant. Want me to patrol the streets in case you flush him out of hiding?" he asked.

She brushed her straight bangs from her forehead, looking in the rear-view mirror as she reapplied her black lipstick. She was procrastinating. A part of her wanted someone else to get to the convict first, take him out before she could enter the murky waters of serious Island intrigue.

'Weak', she chided herself, biting her tongue with her fangs so that she could startle herself back to reality. This was an opportunity to make herself known in House Void Star, and she wasn't going to fuck it up just because she was afraid. The fact that she could even feel fear about something like this pissed her off.

"Play it casual. He has to survive, and the longer he

thinks he's safe with us, the better. You're down there looking for a dog that ran off."

Videl watched her, then looked around.

"All right. Understood. I'll be on the comms if you need me. Astarte guide you." He gave her a lingering stare before he turned, his tall leather boots clicking on the cobblestone road as he made his way to the main street along the water.

That left her to her own business of searching those dark, dreary alleyways.

It was tedious work, but luckily, built into her red contacts was a night vision capability. She could see almost as well in the night as in day, albeit with a rose-coloured perspective.

She made her way up and down vacant alleys, seeing nothing but discarded condoms, used needles, and the odd stray. Maybe her instincts had been off, and she didn't understand the man as well as she thought. She had very little information to go off of, but something about him...

Why did she think that she could get into the head of someone so delicate looking? He couldn't be more different from her.

She worked her way towards the tavern, its loud music thumping and pounding, and as she made her way down the alley, the hair on her nape began to prickle. It was a strange instinct, but one she always paid attention to. A dumpster sat there, which was nothing out of the ordinary. Except this one was too big for the space. It was intended for a garbage truck to lift and unload it, but a truck could never wind its way in between the walls.

The unusual wasn't unusual, not really. Not with all the schemes and secrets her people kept.

But knowing why something was unusual was a skill that kept her alive more than once.

She strolled down the alley as if she owned it, belonged in the deep shadows between buildings.

She inspected the dumpster, walking around in and trying to unlock its secrets. It was too heavy for her to try to move, but she was interrupted by Videl as his gravelly voice whispered in her ear through the communication device.

"Followed a suspicious looking man down the road. He headed into the tavern, lost him. Gonna keep searching."

That meant she couldn't call him back to help her right away; not without interrupting and potentially losing a lead. She'd have to figure out how to move the dumpster on her own, and she began to look around for something that she could use as leverage to push it. The alley was frustratingly well kept, and so she hopped up on the edge of the bin, hoping there might be some discarded wood or metal.

But the garbage inside looked a little too neat. Too tidy. It didn't even stink.

What kind of tavern garbage didn't stink?

She took out one of the bags, and while it was full, she doubted it was actually garbage. It felt too... uniform in there. So, she took out another. Then another.

It was a fucking front!

Hidden beneath the fake trash was a hatch, attached to the building. A smile twisted her lips. She delighted in secrets. Another form of currency that held real meaning.

If this youthful man was spying, perhaps a little hidden nook was something he could have used. Or maybe it was a tunnel for human smuggling. It wasn't an uncommon trade on the island, considering how many people tried to sneak in and off it.

She took the time to collect the garbage she'd discarded and placed it a bit less conspicuously back in the bin to surround her before hopping into the dumpster and inspecting the hatch.

It would've been a tight fit for a big man, but for her it would be a breeze. And as she tested it, the metal began to slide open.

It wasn't even locked!

Amateur hour.

It was narrow for a room, running the length of the tavern, and she could hear the thudding of the heavy metal music more clearly. It was probably built in from very conception to be a hidden space for secret dealings she reckoned. The little village was, just as Videl said, a hot bed for smuggling after all. And tavern owners had no doubt learned a few tricks of the trade from the rumrunners of old.

The chamber had old sleeping bags and discarded supplies as she peered around, confirming her suspicion that they were human smugglers. She quietly made her way down that narrow room, and found that the corner looped around to the back of the building too.

She paused at the bottom of a ladder, looking up towards the darkness above it. Maybe it was a scent in the air, or a subtle warmth, but even over the pounding of the music, she could sense something. Someone was above.

One of her platform heels tested the ladder, and put her weight upon the rung. It didn't creak, and she chanced another, then another. Finally she made it so that she could peer over the edge, and she was bombarded with the smell of sex.

A big, burly man's ass clenched and bounced as he thrust into a smaller man that he was pinning down onto the table.

The husky guy grunted and groaned, the sound of his flesh slapping to the attractive, younger man's filling the air. He gripped the boy's dark hair—it was impossible to tell what colour it was in such darkness through her night vision – and wrenched it back.

"C'mon... that's it... you little bitch," he growled at the smaller man

The other man groaned and whimpered. He was a fit man, nude and pristine, but he was weak and pathetic, not even able to struggle against the violation of his body.

It wasn't an uncommon sight. Do as thou willst, was the core tenant of the island's faith after all. Violence was a natural part of human nature, and as long as the guy wasn't going to kill the younger looking fellow it was largely fair game.

But Valeska was on a mission, and it was do as she willst most of all.

Her eyes darted around the room, seeing no one else around. The thrum of the music would drown out all sounds to the outside world to the point that Valeska thought that this rapist was far more of a coward than he looked. Why gag a victim when no one could hear him scream?

Even the kink of it seemed pathetic to her.

She grabbed one of the sharp stilettos from her side,

weighing it in her hand as she waited for him to be fully distracted by pleasure.

The burly guy began to tense up, and Valeska slithered along the ground so as not to draw his gaze. Patience was a virtue that her House had painfully taught her, and in that moment, it felt natural to breathe into silence, move with the shadows.

The Chimera could contort itself, cut off the useless pieces of its body and replace it with what it needed in the moment without regard to the personal pain it would cause. The only thing that mattered was the mission, and the path of the Chimera was that of invisibility, camouflage, and sacrifice.

She got behind him as he reached the finale, letting the steel of her stiletto graze along his femoral artery before settling the tip at the base of his taint.

Chapter 3

Sweet Boy

Exemplify the chimera; that which can evolve by sheer will alone.

Sever that which no longer serves you, and birth yourself anew.

— House Void Star Motto

"I'll be taking him in payment for not interrupting you sooner," Valeska said from her crouched position, threatening the heathen's masculinity with her weapon.

He gasped, going stone still as that cold steel touched him in such a sensitive area.

"Who th—" he began, but as he looked over his shoulder, the man's face went wide in horror. His eyes were adjusted to the darkness enough to make out the insignia on her lapels, to see the trademark signs of her uniform, even though she'd taken such liberties with it.

"A W-Wolf?! I... I ain't done nothin' wrong. Just takin' what I want," he protested.

"Give me what I want and your statement remains honest," she said patiently, her voice completely devoid of all emotion. That was the part of her that she had to exorcise so many years ago. Countless lessons to dull those pesky feelings that would nag her about how what he was doing was wrong. The Chimera had demanded she amputate those first.

"I'd also like a thank you."

The big guy's eyes were still wide, but he nodded after a moment's pause.

"Aye, of course, Wolf. I mean... officer," he said, swallowing anxiously, before slowly pushing the younger male off his dick, letting that figure slump to the floor with a groan. "He's all yours. I was just finished with him anyhow, I swear."

"I know," she said, letting him move from her blade without a scratch, though the reminder of its presence stung just as deep. "That thank you I asked for?"

She stood, her unnatural red eyes fixed upon him, and even with her delicate stature, she radiated power.

"O-Oh! S-sorry, thank you! Thank you, ma'am. Officer!" he stammered, before hauling up his trousers over his glistening shaft. The light in the room was dim, but she'd be able to see without her night vision, so she let her eyes readjust as she looked down at that nude, handsome young man.

He was just laying there, curled in on himself. He didn't even look traumatized. He just seemed... exhausted.

"I'll... I'll just be leaving you to him then, yeah?" the man asked as he began to back away towards a sliding panel door in the wall. Valeska figured it led into the tavern.

"You had a great time, finished up, and left. No humiliation, because I was never here," she said sternly.

The husky guy froze for a moment, then got her meaning. He nodded sharply as he tied his pants shut.

"You got it. Never here!" he said, as he slid the door open. "Thank you, officer! Thank you."

The man was twice her size, and utterly terrified of her. He couldn't get out of there fast enough. The music thrummed louder and then quieted as he closed the door behind him.

She stared at the young man on the table, and knew it was her mark. She could make out the brown of his hair as her eyes adjusted to the dim lighting of the dangling lamp. Her eyes scanned his lean, muscular body with a lustful desire before her gaze went to his face.

Her hands were gentle as they untied the gag, waiting for his eyes to meet hers.

"You'll be quiet as we walk?" she asked patiently.

The young man's eyes opened, and he peered up at her at last.

"I need to get away..." he said, wearily. Then his hand came to grasp her wrist, not roughly, but... pathetically, a pleading look in his eyes, "Please help me get away. I'm not cut out for this place," he said, in a masterstroke of self-awareness.

"I know you aren't, sweet boy. I can help you. But I

need you to promise that you'll be quiet as I lead you to my vehicle."

He slowly began to get up, and she could tell quickly he would be half a foot taller than her or so. He was nude though, so not as imposing as he might've seemed, but in raw strength, he might be able to overpower her. If she let him get past her array of weapons. In person he didn't seem quite as soft as his photo made him seem.

"Aren't you one of... one of them?" he asked, looking her over as he stood up on shaky legs, cum drooling down his inner leg.

"You don't have a lot of options, sweetheart. You're right, you don't belong here. So, you can come quietly with me, and pass out in my massive backseat, or..." she trailed off, knowing there was no other offer on the table.

But it would be a lot easier if he didn't force her hand.

He looked at her, pausing in silence for a while as he thought on his options. And it gave her a moment to appreciate what a rare little beauty he was on this island too. No permanent scars she could see, though he had some scratches and bruises, probably from escaping prison more than the brute that had ensnared him.

"Okay..." he said weakly, nodding to her.

"Good. We're going down the ladder, then through a few tunnels, then up. After that, you'll need to stay close to me. No one should fuck with us, even with you looking like you do, but I don't know who else is after you."

She looked up at him, and felt an emotion that she remembered from her childhood, when she'd seen a mouse devoured by a snake. It still moved, it still lived, as the snake's muscles contracted it further down into its depths, and she'd felt bad.

"That's pity," one of her many teachers had told her. *"You're sad that the mouse is weak, instead of admiring that the snake is strong. Indulge in those feelings, and you'll soon become a thing to pity yourself."*

Pity.

An indulgence for someone soft.

Another feeling to extirpate.

The young man shakily followed her down the ladder, along the narrow space between the walls. He went without trouble out through that hatch into the dumpster. And as they came out into the dark alleyway... he saw his opportunity and he dashed.

He looked so weary; she hadn't anticipated his revolt.

So much for playing the role of the sweet rescuer.

He ran surprisingly fast as he sought to escape captivity. Perhaps she'd arrived just a few moments too late. Perhaps the betrayal of the last man who promised to hide him had left him unable to trust her.

Whatever the result, he was racing right out onto the water street.

She wasn't surprised so much as she was disappointed. Not at him, no. That was actually pretty impressive. He was feistier then she expected.

She was just disappointed that she had thought kindness could ever be used to get what she wanted.

She began to sprint after him, even as she spoke into her comms.

"He's heading to the water, naked, can't miss him."

"On it," Videl replied after a moment.

She broke out onto the main street, and could see the nude convict on the run past the tavern entrance. And sadly, Videl was just a moment too slow getting out to block him off

The taller man was a good runner at least, and he joined the chase with her, sword in hand.

Their target didn't draw as much attention as one might've thought. Nudity was hardly uncommon on the island, and it was at night, outside a tavern. So doubly so. But still they got a few looks from inebriates as they ran by.

Valeska's hovering drone rejoined her, still offline, despite its eagerness to be ever present. She pumped her legs, using all her strength to race after the escapee. He turned down a side alley, and luck was not on his side.

A wire fence greeted him, but he wasn't cowed. He began to frantically climb it, but Videl wouldn't allow it. He grabbed the young man's hair, yanking him off the fence and onto the ground with a painful thud.

"On the ground, scum!" commanded her second as he put his boot to him, kicking the young man in the side. He then brought down the flat side of his blade, smacking his backside with a loud, painful sounding smack.

Valeska felt that instinctive pity prick up inside her, combined with a dark arousal. The emotions felt like twins at times and she bit down on her lower lip at the show of sadism from her second. He so rarely indulged in violence when it wasn't absolutely necessary, and she wished she could take the time to enjoy it.

But she couldn't risk them getting caught taking him in alive.

"Pick him up. We have him. The cleaner he is when we

deliver him, the better," Valeska ordered, straightening her tank top beneath her leather jacket. She sheathed her weapon, and Videl followed suit.

He grasped the convict's two arms, tugging him to his feet. He was whimpering pathetically as Videl slapped a zip-tie around those wrists, binding them as he began to push him on back towards their vehicle.

"You got lucky, fuckface."

Valeska liked that growl in Videl's voice, that hint of darkness he always kept so tightly controlled. His restraint was impressive, but something about this lamb had teased it out of him. Or maybe it was just the stress of disobeying official orders.

She walked at the convict's side, her gaze drawn over the village, looking to see if any eyes might be a bit more intent than she'd like. If someone saw her taking him hostage instead of killing him, it might cause her problems. Usually, that would be enough to make her want to see him suffer. But she wasn't going to beat him and risk being seen by someone who might know too much about what was happening.

There would be time for suffering later.

Technically you could only hold someone captive for a day. Free will came with caveats about *other* people's free will, but there were some that were beyond questioning. The Elders weren't held to the same standards, and, well... the law only applied so well as you could enforce it.

Her House asking for him alive was unusual enough that she knew laws would be bent in the coming days.

She had no idea why.

Her House had many secrets, of course, even from her.

It fuelled her curiosity.

"Why'd you come here?" she asked as they made their way towards the edge of town, towards their vehicle.

The young man looked at her, bright eyes wide and sad.

"I... I didn't," he said, swallowing anxiously. "I was abducted. And... I woke up in that... that horrible place underground. Where they... they experimented on me or... or something," he stammered.

Videl wasn't interested in his backstory, and he opened the back door to the hummer, pushing him inside roughly across the backseat.

"Want me to drive, Over-Lieutenant?" Videl asked. "Give you some time to... question the suspect."

He said it without judgment, but also without insinuation.

Most officers took liberties with the people they hauled in, and a handsome, naked man would be seen as a banquet feast for hedonistic delights. But Valeska didn't like to mix work and pleasure like that. It was one of the few things she had in common with Videl.

"Yea, you drive. Take the longer route," she said as she jumped in back with their detainee.

She slammed the door shut behind her, her ruby eyes trained upon him.

She was going to unravel why he was worth risking everything for.

CHAPTER 4

FREEDOM IS A LIE

They promise them freedom, but they themselves
are slaves of corruption.

— PETER 2:19

"What's your name?"

Valeska figured that was as good of
place as any to start her interrogation.

He looked at her sheepishly, flinching a bit as the door
slammed. The back half was sealed off from the front, with
a sliding metal viewing window. But Videl had slid that
shut in the process of saddling up to drive.

"I'm... I'm Cole," he said, his big, bright eyes fluttering,
his head hanging a bit low as he sat there. In the light of the
backseat, she could see he had some bruising and puncture
marks on his inner arms.

"Hey, Cole." She frowned thoughtfully at the markings, leaning in to inspect them a bit closer. They looked like something you'd leave a hospital with, more than one of the island's many drug dens. "So, you weren't using experiments as a euphemism? You're not just shooting up and living your best life?"

He looked down at his arms, then back at her.

"There were drugs, yeah." He wasn't the most talkative of prisoners, even with that new bruise in his side developing from Videl's boot. "I don't know what they were though... I just know I felt like hell in here the entire time."

Nothing he'd said so far made her understand why he was special. Why he was worth the risk of disobeying an order.

"How long have you been here, do you think?"

His head shook as it hung low, and he shrugged his bare shoulders. His body was lightly tanned, smooth, and—but for the recent markings – unblemished. He would've been quite popular with women and men if he came as a tourist, that was for certain.

"I have no idea... it feels like forever. But... But I think that was the drugs. They keep making me slip in and out of consciousness... I couldn't tell me how much time was passing." He didn't even sound angry about it. He was confused, but if anyone had done that to Valeska, she would have been filled with unbridled rage, eager to get revenge on every last mother fucker who touched her.

"Did you have a lot of visitors like the last guy?"

He shook his head quietly, not saying a word at first.

"No. Usually... people in white medical suits. I couldn't see their faces," he explained.

"But always in that room? With the music playing?"

His brows furrowed at her, struggling with his memories.

"Huh? No. No, that's not where I was held. I... I escaped and tried to get out. Someone helped me. Told me that village would be the best place, that I could find someone to assist me there. But... but I think it was the wrong guy. Because he didn't assist me at all. He just..." he trailed off.

"I figured. It was good of you not to trust me. But I am your best hope, all the same. And at least you can have a little reprieve from suffering for now," she offered as she leaned back in the seat, pushing her fishnet knees into the divider in front of her. "Always go down with as much fight as you have in you. It might not save you, but the struggle is what's important."

He swept his gaze over her, and she didn't care for the expression of... Was that pity? Was *he* pitying *her*?

"How can such a... such a pretty little lady be involved in so much nastiness and evil?" he asked in disbelief.

The hummer bounced along some rough patch on the country road. Videl was buying her time, taking the long route. It was a risk for both of them in dallying, but he knew that once her mind was set on something, there was no chance in changing it. And secrets were her opium.

"We're little more than animals, you know. We work so hard to deny it, but the only thing that separates us is our ability to judge our behaviours, and deny ourselves what it means to live," she said in words that weren't all her own. It was just her interpretation of the many, many things she'd been taught.

"Your world seeks to cage you, mine seeks to free you. Both are deadly, but yours pretends it's not."

He listened, but as she finished, she could see that look of disbelief, shock and... even amusement, take over his face.

"Free me?! They... they took me away from everything I had! Locked me in a dungeon! Drugged me for God knows how long! You call that freedom?!" he stammered.

She smirked a little, her fangs glinting in the dim light. He was getting angry. That was something she could understand, and she relaxed back into the seat again.

"Well, there's technicalities, I guess you could say. You're not supposed to hold someone for more than a day, but if no one knows..." she shrugged her shoulders. "Become the one who can bend the rules instead of the one that is bent by them."

His handsome face twisted and he looked her over as if seeing her for the first time.

"How can you live like this?"

"I live like this because I've seen how I could die, and I refuse."

"Getting close to town now. You want me to take a detour again?" Videl interrupted through her earpiece.

"We can head to the house," she replied, never breaking her gaze with Cole.

"You're a beautiful man, and I wish I was strong enough to take you for my own. Maybe even offer you a chance to..." she trailed off with a sigh. "You're like a prized ornament, meant to be admired, but a delicate rarity is always at risk for being destroyed. If I can offer you a piece of advice, tell my House what they want to know. Someone saved your life tonight, and as much as you might hate the situation you're in, your hate won't change it. Bend just enough so that they won't break you."

Her words did not comfort him. She could see the confusion and conflict in his face, and his gaze slid down to the floor. Silence reigned for a while, until she felt the vehicle come to a halt.

"Will I see you again?" he asked her as the door was pulled open, and Videl stood there, dutifully waiting for them.

"I don't know, sweetheart," she said as she got out her own door, walking around to join Videl. "I don't know why they want you. I've never been asked to save someone's life before." She looked at him for a moment longer, committing his beautiful face to memory. He felt familiar, in a way, though she was certain she'd never seen him before. Men like him didn't exist in her world.

"I'll escort you to the formal chambers."

Cole's eyes went past her to the front entrance of that manor.

Her House's headquarters.

It towered over them; pitch black against the night sky. House Void Star was an oxymoron, an impossibility. Darkness where light should exist. Valeska always felt that the estate reflected that well.

The main manor was partly constructed in a gothic style, with large, black marble columns flanking the stone stairway. There was a wrought iron fence, towering high at five meters, showing the excessive caution of her house.

At the top of the stairs stood armed guards in full formal uniform with rifles held. Giant black braziers illuminated the giant marble statues of Dark Goddess Astarte, her ruby eyes glistening in the night.

Cole was frozen in place, and she reached into the vehicle, grabbing one of his zip-tied arms and tugging him out. She could see that the other hovering drones in the area were all offline, reminding her of the effort her house had gone through to arrange this.

And she still had no idea why.

"Shall I accompany you, or stand watch at the vehicle, Over-Lieutenant?" asked Videl, slamming the door shut as she began to take the sullen Cole towards the stone stairs.

"Wait here; we might need to do some cleanup after."

Valeska took the steps slowly, her voice growing quiet.

"Who were you, Cole? Back in your world, I mean. There's something special about you, something important," she trailed off as they made their way up the stairs.

"What?" he asked, broken out of his stupor. "I... I was nobody. I was at college, my first semester, and... I hadn't even gotten a chance to start life yet," he said with a stark realization.

The guards at the top broke their rigid stance as they reached them, and they clicked their heels and saluted her.

"Hail Satan!" they chanted, as two more guards emerged from behind the giant doors, going right for Cole, grasping him by his arms and beginning to haul him off.

Valeska wanted to intervene, to say that she'll deliver him personally, but a third officer intercepted her.

"The Magister would like a moment of your time. If you can spare it." The scar across his lip stretched as he smirked, phrasing it so politely but knowing she couldn't refuse. Nobody turned down the head of the house.

Least of all her, since she owed her fast rise to the man. Him and what she'd done for him at least.

"Yea, I can clear my schedule," she said casually, though her eyes still drifted towards Cole. It was so strange. Sure, he was handsome, like a delicate bird that looked best when freshly preened. She'd describe most people on the island as... rugged.

But that couldn't be why he was chosen.

"This way, if you're coming," the officer said as he led her into the grand interior halls, and up the stairs.

She followed the officer, knowing that, no matter what, Cole was out of her hands. Above her pay grade. Not her business.

And still her curiosity could not be stilled.

She hoped the Magister would offer answers, even knowing that he rarely did. At least, not an answer that satisfied.

The inside of the manor felt at once cavernous and claustrophobic, the lights dancing on the walls in an eerie way. The island had full electricity, but still they preferred older lanterns and lights, shrouding everything in mystery.

Cole was out of sight soon, swallowed by the void as he was led in the opposite direction as her. She didn't need the officer to guide her, but protocol was an important custom to be rigidly upheld, and she didn't fight it.

The ominous halls of that beautifully constructed estate wound up and around, the walls covered in curtains and old paintings of people, of beings from other worlds, of rituals, and of things she never quite understood. She looked at them as she passed, lost in thought, until she came to the great double-doors of the Magister's office. The officer nodded to the two guards there, and the door slid open as if by itself.

"Enjoy," the officer said before he left, and Valeska sneered a bit at his back.

What a petty dickhead.

She was quick to correct her expression, turning it icy cold as she turned towards the great desk; made of stone, it looked like a sacrificial altar. Behind it was a great stonework carving of a Void Star, the symbol of the house. Its rays jagged and powerful, carved so hideously beautiful.

The doors slammed shut behind her, the darkness of the room with its two-story tall red drapery all around enveloping her. She let out a soft breath of relief at being alone, but the feeling was short-lived as the skin on the back of her neck began to prickle in warning.

Chapter 5

Daddy Issues

Whoever spares the rod hates his son, but he who loves him is diligent to discipline him.

— Proverbs 13:24

"Ahh, the pride and joy of the Void Star does me proud yet again, yes."

Valeska startled as the Magister's hand rest atop her shoulder. He had been so silent that she'd not even heard him emerge from the adjoining room, and inwardly she scolded herself for failing.

His praise was all but ignored, wiped out by the realization that she'd let her guard down.

But when she turned towards him, there was a smile creasing his cheeks. His jagged-looking black overcoat looked almost like a robe as it hung over his broad-shoulders. His hair was long and white, framing his stern face. He was undoubtedly a very handsome man in his youth, and in his advanced age of—she would guess fifty—he looked stately and imposing. Just as a House Magister should.

"How was it, my beautiful Over-Lieutenant?" he asked, and she was reminded of the last time she'd met with him.

The Magister had always terrified her as much as he delighted her. Outside of his presence, she had desires, needs, plans...

But when she was near him, that all was chased away by a singular compulsion to make him proud. He'd been with her all her life. Usually in the background. But they'd had meetings like this periodically, him grooming her for greatness. Or so she was told. Her recollections of their times together were faint, as if he was a Dark Lord himself, and her mortal mind couldn't quite grasp him.

He was the closest thing to a father that she had, and he reached out to caress her raven black hair, her cheek.

"The task itself was easy. I don't believe there were any suspicions raised. The challenge is always in seeing the tapestry being woven just out of my view," she said with a confident grin. Respect wasn't the quiet and mewling type of the old world, and she stood tall as he graced her with that tender touch.

"Indeed," he said, as his thumb caressed her cheek, then along her jawline. "I covered your tracks. And when you're done, you'll be given all you need to prove it to your superiors. The appropriate video is being prepared to replace the... unfortunately interrupted stream. I hear you'll have killed him; fired so many shots into him there was naught but pulp and a few digits left," he explained to her, his voice warm but brimming with that edge of power beneath.

The story was so much like the one she'd teased Videl with, knowing they'd have to be more surreptitious than that. House Void Star didn't like sending loud messages, as he'd said.

"Good for me," she said with a relieved sigh before stiffening. "So, this is some serious shit, huh? Videl obeyed me without question, as expected. I took the boy from someone in the tavern, but that won't raise suspicions. He ran towards the water, got to the fence, and we brought him back to the hummer. Doing it there would've been the natural choice. Less messy and disruptive."

"No worries, my child of Astarte," he remarked, letting his hand slip from her face. "It will all be taken care of soon."

He turned and walked towards his desk, his boots now clicking on the marble in a way they hadn't upon his entrance.

He uncorked a jewelled decanter and poured up a glass; then another. It was a rich brandy, and he brought her a glass, offering it.

"I would love to keep you here a while, but you have to report to your superiors as soon as the pieces are all in place. So in our precious little time, tell me... what do you wish for next, dear child of darkness?"

It was a strange question, and she mulled it over as she took a sip of that thick, strong liquor.

"I wish to know all the secrets," she said thoughtfully, before grinning fiendishly up at him. "And the power to wield them. The other Houses are only as strong as their loosest tongue, and once I start tugging at a thread, it will turn to wire to garrotte them on. If the time comes for that, of course."

Bold plans always had to have the edge of obedience and loyalty to them. It was a difficult line to walk.

He listened to her, lightly swirling that dark amber fluid around in his crystal glass. A grin formed on his striking face, and he looked both amused and pleased with her response.

"A very big wish indeed," he said, before sipping the brandy, his eyes narrowing a bit as he inspected her, from head to toe. Her leather jacket was open, her tank top revealing her cleavage and a slip of bare skin along her lower stomach, just above the waist of her shorts. It felt so informal, compared to his carefully tailored outfit, but it was perfect for the field.

"You'll have to do a lot to earn all that. But... in time, I can oblige," he said calmly, sitting back on the edge of his stone desk and scrutinizing her for a moment. "For now, know you did our House a great service. A great service indeed. And I want to reward you for that."

He sipped his drink again, taking just a moment.

"You will have to go now, I'm afraid. Our time is about up. But I will see you again soon. Sooner than you'd usually expect. So, for now, go. Do your duty. Celebrate. Ponder what you want your future role to be," he said, as she saw him press a button, and heard the doors unlock behind her.

"Is this secret worth knowing?" she asked before tossing back the rest of the liquor, feeling that pleasant burn chase away the pity that still seeped insidiously into her mind. "He didn't seem worth the trouble to me."

It was the truth, but it felt like a lie in the moment.

He came and took the glass from her, smiling unevenly down at her.

"Not yet. Not for you. It would just put you in danger. It is best you know nothing more. In fact, it would be best if you knew even less for the time being. At least until the matter is settled with your superiors," he said, reaching up to pat her cheek paternally. "And if you are merely lamenting the loss of a pretty play thing... I could remedy that. Have another sent to you. Or replace that second-in-command of yours with one more appealing if you like," he said, turning back to his desk.

She shrugged her shoulders at him as she began to step backwards towards the exit. She didn't let on how much him replacing her Second bothered her. Though she couldn't quite remember why, she knew that revealing any connection to another was not something the Magister could ever find out about.

"Don't worry, Magister. I wouldn't ask a favour from you that's so frivolous. I'll keep my curiosity caged, and look forward to our next meeting."

"Excellent. Until next time, my rising dark star," he said as the doors opened on their own.

The officer from before was there to greet her as she left, a package beneath one arm, and a tablet in the opposing hand.

"Here is the footage of what you did tonight," he offered, holding out the tablet.

A series of videos from different camera angles played, all portraying her doing something that absolutely did not happen.

The vehicle stopping by the cliffs where she'd been idling earlier that evening.

Her pushing the frightened Cole to the edge.

She was smiling and laughing, and she realized it must've been spliced from other footage. She couldn't quite place from when. It had to be recent, though, as she was wearing her new insignia.

She gave an order, and Videl opened fire, just as she'd joked with him about doing. Spray and pray. He'd told her that it would be risky, yet that was to be their cover for the evening. It was ironic.

A massive spray of bullets blew the poor, cowering Cole into a billion pieces, his body becoming little more than pink mist and a few chunks.

Videl was crueler than usual in this video, and didn't stop until a chunk of rock was torn from the cliffs, and nothing except two fingers remained of Cole. She crouched down then, and took them up, before wrapping them in some cloth.

"And here," said the officer, giving her the package, which she now realized was a cloth bundle, like that in the video. "I trust you need no instructions or further information from me on this matter," he said to her, arching a brow at her beneath his military cap.

"I know what happened tonight, I don't need a recap," she said, taking the bundle brusquely. "Videl really needs to get laid and work out some of his aggression; I'll talk to him about it."

She should be relieved that the House had handled everything for her, but the prickle on the nape of her neck would not dissipate.

It was late in the night by the time they were relieved on duty after filing their report and attending their debrief.

"You did the isle a great service today, Over-Lieutenant. Keep this up and you will outrank me before long," said her commanding officer before she was let loose.

Her and Videl stepped out of the bunker-like fortress that housed military command richer than before, and she was confident that the skills of House Void Star were proven superior once again.

Neither said anything for a while as they went down the lively street. Night was when things came alive as the ominous and festive storefronts and establishments were at full tilt. Locals and tourists alike came out to party, drink, fuck.

"I guess we're officially off duty until tomorrow," Videl said, almost sounding disappointed about that. He was always a workaholic.

She rolled her eyes at him.

"No wonder you blew that guy into the next world. We live in paradise, and you can't even relax enough to enjoy it," she chided him, believing the lie they told. "Fuck, what was it that made you want to be here, huh?"

Videl looked to her with a raised brow, the scar along his eye rising with it.

"Beats working some shit job for no pay, just to keep up on debt payments. Only you never keep up on them, they just get worse and worse," he said with a shrug of his shoulders. "The mainland isn't any fun. It's just dreary, pointless work. Filing folders. Refiling folders. Punching numbers into a computer. At least this stuff is... real," he said, looking around as some other Wolf stumble out of a brothel—drunk—an arm around a topless, busty woman. Their laughter filled the air, maniacal, before it was silenced as their mouths met each other's skin in a frenzy.

"Yea, it's real, but that place must have really twisted you if you're here and all you can think of is still *work*." She nodded towards the brothel, "At least he's doing something else to blow off some steam, experiencing something that isn't just following someone else's wishes."

Videl was a handsome man in his own way, the scar on his face didn't even diminish that fact. It made him look more rugged in a way. He wasn't like Cole, but then few were on this island. No, his main issue was just that he was too stuffy and work-oriented.

But he looked to the brothel with unmasked interest.

"It's not as if I don't visit such places," he said with a shrug. "But I want to do well. To rise up. To belong here," he said to her, hands going to his belt. He was at least a decade older than her, and she pegged him for mid-thirties, but she would always be his superior. She was born here. He was a mainlander. Maybe that was why he always felt like he had to prove himself, and separate himself from the lowly tourists that immigrate to the Island before fleeing back to their normal lives.

He had already proven himself to her, for whatever that was worth. He was a Satanosite as much as he could be one.

"Belonging here and doing well here means getting in touch with your carnal needs," she said sternly.

"I might visit a whore house I like on the other side of town before calling it a night; I could use a chance to blow off some steam."

Valeska got the impression that he was just doing it for the Eyes that were once more observing their every move, but she still smiled triumphantly at his decision to obey her command. Even if it wasn't *really* a command.

"You're gonna make someone very lucky tonight. I'm almost jealous," she teased, and his stern expression broke as he chuckled, his gaze tilted down towards her.

"What about you? What are you gonna do now?"

"Well, that's a secret," she grinned mischievously. "Good work out there tonight. It's nice to know you have my back. I made sure to pass that along up the chain."

"Thank you for that, Over-Lieutenant," Videl said, with a tip of his head. "It's a privilege getting to serve you," he said, sounding quite serious. "You're not only a good commander, you're... easy on the eyes too," he dared. They had worked together for so long, but he was always so stuffy that his comment was almost raunchy coming from him. Her ruby eyes widened with delight, and her heart thud a little bit heavier in her chest.

"Obviously," she agreed with a playful laugh. "Now go get laid so that next time I can bring something back to command that is a bit more substantial than a quarter of a hand!"

She watched as he left, his shoulders held straight, his gait filled with a casual confidence. He was so appealing, but she could never take a chance like that. Loyalty had ways of getting complicated once sex was involved, even in the hedonistic world of Satanos.

No, she needed something to take her mind off the night. She wasn't going to get any answers, and nosing around would only be suspicious, but as she considered her options of usual lovers, she knew none would suffice. Not for what she was looking for.

She'd need a tourist.

It wasn't like she was looking for Cole, or even a replacement for him.

He's nothing, she reminded herself, *a nobody.*

She just didn't want to have to deal with someone she had a history with. Someone she'd see again, and have to play those little power games with. She wanted the upper hand, and a fresh face was the only one who'd do.

She tended to sleep through the day, so she still had a few hours of energy left in her, and with her recent promotion came privacy that she'd never known before. For the first time ever, she had her own house on the estate, a place where she could indulge in some of her own carnal needs, away from prying eyes.

Despite the chaotic nature of the island, it still managed to attract its fair share of tourists. Mostly either young people seeking adventure and forbidden drugs, or older, richer people seeking hedonism and an escape from their dull lives. It kept the bars, brothels and clubs quite busy, their cash adding to the flow of wealth on the island.

Not that they were needed, since the island's drug business fuelled the international flow despite all attempts by foreign governments to stop it. Those riches kept the island powerful, secure, and with all the fanciest new gadgets and gizmos one could desire.

She began walking down the strip of bars, hunting for her prey. It didn't take long to spot him. A tall, dark-haired man with an intense look was peering around, trying not to look intimidated by the island.

But she could spot a lamb from a mile away, and this one was fresh.

She felt like a wolf when she smiled at him, revealing those polished fangs between her dark lipstick.

CHAPTER 6

THE WOLF'S DEN

Astarte has come again, more powerful than before.
She possesses me. She lies in wait for me.

— JEAN LORRAIN; MONSIEUR DE
PHOCAS

Her finger crooked as she beckoned him to her. She was still in her work uniform, but with her tits pushed up, her shorts sinking into her ass cheeks, and the fishnets climbing her thighs, he could be forgiven for not realizing what line of work she was really in.

It didn't matter either way.

His surprise and intrigue were instantaneous as he let his gaze sweep over her. The tourists were always astonished by her, looking hard as fuck, toting weapons and an air of authority.

He was dressed in black pants and shoes, with a dark top, undone and showing his lightly tattooed chest. She could see some of the markings there, and tell that he thought himself like her and the denizens of Satanos. But while it may have fooled the people back home for him, she could see the tell-tale signs of a poseur. He was a visitor. Aspiring to be what she was, but never going to have the guts to follow through.

They rarely ever did.

His companions had continued on without him as he gawked at her, so he approached, hands in his pockets.

"Yeah?" he said simply, arching a pierced brow.

She stared at him up close for a second, letting her unnatural, red eyes dip down over his body, inspecting him like a piece of meat.

Or at least letting him feel like he was.

Tourists loved being objectified. Up close she appreciated his lightly toned torso, those visible abs, and knew that it wasn't just an act for her. He'd make a perfect sex toy.

"You found a place to sleep tonight. Lucky you," she smiled fiendishly. "What's your name?"

He looked surprised by her directness, as tourists so often were. They weren't usually used to women being so assertive. The mainland sounded like a shit place to be to her, to be honest.

"Abel," he said after a moment's delay. "Who're you?" he asked, sounding a little awed frankly. But she was used to that.

"Abel," she laughed, her eyes twinkling with amusement. "God's favoured son? I can't tell if that's a hilarious pseudonym or if your parents are just very disappointed in you."

She began walking in the direction of the car she was using for the night, expecting him to follow.

And he did. With his eyes glued to her backside as they were he felt like a dog on a leash. Only the leash was his innate desire for her flesh.

"I didn't pick the name. But there's a very good possibility you're right on that last point," he said in his deep voice, taking his hands out of his pockets. He wore several big, silver rings on his hands. "So, you're not gonna tell me who I'm going with, huh?"

"My name is Valeska, but I doubt that tells you who you're going with," she said with a playful glance over her shoulder, her black hair catching the light as it bounced in its ponytail. "Besides, you're on the Isle because you like playing with danger. You should just be grateful that the danger that found you is me."

Tourists were such suckers. She could so easily have much worse plans for him, and he'd be walking right into her snare. But he was, as she said, getting off quite lucky.

All the same, the handsome stranger only paused just a moment, before he opened the passenger side door, then moved to get in with her.

"So... you're one of the islanders, huh?" he remarked, brow raised, as he sat in that seat, curiously looking around the car, before settling his uneasy gaze back on her. "How long have you lived here?"

"I was born here," she said as she closed her door and started the ignition. "So, I'm a full-blooded islander. A real story to tell your friends back at the yacht club or whatever." She pulled the car onto the road, following the familiar path to the House Void Star estate.

He laughed with a hint of derision there.

"Yacht club? Hardly. Just... taking a vacation to some-where... interesting," he said, wetting his lips. She got the vibe he was used to feeling in control. He was going to have to get over that fast. "I work in construction back home. For now, I mean. Pays well enough," he remarked, yammering a bit in the awkward silence. "What about you? What do you do... here?"

"Kill," she said simply, letting that word hang there in the air like a noose. She let her words hang in the air threat-eningly before she smiled. "I keep the peace. But lucky for you, I'm off duty. This is just pleasure."

She was a little surprised to see he didn't piss himself in fear. Instead, his surprise merged into respect as his eyes wandered her body.

"You don't look anything like cops back home," he said with a wry laugh. "But I guess even a Satanic paradise needs some folk around to maintain some... peace. Is it a rough gig?" he asked, leaning back in the corner of his seat, legs splayed as he watched her drive.

"No, not usually. There's not a lot of laws to break. I'm guessing that's part of why you're here, huh?" she said, glancing to him. The roads tended to be pretty quiet outside of the main areas, but joy riding was a common past time, so she was always on alert.

The island was large, but with a volcano in the middle of things, there weren't a lot of roads, so it was an easy drive back to her neighbourhood. They were surrounded by pointed, iron fences that walled off homes with bars on the windows and doors of steel.

Security was a serious matter in her neighbourhood, since everyone there was military and house affiliated; two distinct factors that made for great privilege and responsibility after all.

"Shit. You live around here?" he asked. And though the houses weren't huge, they were beautiful monuments to the island's harsh, eclectic style of gothic menace.

"Yea. Got my own place a while back as thanks for some messy business I solved," she said, pride tinging her voice. "Still working on getting it decorated, but it'll be better than some inn your friends are going to end up crashing in. By, like... a lot. Obviously," she added on. "Not to mention the company."

"Obviously," he said, finally loosening up a bit as he cracked a smile at her words. "There's a lot of lookers on this island. But you stand out even among them." His gaze lingered on her appreciatively as she pulled up to her front gate, two gargoyles staring down at them.

The gate opened at the press of a button, the metal screaming in protest against the pavement. She drove inside, parking in front of a house that felt *made* for her.

It had sat empty since before she could remember, but it was maintained through the years. As she started taking on more responsibility, she noticed that more work was being done on it. She'd even fantasized that it could be hers.

It still surprised her when she got it.

The style kept with the aesthetic of the place, dark and a bit foreboding, even though it wasn't particularly large.

She'd taken care to hang up some dark velvet curtains,

which were almost always drawn. The only light that greeted them was the security lamp that crawled over them as they approached the heavy wood door. Unlocking it, she pushed it open for him to step inside.

"So, is this a normal way of hooking up here? Just hauling a random guy off the street?"

"Oh, usually when a girl hauls a random guy off the street, it's not for a hookup."

He had followed her up, but her last words made him pause at the threshold. The tall, handsome man paused before he finally relented, and did what any guy not raised on the island would in that situation: he put all his very real and founded doubts aside, and stepped into her lair.

Even though it was sparsely furnished due to her newly moving in, it was still beautiful inside. It was a perfect blend of the old and the new, with hand-carved mouldings and fresh new paint. Dark hardwood was covered with a few heavy rugs, and an electric chandelier swayed in the entry way, its dark metal absorbing some of the pale light.

She shut and locked the door behind them, put in her security code to silence the beeping, then started up the stairs. "We don't have time for a tour."

"Shit, this place is awesome though," he said as he tore his gaze away from her ass to glance around. "I don't know anyone with a place this nice."

"I thought you worked in construction?"

"Yeah, I just help build them. I don't know the people who end up living in them. It's just shitty suburb homes thrown up cheap and fast, to be shilled out to people for way more than they're worth. We don't get a chance to put up quality construction like this..." he said, gripping the ornate railing with appreciation for its craftsmanship.

It was so confusing to her, the ways that his world undermined and harmed each other without a care. Cole had easily found the hypocrisy in the Island's law and its application, but how was this any different?

The heavy rugs softened their footsteps as she guided them down the hall.

Her room was the one she'd spent the most time decorating. After having nothing more than a bunker for so long, she wanted a sanctuary, some place she could be herself.

The walls were painted ombre, the top of them purple before bleeding down into black, and she had a few paintings up. They were mostly erotic, though all were moody and painted with affection rather than lust.

A large bed sat in the middle of the room with solid wood columns leading towards the steepled ceiling, draped with a heavy, violet comforter. Built into the headboard was two restraints, old fashioned iron cuffs that could only be opened with a key.

She took off her jacket, tossing it atop a reading chair next to the bookshelf.

"Make yourself at home. I'm going to wash the blood off my hands," she said casually as she moved into her bathroom. She shut the door behind her, flipping on the light switch and starting to run the hot water.

She pulled her hair from its elastic, shaking it free and giving the overly straight strands a bit of a tussle to wake them up. She washed her hands and then looked to the mirror.

She had managed to remain blemish free, even after living here all her life. She knew it wasn't all her doing. People had protected her, kept her safe in her younger years, and were careful to discipline her only in ways that wouldn't mark her permanently. Her youthful looks were one of the tools in her arsenal, and the House knew that just as well as she did.

She freshened her lipstick, putting her mouth around her finger and tugging any excess away from her teeth before she smiled at her reflection.

It was just a normal night, and she was celebrating a job well done.

That's what she told herself.

She returned back to the room to find Abel studying her artwork. His eyes were sweeping over an erotic painting of an orgiastic consecration, much like the one that ushered her into adulthood and full membership of the island's faith.

There were many interpretations of the code, many thoughts on who the true Dark Lord was, and each house represented at least one of those views.

But hers, of course, was the right one.

He turned slowly to look at her, his shirt undone, the light of her bedroom doing a better job of highlighting those dark, Satanic tattoos of his, decorating the hardness of his abs and pecs. He was definitely someone who knew work and labour, she could tell just by looking at him.

"You haven't decorated much of the rest of the house, but this room..." he said, gazing around once more, then letting his eyes stop momentarily on those cuffs. "Well, you prioritized, I guess. And it paid off. Did you do these?" he asked, pointing to the paintings.

"Some of them," she said, joining his side. "I did this one. My birthday," she said with a faint smile, true fondness in her tone, more than desire. "Not the day I was born, of course, but the day I was reborn. When I became something worthy."

She turned towards him, her head tilted back to look at him, her ruby eyes roaming his face.

"Why did you really come here?" she asked, her hand reaching to his shoulder, pushing back his shirt from his frame.

He didn't resist, and instead let his shirt slide back, revealing his broad shoulder, his bulging bicep that must've swung many a hammer, and lifted many a load of lumber in his work. He wet his lips as he looked down at her, so much taller than her and yet she was the one in control.

"The easy answer would probably be... you don't see 'no' to a hot girl that beckons you," he said, reaching one hand out, touching at her waist, caressing her side down to her hip. "The longer answer, I guess is that I came here looking for... something different. Something that would make life feel more worthwhile. And as beautiful as the island is, I was growing tired of being around other tourists. Acting like wannabes..." he said, stepping in a bit closer to her, speaking lowly.

On any other night, she might have laughed in his face, called him just as big of a wannabe. But, in that moment, she thought it was almost sweet.

She smiled, her fangs poking out from her dark lips as she continued to push his shirt back. As he got closer, her hand went to the other shoulder, until his shirt was drifting off and down to the floor.

"I'm surprised someone didn't snatch you up already, sweet boy," she cooed.

His shirt pooled to the floor behind him, his muscular physique on display, his pants hanging low and heavy, revealing just a hint of his treasure trail at the cusp of them. His two hands went to her sides, touching her, feeling her body, before grazing the bare skin of her hips, his fingertips sneaking in beneath her top.

"Who's to say they didn't try?" he responded with a cocky little smirk, as if he knew how to play the game on the island. "I guess they just didn't excite me the way you do," he remarked as his hands guided her tank top upwards, peering down at her with longing in his eyes.

And a throbbing through his black pants.

He stripped off her top, revealing a black, lace bra, and she stepped away.

"Aren't you greedy," she mused, folding her arms beneath her chest, pushing her cleavage up even more. Without her top, it was easier to see the several blades that were attached to her belt, the hilts pressing in along the edges of her hips.

"You can't get into a killer's car and then take what you want."

It was clear he didn't get the full danger she could pose if she wished. Because he smiled like it was all so innocent, and stepped after her again, pressing up against her.

"Fuck that's so cool," he said, admiring the sharp daggers, letting his fingers caress one, only to find it was truly sharp and deadly as he pricked a finger. "Damn," he said, suckling at the finger, cleaning away that blood. "These aren't just for show at all..."

"Haven't you heard of the wolves, sweet sheep?" she scoffed. "I wasn't lying. I held this one against a man's sac tonight," she said, pulling out her stiletto, flipping it in her fingers with a practiced skill.

His eyes flared wide, his body frozen in place. It was clear he still didn't know how to act entirely.

"What'd he do to earn that little favour then, huh?" he asked, tonguing the seam of his lower lip anxiously.

"Oh, nothing. He just had something I wanted. Someone I wanted. So, I let him know I was serious," she said lightly, though that only made her words sound more menacing. "That's how things are done here. Really done here."

His dark eyes flitted over her, from her blade to her eyes, then back again.

"I wasn't assuming you'd need those to get what you want from me. Unless you're planning something different..."

Valeska smiled at him, her darkness welling up inside of her.

Chapter 7

Don't Touch Me

Now the works of the flesh are evident: sexual immorality, impurity, sensuality, idolatry, sorcery, enmity, strife, jealousy, fits of anger, rivalries, dissensions, divisions, envy, drunkenness, orgies, and things like these.

— Galatians 5:19-21

He gingerly reached out for her, and she batted his hand away, though not with the dagger hand; lucky for him.

Her smile was just as dangerous, though.

"I think you like it," she teased, stepping away from him once more.

He wasn't entirely sure what to make of her. But he cracked a slight smile, and stepped closer after her.

"You're really a killer... huh?" he asked her, tonguing his

lower lip again as she could see that the little game she played hadn't inhibited the bulge in his pants at least. "Are you planning to off me when you're done?" he asked, reaching out to grasp her hip with one hand.

"Depends on how good you are," she grinned. He really was proving to be a good distraction, at least. Even if she did dodge to the side to avoid his grasp. "Get to the bed. And if you keep grabbing, I know that *you* know what I'll do with your hands."

He seemed to take that last threat seriously at least, and put up his hands. He stepped back and went to the bed, undoing his pants and letting them drop. He stripped out of his socks too, leaving just his boxer briefs on, as he got up onto the luxurious bed.

Those bare calves and thighs were thick with muscle too. It was clear he really was a working man, and not just some gym-bro who skipped leg day like all the others.

"You win. But I'm sure you're used to that," he said with a slight grin.

"Just because I'm used to a thing doesn't mean I can't still enjoy it," she said cockily. She went to the edge of the mattress, peering down at him as she leaned against the banister. The Satanic inkings he wore were quite well done, even if they weren't according to the proper rites of the island.

"You really are well made, aren't you?" she hummed, her gaze lingering on his hard-on.

He lay back against her large headboard, folding his thick arms behind his head as he looked to her.

"I certainly like to think so. But then..." his eyes swept over her and his cock throbbed. "So are you."

"Mm, I was blessed to be who I am. You, sweet Abel, are an aberration." One knee went to the mattress as she leaned over him, her hair tickling his face. Her nose was just an inch away from his, and she lingered there, testing him.

It was clear he was having trouble with this game of hers. And it was no surprise. Built as he was, looking as he did, he was probably not used to being the passive one in a relationship or sexual encounter.

But under the circumstances, he just partially lunged for her lips before stopping himself. As if she'd put a slice of juicy meat before a mostly trained dog.

"I probably should've asked what you had in mind to do tonight... huh?" he asked lowly.

"You should have asked a lot of things, especially if you're being so picky with the others," she agreed, her hand lightly stroking along his jawline. "I doubt you were really hoping for just some sweaty missionary before passing out."

His eyes locked on hers, and he unfurled his arms from behind his head. He didn't go to grab her this time, he let them rest there, as he got lost in her gaze.

"You're right," he remarked softly. "But if I'm being honest, I'm not exactly sure what I want either... except to not be killed. I think I'm against that firmly."

"But you're already using a qualifier," she teased, her eyes dancing with amusement and delight. Still, she set aside the stiletto before crawling on the bed fully. He audibly exhaled as he relaxed, and she threw her leg over him so that she was straddling his stomach.

"Do you actually believe?" she asked, her fingertip tracing one of his satanic tattoos, a sigil that was supposed to be for Lucifer, though the angles were a bit off.

He was utterly entranced by her, and he anxiously wet his lips again.

"Yes. I mean... at first it was just something to piss people off, rile them up," he confessed, watching her finger trace over his hard body, feeling those bulging muscles. "But coming here... getting a glimpse of how you all live... what you've done just by adhering to the code. Fuck. I come from the richest country on earth, and we don't make shit anymore. You all transformed a volcano into a God. You can't do that shit without being blessed."

It actually kind of impressed her. A lot of tourists talked the talk, but he wasn't just focusing on the hedonistic shit. The rock-and-roll version of Satanism.

Her finger lifted, her pointed nail beginning to trace down his body, teasing his nerve endings with a practiced pressure. He shivered and bit his lower lip in ecstasy.

"You got anyone keeping you back there? A girl? Family?"

"Family, yeah. But they don't even live in the same city as me. I had to move for work. And as for a girl..." he gave a shrug. "She talked a big game about being into this stuff. But when the time came for us to go, she not only chickened out, she begged me not to come. Said this place was crazy. That I'd get killed or worse," he remarked so casually about that rift. "She told me not to come back if I go. I bet she's just hoping you'll kill me," he said with a hollow chuckle.

"And you?" He reached out to touch her again, but he successfully stopped himself, restraining his big, strong hands. "How many men like me you keep danglin' on the line?"

"People know where they stand with me at the end of the day," she said as she leaned back, her ass pressing against his throbbing package delightfully. He shivered as her round backside pressed upon his girth.

"You are a pleasant and good-looking distraction after a strange day. I picked you because you were new. Handsome. Obedient. Someone that was... uncomplicated, politically speaking."

She kept tracing her fingernail over his body, causing a line of pinkened flesh to chase it.

"You clean?" she asked with a tilt of her head.

"Huh? I mean I've done some—"

His mouth dropped open when he realized what she actually meant. "Oh! Yeah, yeah, I'm clean. Only ever done it raw with my long-term girlfriends," he explained to her, groaning a bit as his hands clearly wanted to grasp and feel her thighs as she sat atop him.

She lifted her arm, pulling up the holographic keyboard for her watch. A few keystrokes and a database search reported back his entry passport, complete with his health records. STDs were a serious issue that they kept stringently controlled for tourists. They didn't pair well with hedonism.

And sure enough, his health report had been clean when he arrived four days ago.

"Fuck I wanna touch you so bad..." he rumbled, not paying much attention to what she was doing on her smartwatch. She exited the program and gave him a smile.

"I want you to want to touch me," she said simply. "And it's been a while since I indulged in what I want in the short term."

She shifted down his hips a little more until she was sat atop his package, her tight shorts stretching as she spread her legs to accommodate his powerful hips. She reached back, her torso contorting as she reached for one of her boots, tossing it aside. She leaned the other way, repeating the motion, and then wiggled her toes beneath the fishnets.

"It's to both of our benefit to give me what I want tonight."

He watched her with such intensity, his fascination written on his face. And his chest heaved as his breathing grew heavier.

"I want to give you that," he said, licking his lips then biting the lower one, as he clenched his hands into fists.

"Fuck I want you. To grab you and pin you down. But I'm honestly fuckin' afraid you're the real deal and I'll end up like a stuck pig instead," he confessed.

"It's good you know that. Good you're afraid of it," she agreed, her hips beginning to rock back and forth along the underside of his shaft, separated by their clothes. It did nothing to reduce the friction, though.

"I had to kill someone tonight, and I don't want to again. Especially not in my house. I'm not keen on already having to redecorate."

He groaned, moaned, shuddered all over and visibly struggled to resist touching her again. But he let his tensed-up muscles relax as she rocked atop his steely hard cock.

"I want you to tell me about it... would you?" he asked, his breathing heavier. "I came here to do the shit I couldn't admit to anyone that I wanted to do. I wanted to pin a hot girl down and ravage her, no matter what she said. But fuck..." he groaned, "I couldn't do it. And here I am instead, with you in charge. Dammit I'm fucked."

"Sweet boy," she sighed, reaching around her back and finding the clasp of her bra. She slipped an arm through, then the other, before letting the lace drift down from her firm breasts. She barely needed a bra at all, despite the heaviness of her chest, still graced by youth. Her pink nipples stiffened as they were exposed to air, and she tossed the bra aside.

"Murder isn't something we take lightly, you know. It's the most serious thing you could do to someone else. To infringe on someone else's freedom forever? It's not enough to just want to do it," she lectured, even as she ground against his dick, feeling the rush of blood flow through her.

He shuddered and groaned.

"I know," he said, his voice huskier, laden with lust as he watched her, his eyes rolling back at the sight of her large tits. "Fuck those are amazing!" he shuddered.

"And... I didn't wanna kill anyone. Not really. Just... you know..." he said with a grunt, his pecs twitching, biceps bulging.

"It's different than you expect," she said, leaning forward, gathering his thick wrists in her dainty hands. For a moment, it seemed she was going to guide him to her chest, finally letting him have something he wanted, but instead she pushed them back to the mattress.

"If you want me to fuck you, you'll show me you deserve it by controlling yourself," she said simply. "You can't take what you want from me, and you know it. It's easier if you don't fight."

He bit his lower lip again, as if having to restrain himself intensely from saying or doing something unwise.

"I'm pretty confident I could overpower you..." he said, but his eyes drifted to her daggers. "But I'm not so confident when you're wielding one of those," he admitted, letting her keep his arms pinned as his eyes clung to those tantalizing breasts. The sight of those ample mounds so close to his face made his cock thicken and pulse even more incessantly.

"Even if you did overpower me, you wouldn't leave the island without repercussions," she smiled, her tone so girlish and sweet.

"Are you ready for your final test?"

"Fuck I hope so."

She pulled away from him, slinking off the bed. Her fingers wound into her belt, unfastening it. She stepped towards the bottom pillar of the bed, wrapping the leather around it, letting the other dagger hang away from them, but keeping it in reach. Then she went to her shorts, and unbuttoned them, tugging the tight material down over her fishnet clad thighs. She wore no panties beneath, just the tights, and even in the dim light he could make out the hole she'd ripped there, her bare pussy glistening between her thighs.

She climbed back onto the mattress, her fingers then guiding his boxer briefs down over his ass, letting his cock bob free from its confines.

Though it might've been more accurate to say it leaped out at her. That thick, veiny girth eagerly excited to find a place inside her. His eyes never left her, but they were finally able to leave her tits, to instead stare at her glistening slit.

"You're so god damned hot," he groaned, his big hands gripping the blankets in restraint. "You don't need those daggers to get any man you want, that's for fucking sure."

"I know," she said as she crawled back over him.

"All of your friends will be jealous when you tell them a Wolf brought you back to her den to fuck. But I'm sure you won't tell them that I made you beg for it, because baby, you're gonna *mean* every word of it."

CHAPTER 8

PRAY BETWEEN MY THIGHS

And the L*rd Wolf was pleased with Abel's offering.

— GENESIS 4:4

S he brought her bare pussy lips to the underside of his cock and began to get him wet from her juices, teasing him to the point of torture.

"F-Fuck! Holy shit! I didn't think you'd actually go this far without a condom," he husked, staring at her body with such rabid desire. He swallowed it down though, ran a hand back through his dark hair and tried to steady himself. "Holy hell... please," he grunted, his dick spurting some pre onto his treasure-trail. "Fuck I want you so bad... please, don't fucking send me away without letting me know what it feels like inside you."

She smiled, his words like a soothing balm along her tensed shoulders.

It was so rare that she felt truly in control. Not as a temporary thing that could be snatched away later in a game, or as a trade for something else, but truly in charge of how things played out.

And she needed that after the night of lies.

His words were honest and from the heart, and that pleased her enough that she moved up his cock, until she was grinding just below the lip of his crown.

"Will this make you really commit to your faith?"

She watched as those glistening petals of her pussy made this big, strong man tremble and shiver. To bring such a brute to heel with so little of her power... Intoxicating.

He groaned and shuddered, his eyes shutting for just a moment as his cock throbbed.

"I'd commit to Lucifer for you. I'd... I'd do anything you asked for this," he said with such an air of honesty, his desperation for her bringing out that sigh of sincerity. He had to grip his hair and the bed to not grab her body though, his eyes rolling back into his head as he groaned.

"What do you want of me? Just tell me, please."

"You're swearing that on sanctified grounds," she said, leaning in over him, her mouth just barely grazing against his. "I want to know you mean it. That even after seeing all this, knowing who I am, that you pledge yourself to the Void Star."

His eyes narrowed as she got in so close, and he trembled again, truly shook beneath her. While her muscles relaxed, his tensed.

"How can I prove it any more?" he asked, his voice hushed, intense.

"I pledge my soul to Satan. To Lucifer. The Void Star. By your bidding. For the meaning it might give me, for the pleasure of your body. Because you asked me to. All those reasons and more. Consecrate me, make me more than the hollow shell of a man I was back on the mainland," he begged.

She let out a breath as she pushed down upon him, her breasts gliding along his torso as her wet slit kissed the crown of his cock. She reached behind her and grasped his shaft, teasing her clit on his tip.

"Don't buck up," she commanded, the dainty woman in full control, and wanting to keep it that way.

Every one of those little touches, or grazes, were electric. They sent his body into spasms of titillating pleasure. And he got to experience carnal excitement like never before. Somehow all that restrain, that resisting of touch, made each bit of contact all the more intense.

He shut his eyes tight as he nodded to her sharply.

"Okay," he said, breathing heavily already, just from sheer desire. "F-fuck... are you on the pill or anything, or should I...?"

"You should stop thinking you have any say with what happens here," she taunted him, descending down his shaft with an achingly slow pace. She was so wet, her shaved pussy flushed with blood, the scent of arousal swirling around them in the ornate room.

Despite his obvious attempts to watch that glorious sight of her pussy swallowing up his shaft, his eyes rolled back into his head. His whole, strong body tensed up and those muscles bulged delightfully. But inside her, his cock throbbed thickly, stretching the narrow walls of her pussy out more, twitching and pulsating wildly.

His hips began to roll up into her, but he reined them back in, as he ground his teeth with an audibly grinding sound.

"F-Fuck..." he choked out.

"You don't cum until I say, or else," she said, not even bothering to think up a threat. It hardly mattered. Maybe it made it better to leave him wondering what his punishment would be.

She sat upright on his lap, her delicate body pressing down upon him until her pussy was strained to its limits, and still she fought against it. She needed him almost as much as he needed her, and the pain was delicious. Her ruby eyes rolled upwards as she ground against him, forcing her body to yield to him.

Abel grunted and groaned, his body tensed up so much it looked like he was bench pressing 500 pounds, and not taking her tight pussy to the hilt and resisting the urge to do far more. He gasped and swore, and very nearly grabbed her thighs in his delirious state.

"Fuck! You feel... sacred," he gasped out, as his eyes were forced back to her body, soaking it in with such hunger.

When she knew that she couldn't force her body to bend any further, she began to ride him. Her pace was slow, at first, luxuriating in how he felt. How he stretched her open and teased at all her nerve endings.

But it didn't last long before the ache of frustration built within her, and she began to tire at the tease. Her pace picked up, her breasts bouncing on her pale chest as the sounds of slapping filled the room.

Her victim for the evening grunted and moaned, his pleasured sounds filling the air as he struggled with his inability to do anything but lay there and take it. And he reached back, both hands gripping the headboard as he watched her tits bounce through strained eyes.

The wood of the headboard creaked in his grip, and his dick twitched excitedly inside her as he huffed and panted. But the more she rode him, the more he struggled. She could feel his dick throbbing inside her, that tell-tale excitement of a man close to losing control. But he grit his teeth and obediently deprived himself as he watched her.

"You're glorious. Please, just let me touch your thighs at least," he begged.

"No."

Her eyes closed as she focused on her own needs. He was little more than a dildo at that moment, albeit a flesh and blood one.

And the fact that she was depriving him only made her feel more powerful, more seductive. She rode him with expertise he'd surely never experienced before, a confidence in her motions that belonged to a much older woman.

Her breathing began to pick up, and involuntary whimpers began to escape her.

He was doing his best to be still, to be her personal little flesh toy, something for her to bounce and ride atop for her own pleasure. But his hips gradually rose up of their own accord, as he gripped the headboard, and resisted that insatiable natural urge to cum inside her.

"Oh Hell," he gasped, trembling beneath her, his dick swelling thicker as he could barely keep that fiery tide of his orgasm at bay.

It was a rush to keep him perched at that precarious edge so long, but she didn't care to deny herself of her own pleasure any longer.

When she finally said the word, "Cum," it was a command for her as much as it was for him, and her body eagerly obeyed.

Her pussy tightened around his bare cock, her head thrown back as she screamed, her own sounds completely unrestrained.

He joined her in almost perfect unison.

All his teeth gnashing and withholding was ended, and he let loose a loud, bellowing shout as his cock erupted. Thick strands of his virile seed shooting off into her as he came hard. The most intense orgasm of his life racking his body as he let loose so many strands of pent-up seed. He shook and moaned, yelled and cried out as his orgasm drew on long, draining him dry.

She was a succubus sucking the life from him.

An involuntary buck of his hips sending a jarring thrust of his dick against her utmost depths, hitting her hard in that moment.

Earlier it would have been enough to find himself punished, but in the throes as she was, it only added to her own ecstasy.

"Sometimes denying yourself what you want can give you greater pleasure than unrestrained indulgence."

It took her a long time to come down from those

heights, her forearms leaning on his chest as she caught her breath. As she looked down at his handsome face, for a brief moment, she thought she saw a familiar scar over his eye.

The momentary illusion forced her to look away, towards the dagger that hung on her bedpost within reach.

CHAPTER 9

I WANT A ROCKET LAUNCHER

From the beginning you are immortal and children of eternal life. You wished to distribute death amongst yourselves so as to consume it and annihilate it, and so that death might die in and through you. For when you dissolve the world and are not yourselves dissolved, you rule over creation and over the whole of corruption.

— GNOSTIC FRAGMENTS FROM
VALENTINUS FRAGMENT; FRAGMENT 4:
ANNIHILATION OF THE REALM OF
DEATH

Her body was still wet from the shower, and she towelled out her hair before tossing it into the tub to wash later. Returning to her bedroom, she smiled at Abel, still sleeping with one hand cuffed to her bed.

She really wore him out.

She crept towards him, over the heavy rugs, not making a single sound. She was just about to reach out and grab his cock when her wristwatch buzzed.

"All officers report to duty stations and muster your unit."

"Damn it," she cursed under her breath. She turned towards her dresser, tugging out a fresh change of clothes. Before she could even pull on her fishnets, a klaxon siren wailed, warning of a potential air raid. She grabbed her shorts, tugging them up before making her way to the bed.

"The hell is going on?" Abel gasped in alarm, bolting upright in bed only to find himself still cuffed. Her watch screen lit up again with more details.

"UNIDENTIFIED AIRCRAFT OVER SATANOS."

"Sorry lamb, time for you to go," she said as she went to his cuff, freeing him.

Valeska opened the app to contact Videl directly.

"Hey, you far?" she asked, tugging the tank top on over her bra, her outfit almost identical to the one she wore the day before.

"I'm between you and the barracks," came Videl's voice back, the man wide awake and alert. "What's your command, Over-Lieutenant?"

"I'll meet you there, get the guys together. But send one to my place; I have a tourist that'll need an escort back to town."

She was practically a Saint. She gave him a place to stay, fucked him raw, *and* didn't eat his sweet little heart out the morning after.

In short, she was grateful she'd never see him again. It wouldn't do for anyone to know how soft she was.

Abel was getting dressed at a much slower rate than her. He looked at her with surprise before it was chased away by a light, sheepish smile as he tugged his boxer-briefs up over his package that had served her so well the night before.

She would have liked another go at that before she sent him packing, but this was an emergency.

"Yes, Ma'am," Videl replied, and then cut the communication.

"So, is this like... serious?" asked Abel, looking at her as he got his pants.

Valeska shrugged.

"Impossible to say," she replied easily, though she dodged his question with skill. "You're gonna sit on the front step until my guy comes for you, and you're gonna be very respectful, and not indulge any details to him. You'll see that the door is locked, and your lips are sealed. I don't give a shit what you tell your friends, but you don't put any thoughts in my man's head that I don't want there."

She pulled on her jacket, then grabbed her knives, strapping them back onto her body.

"Will I see you again?" he asked a bit hesitantly, afraid of overstepping or being too clingy.

A further buzz came from her watch, this one a command alert only.

"Action Overhead IMMINENT."

She didn't bother answering. She was dashing out the door, down over the steps, and towards the front porch.

A powerful boom shook the air, as if something had exploded just above her, but she knew it was a rocket firing from one of the island's Surface-to-Air Missile batteries.

She watched the streak of white up into the sky as she made her way to her motorcycle, hopping on it. She wanted something sportier that would let her see what was going on, and as she tore out onto the main road, she caught the sight of an explosion from the corner of her eye. Whatever it was that the rocket hit was too tiny to be seen, but the detonation was sure as hell obvious.

That was something she'd not seen in a long, long time. Not since she was a little girl, in fact, before her time in the Youth Brigade.

She parked her bike at the barracks, entering it and inspecting her troops. They were all dressed and in full uniform, men and women alike, standing in a stick straight line, as Videl turned and saluted to her, hand out straight, across his chest in the service's style.

"Alright, kids," Valeska said, her small voice sounding more commanding than any could expect. It was another thing that she was taught. How to make herself seem bigger in moments of crisis. The condescending tone helped, considering she was one of the youngest in her order, despite her position. "You all know what to do. Defensive positions. Ready yourself for anything, and await further instructions. It's your chance to prove you can think under pressure so don't fuck it up."

"Yes Ma'am!" they shouted in unison, arms across their chest in a salute.

Her and Videl often worked as a pair, the rest of her unit assigned to different strategic locations around the island. It was never good to consolidate a unit too close together, since the Island was so large, and the competing interests of the Six Houses were of constant concern.

"You heard the Over-Lieutenant! File out!" barked Videl, and they all rushed off. Their position was overseeing a segment of the island just at the edge of the city. It was usually an important spot, though unlikely to be involved in anything via the air. After the rocket, she wasn't really sure there was anything more to do than pick up the trash.

"Our vehicle is warmed up and ready, Ma'am," Videl said as he headed over towards that usual armoured vehicle of theirs.

"You drive. I want to keep my eye out for anything weird," she replied, bouncing into the passenger seat. "Did you see anything on your way?"

"No," Videl said, as he hopped into the driver's seat, and began to pull out. "Certainly saw that plane blow up though. Or whatever it was. Might've been a drone."

The usual flood of tourists was gone as they drove down the street, though the early hour likely had more to do with that than the klaxon sounding.

"No rumours among the unit either. Whatever happened, nobody had a clue what it is yet," he said, as they wound through those sturdily paved streets. Videl was not making as much haste as she might've, but he was a cautious driver usually. "I was hoping you might be able to enlighten me."

"Wouldn't that be nice," she said, sticking her head out the window a bit. "Probably threat's passed anyways.

Maybe a spy drone. Probably cost whoever sent it a pretty penny to lose it so fast," Valeska said with a frown. "Was kind of hoping for some action this morning, seeing as I was woken up early."

"I prefer to sleep through the fucking day if I can help it," he said, as they took a sharp turn, but rather smoothly, thanks to Videl's driving. It wasn't long before she could see their own post up ahead.

It wasn't much to look at, just an empty lot at the edge of town, overlooking the main road of entry into the city. It was an important strategic location that had never been attacked. Not in Valeska's time anyhow.

"Yea, last night was weird, too. Would've been nice to sleep through the afternoon," she mumbled, not really paying a lot of attention to their conversation. She was looking around, trying to see if there was any sign of anything around their post.

Videl parked them into the lot. The ocean cliffs were to her right, and the forest was off to her left, looking dark and mysterious, even in the daylight. Straight ahead lay the road winding off out into the mountains.

"Everyone's about in position, Ma'am," he said as he checked his watch. "Did you wanna get out, stretch our legs? Or sit tight here in case?" he asked, looking to her with those red eyes of his.

"We should take a look around. You get into the cupola; get ready in case we see anything. We wanna be ready if we're under attack," she said as she hopped out, grabbing a sleek black assault rifle; a modified AK-470, the latest model of the Kalashnikov variant.

It was a solidly built gun, sturdy and reliable. It operated as a sort of rail-gun, using magnetic fields to propel its bullets at intense velocities. It was cutting edge stuff, but then, only the best for the forces of Satanos. She slung it over her back, avoiding looking at Videl as she tried to forget the previous night's brief flicker of a fantasy she had denied herself for so long.

Videl popped his head up through the cupola, grasping the machine gun in hand.

"I'll keep my comms open, Ma'am," he informed her, as their Eyes silently hovered around them.

The sun was out, but there was intermittent cloud cover that blotted it out periodically. That probably helped obscure whatever it was that flew up over head.

It also meant that the day was not too hot as she stepped across the asphalt, seeing the cluster of buildings there at the edge of town. The area mostly consisted of quiet businesses or warehouses, not open yet, or shut down for the time being, with a few scattered little homes.

It was the industrial side of town where much of their money was made, and tourists never visited. It was also more run down than the glitz of main street.

She paced, keeping close to the vehicle, but trying to work out some of her excited energy.

Abel had been a good distraction from her House intrigue, but she found her mind wandering back to the man from the night before. Cole. The special boy that was saved from death for who knows what reason.

She was looking at a potentially long day, watching out for... in all likelihood? Nothing. She didn't care to ruminate about his fate a moment longer.

"Did you get laid last night?" Valeska asked as she

pulled out a cigarette, but before Videl could answer, a notification of a command level alert grabbed her attention.

"Events still unknown. Siren ended for now. But investigation continues. Maintain high alert. May have been a distraction."

And just like that, the klaxon siren stopped its wail.

Shit.

Yeah, that meant a long day.

She turned back towards Videl, about to relay her orders, when she caught a brief glimpse of someone. They were between an empty storefront and an old warehouse, though Valeska couldn't get a good look before they'd moved back into the shadows.

She was already on alert, and she started off in the direction without a second's thought.

"Someone's lurkin'," she said to Videl as she passed him, nodding towards the buildings. "I'm gonna check it out."

"I'll come cover you," Videl said, as he exited the vehicle.

She was already well ahead of him by that point, almost at the shadowy alleyway that she'd spotted them. She began to track them as the figure ducked down another bend in the maze of alleys, and the figure began to run, clearly in a hurry.

"Don't make this worse on yourself," she called out. It wasn't any use to treat this mission with stealth. They knew she was there, just as much as she knew they were there. "I just have some questions."

But they didn't stop. Of *course* they wouldn't make this easy on her.

"I think I can cut them off if I'm gauging where you are right," Videl said over the comms. "Do you want me to try or should I just catch up?"

"Cut them off," Valeska commanded, her tall boots never pausing as she ran. The platform heel gave her four inches in height, and she was so used to them they never bothered her. Even when she was having to chase after some asshole through the rough alleys.

"Yes Ma'am," was the last thing he said as they both picked up their pace.

Whoever this was, they were spry and fast. Valeska struggled to gain ground on them, but she was slowly catching up, and she caught a peak of long hair as she ran around a corner.

Valeska turned to follow, but there was no one there, and the path branched off in multiple directions. She was just about to ask Videl if he had eyes on them, but the sound of a cut-off shriek told her which way to go.

She hurried on, just in time to see the woman trying to climb through an open window into a warehouse. Videl grabbed the back of her shirt and yanked her out onto the ground without hesitation.

"Get down!" he shouted at the suspect, as he pointed his own assault rifle at her. He got atop her, pinning her down, both arms beneath his legs.

"Fuck," Valeska panted as she made it to them, smiling at Videl. "Good job. Now, those questions I had for you that you forced me to work for," she said, her tone growing dark as she looked down at the pinned captive. "I'm not feeling so friendly anymore."

Videl put his gun over his shoulder and back, then took

out some zip-ties to bind her. Valeska crouched down, staring at the woman, and the hair on the back of her neck stood straight up.

CHAPTER 10

FILTHY MOUTH

The mask of self-deception was not longer a mask for me, it was a part of me. Night lifted it, laying bare the stifled truth below; but there was no one to see except myself, and when day broke the mask fell back again of its own accord.

— ROBERT W. CHAMBERS; THE KING
IN YELLOW

Videl rolled the woman onto her stomach, grabbing her arms and tying them with the handy zip-ties as Valeska stared at her pale face. Valeska had never seen her before. She knew that much. She had dirty blonde hair and bright blue eyes, but she was a little too skinny. Her hollow cheeks would be perfect for a heroin-chic look, and Valeska's index finger guided the hair off her face.

Staring at her felt so... curious.

"Please!" she said, her voice pleading. "I was just lookin' into what was going on! That's all!"

Truth was, they didn't have much to hold her on. She was out during a siren warning, but... by the time they'd seen her, it was off. It was a technical violation at worst.

The real violation was that the woman had pissed Valeska off by making her chase her.

Valeska squat down, elbows on her knees, legs slightly spread, her black shorts riding up between her thighs.

"Why'd you run from me?"

Something about her face just really felt off to Valeska. It was driving her mad as she stared at her up close in the shadows. That pale skin was beautiful, and yet...

"I didn't want any trouble, and when I saw you were soldiers, I panicked," she said, pleading as Videl kept her pinned nice and tight. "Please, I'll do anything, if you just let me go."

"I can think of a thing or two she could do," Videl muttered as he grabbed the back of her head, gripping her hair and keeping her face pointed at Valeska despite the girl's efforts to look away.

"Please, I'll give you money! I'll... I've got some powder. The good stuff, you can have that! Or... or I'll let you two fuck me, whatever you want," she offered insistently.

Videl pushed his watch against her, and it scanned her for an ID tag.

"Name is... Valerie," Videl repeated. "Valerie Delin. Agricultural worker." Valeska looked at him, noticing the curious little tick in his expression.

"Valerie, you need to shut up," Valeska said, her gaze

stuck on Videl. "There's something off about her, isn't there?"

Videl stared at the screen a bit longer, then seemed to snap out of it and look to Valeska.

"Her ID file all seems in order. Born and raised here. There's just something about her. She looks familiar."

And Valeska had to agree. Where did she know her from?

"Cmon. I'll suck your dick, let you fuck me, or... or whatever," Valerie offered again, insistently.

For the first time ever, she got a curious feeling Videl was actually interested in something more than just his straight duty. It made Valeska smile, for just a moment. Despite her momentary fantasy that it was him she was riding the night before, she knew that she'd never fuck him. The politics were a minefield she wasn't interested in navigating, but keeping him happy was a way to keep her loyal. If he was tempted to indulge in some hedonism, she wasn't going to cockblock him.

"Anything you want to hold her for? Or did you want to take her up on any of her offers...?" he asked.

"Something's off about her for both of us, and we're still on alert. She shouldn't be out. Where's her file say she lives?"

Videl looked back at his watch.

"She's staying in a bungalow with other agricultural workers, outside of town. Nothing fancy. She's a Lamb, if ever there was one. It's on the north end of things," Videl said. "Way out of our unit's posting."

"Way the fuck away from here. If you were curious about what was goin' on, why would you head here?" she asked Videl, not expecting an answer. "Put her in the hummer. If she doesn't cause us any more problems, we'll bring her back after we're relieved of duty for the day."

"Aw come on!" Valerie whined as Videl began to get up off her. A good strong yank pulled her up horizontally, then put her down on her feet, and Valeska admired his easy power. "I was just out all-night partying and... and making some extra cash, that's all!"

Valeska stood, sizing Valerie up. She was of petite frame, wearing a tight skirt, thigh high stockings with no shoes, and a tight short-sleeved top over her chest. She was thinner than Valeska, with a petite chest and small hips, but if she was carrying 'powder', there was a good chance that was why she was so slender.

"The correct response to my not turning you in is: 'Thank you, Wolf, for not devouring me even though I know you could,'" Valeska chided her.

"Selling the island's crop on your own is a violation, you know?" Videl said. Though of course, it was well known that everyone who worked in those places did it. It was mostly just a crime to get caught.

"I never said it was the island's stuff. I don't even work with the cocaine," Valerie protested.

"How long have you been on the Isle?" Valeska probed.

"Didn't you listen to your lapdog? All my life!" she protested. Videl gave her a good shove forward, causing her to stumble as they made their way back towards the vehicle.

"I dunno, Over-Lieutenant," Videl remarked. "Maybe we should do more than just hold her a while. She seems to have an attitude problem for a lamb," he said with a tinge of deviousness as they neared the lot where they were parked.

"Valerie, I wanted to hear it from you, because something isn't adding up about you. As he said, you have an attitude problem for a lamb. Especially for a first gen. I had hoped you'd confess that the records were fudged and you're new here, so at least you'd have an excuse for being such a pain in my ass. But as someone born here?"

Valeska shook her head.

If Valerie was one of the first generation, the people who raised her had to have believed in the project. Believed in the Isle's future. Perhaps not in the same way Valeska was raised, but it would have had some similarities.

She ran her hand through her glossy, black hair.

"Maybe you can prove to Videl that you really were born and raised here. Your client went home when the sirens went off?"

"I was partying all night. Drinking, having fun. Selling some blow, getting paid some money to suck dick, it was a good time, that's all," she protested as they got to the vehicle. She definitely looked a little too saucy for a lamb. But that only seemed to heighten that sense Valeska had about her.

"I was sleeping it off in some dude's place down the road when those fucking sirens went off, and I realized I'd be late for work. That's all! I don't have a car or nothin', so I was having to walk back in a hurry."

"You won't get in shit for missing work," Valeska said with a tinge of annoyance. "You'll be escorted back, and told that we held you up on official business. So just... relax."

That seemed to help calm this blonde down a bit, and

she didn't look quite so lippy. But of course, she was still bound and held by the towering Videl.

Valeska knew better than to dismiss her gut feelings, and something was off. She was going to buy enough time to figure it out, at least.

"Oh," Valerie said to Valeska. "I'll still let your boy fuck me in the back seat if you want. Y'know, just to smooth things over. You can help yourself to some blow," she said with a cheeky smile, some charm seeming to come out. "I know how the island works. Like he told you, this is my home."

Videl looked curious, but his interest was undeniably a bit more intense than his curiosity. For once.

"I'm not opposed... if it pleases you, Over-Lieutenant." He was trying to sound so professional, but he couldn't help but betray a slight hint of a smirk. The Eyes hovered around them, but Valeska paid them no mind. If they weren't making work for the higher ups, the Wolves could get away with almost anything.

"After last night, you need to blow off some steam," Valeska agreed, meeting Videl's ruby gaze. "Just don't get too distracted if I need you. And no coke. We're on duty. I'll get a status update from the others."

Videl opened the back door to the hummer, and Valerie casually bent over the back seat, lifting the hem of her skirt.

"No worries, Over-Lieutenant," Videl remarked as he began to work open his black pants. "It wasn't the coke that interested me in the offer. Now. Valerie. Turn around. I don't wanna stare at the back of your head."

CHAPTER 11

PERKS OF THE POSITION

> The one who does what is sinful is of the devil, because the devil has been sinning from the beginning.
>
> — JOHN 3:8

"Fuck, you're one of those needy guys," Valerie muttered as she got up, and then scooted her backside onto the seat. Videl wasted no time pulling her skirt off, tossing it to the ground. "I hope you're not gonna want me to kiss you and go meet your mother too."

Valeska softened at that, an unwitting smile tugging at her lips. She gave the two of them another glance before she walked off towards one of the buildings to give them some privacy.

"Reports, now," she barked into her watch.

The routine reports came in. Every single one was dull and uneventful, and did nothing to hold her attention from the scene playing out not far from her.

She found herself beginning to wander back towards the hummer, and glanced up to catch a glimpse of Videl's manhood. For such a lean man, he had a generously proportioned girth, and a heavy sac to match, all nicely shaped.

"Wasn't anticipating you to be such a big boy," Valerie remarked in that saucy voice of hers, right before Videl helped himself to her. "Ah! Shit, you soldier thugs never volunteer a condom, huh?"

"Do you behave like this with all your clients?" Videl asked, his voice a bit breathy as he began to fuck her on that back seat. But he didn't sound half so annoyed as he was trying to be.

"Ma'am," came in another report on her private line, and Valeska forced herself to walk back away from her Second. "I heard some rumours from a friend up in Z company." Aran was almost forty and had been on the island about ten years. He was a man who definitely seemed to 'get it', unlike so many who showed up, and his intel rarely disappointed. He wasn't going to waste her time with some stupid bullshit, unlike some of the others assigned to her.

There were those so desperate for praise and approval that they'd forward on anything they could get their hands on, in case it panned out.

"What kind of rumours, Aran?"

Valeska turned back towards her Second and his new catch to see Valerie's legs hooked around Videl's waist. It gave her a rather lewd view of the two of them, and the way his thick, veiny shaft pistoned in and out of her. The sound of her moans and his grunts were distracting, and Valeska had do close her eyes to focus on Aran's words.

"Says that he got a lead on something that happened up north-side of the island. That someone came ashore today, about the time of that business above. Says command seems confident they dealt with it, but he saw someone slip away. Knows where they might be hiding out," Aran said.

The entertainment Videl was providing her got better as his pants slipped down, showing off his round, tight ass as he pumped away. He was going at her hard, her moans and intensifying squeals were evidence of that.

"You're a hot one," Videl groaned out as he reached forward to grope Valerie's chest. Valeska's heart began to pound harder, and she had to force her attention back to Aran.

"Up north, right." As far from them as possible. "Where are they looking?"

"Thing is, my buddy is on the outs with his commanding officer. He won't trust what my buddy says, so they're not looking at all. My buddy offered me the information, for a price, of course. Doesn't mean anything to me, though. Not worth breaking ranks over. But if you're interested..."

"If there's a threat and it's ignored, it's all our asses on the line, starting with your friend's officer," Valeska said sternly. "Find out what he wants. If there's an actual lead, it should be investigated. But if your buddy is full of shit, the interest on what I pay him will be expected in full."

"You got it, Ma'am. Will report in as soon as I have more," he said, signing out.

"Fuck, how long are you... you gonna last?" Valerie panted out, groaning. And he grunted.

Videl – for the first time in the many years she'd known him – helped himself to some perks of the position on the job, and Valeska was reaping the spoils.

"You're getting off easy compared to some," he chastised her, his own voice breathy. He was drawing the moment out, holding back his orgasm. Abel could only dream of his level of self control.

Valeska walked back towards them once more, watching the show with a casually growing arousal. Valerie had no idea how lucky she was.

"Got it." It must have been at least twenty minutes, and Aran's voice startled her from her dark little fantasies. "He says there's a little shack up on the north-east corner of the island. Coordinates coming your way. I trust you won't forget me if this pans out, Over-Lieutenant. Paid a nice chunk of my salary for this."

"You know I won't, Aran."

It would give her something to do once Videl finally finished up. She was actually surprised by his stamina. He'd always been such a closed book, a loyal friend and companion. She had no idea he could be so... relentless.

"I'll check it out myself once I finish here. How do you feel about taking over for Videl and I and keep watch at our post?" she asked Aran as she began to make her way back to the hummer.

"Of course, boss," Aran came back, his voice a little self-satisfied. "Anything for you. I'll head right over."

Valeska jumped into the passenger seat of the hummer, slamming the door shut. Sensing it was almost go time, Videl picked up his pace, hammering into that saucy woman harder, faster, as he grabbed her by the breast.

"Fuck, I'm cumming!" she squealed.

Good timing.

Valerie's toes were curled as she came on his dick. She wasn't even faking! That was impressive.

Valeska repositioned the right-hand side mirror so that she was able to watch Videl's final thrusts.

Objects may appear closer than they are and all that.

But Videl caught Valeska's gaze in the mirror, holding onto it a bit too long. It was only when she smiled at him, revealing her fanged teeth, that he shuddered. He tugged his hips back, that bulging girth swelling up before he shoved into Valerie.

And she knew, in that moment, that he was fantasizing about cumming in her.

CHAPTER 12

TOSSED TO THE GRIND

> Every foundation has a crack, and the shadow can penetrate all.
>
> — HOUSE VOID STAR MOTTO

"You never even thought of pulling out, did you, you jackass?" Valerie remarked as she was left gaping, and Videl smeared his slick cock onto her inner thighs.

"Not even for a second," he said, running a hand back over his head as he slipped his uniform cap off for a moment. He didn't waste any time. Duty was calling, and he zipped up his pants, shutting the door as the bound Valerie only slowly pushed in on the seat further.

"What's the deal, Over-Lieutenant?" Videl asked Valeska as he opened the driver seat door and got in, sounding perkier than usual.

She grinned at him, her fangs showing for just a moment, before she glanced ahead.

"We have a lead someone else isn't following up on. I have Aran coming to take over for us. We'll drop your new friend off on the way," Valeska said, her nostrils flaring a little at the scent of sex that was still thick in the air.

Despite being done with the girl, Videl's pants were still looking tight in the crotch, and he shifted a bit in his seat as he adjusted it.

"Yes, Ma'am," he said as he started the vehicle up.

"Hey don't go giving him ideas. He has a great dick and all, but we ain't friends. If he wants another go, he's paying. A gal can only be so generous. Especially when the prick doesn't pull out," Valerie said, kicking the back of Videl's seat.

He rolled his eyes and began to slide the glass divider shut to drown her out.

"You remember where you seen her before?" Valeska asked when they had their privacy back. "She certainly has a mouth on her, not someone I figured I'd forget, but..."

Videl's brows furrowed as he looked off, thinking. But then he shook his head.

"No idea. I thought she looked really familiar. I mean, still do, but... in a vague way. I never felt seriously tempted to do that kinda thing before. Hope you don't mind, Ma'am," he said as he pulled out of the parking lot and onto the winding road. They were overlooking the cliffs as he started in a round-about way northwards.

"Of course not. I'm just glad you're finally getting into things here. Like I said last night. Fitting in is more than just doing your job well," she said, giving him a lingering smile. "Besides, you saved her from my wrath at being forced to run for no good reason."

Videl gave a light laugh at that as he drove along, moving a bit more speedily than usual. He really did seem to have loosened up.

"I wasn't really concerned with saving her from much of anything, to be honest. She was just more appealing than the women I was used to seeing in the brothels," he confessed. "So where are we going after we dump her off? If it's okay to ask," he tacked on that last part, worried he'd gotten too informal with her.

"It might be nothing, but they caught someone up north, and someone says they saw another suspect escape. We have the coordinates." Valeska paused, licking her lips a little. Her heart was still racing with excitement from the free show she'd gotten, and she hoped he couldn't tell.

"And Videl... I know you respect me. I'm glad you were assigned to my unit. It's fine to not be so uptight when we're alone. Unless I tell you that I want you uptight. Then you best obey," she teased.

A flash of surprise tore his gaze from the road for a split second, and Valeska wondered if she wasn't getting too soft with him. It was true, but... she shouldn't indulge in such childish fantasies of trust and friendship.

He pulled off that main road and they began to drive past farmlands, and the neatly arrayed rows of sheltered hydroponics gardens. They were all pumping out the cash crops that kept the island not only alive, but thriving. Off in the distance, at the very back of it all, were some rather rundown bungalows that were almost shack-like.

"I'm glad I was assigned to your unit too," he confessed

after some time. "I know what some of the other officers are like," he said, squinting a bit as he peered out his side window for a moment. "And I know I'm fortunate. In more ways than one."

"I guess we're both a bit reserved in our own way, huh?" she mulled over thoughtfully. "Or maybe you just figured fair is fair after last night?"

His gaze snapped back to her.

"Wait, are you saying you fucked that guy?" he asked.

She let out a laugh, her devilishly red eyes twinkling in amusement.

"No, but the fact that you knew I didn't is a real buzzkill. Driving us around the long way, and still you didn't think I was having fun," she teased.

Videl pulled up in front of one of the bungalows, and the muffled voice of Valerie in back – utterly unintelligible – rose up. Valeska gave Videl one last lingering stare before turning around and opening up the back window.

"What is it?"

"This is my stop," she said, and Valeska rolled her eyes.

"We know," Valeska replied as Videl walked out to the back door, grabbing Valerie and tugging her out of the vehicle. She'd managed to put her skirt back on, even with her arms bound. Valeska was almost impressed as one of the supervisors of the farms came over to cut her free.

Despite her strange suspicions around the woman... everything checked out. Yeah, she definitely worked there. Yeah, the supervisor knew her. She'd been there for ages, before him even, as he was an immigrant, like most islanders were.

"Alright, thanks a lot for the great fuckin' time," Valerie

said with a roll of her eyes. "Gonna get my pay docked because of you two, I just know it," she said, shooting a glare at her supervisor as she rubbed her wrists.

"You're welcome, Valerie," Valeska said, her voice a bit cool.

She really had a feeling about her, and so rarely were they wrong. She chalked it up to the strangeness of the last day, and the lack of sleep. It was making her jumpy.

But for all her sass, Valerie did give Videl a lingering sort of look before she headed off, straight to work, ushered by her supervisor.

"Yeah yeah, I know," she could be heard in the distance, as Videl watched her backside.

"Strange fucking day," Videl remarked, hand on his hip as he looked at Valeska. "Shall we get going then? Or were you still suspicious and wanting to look around?"

"I mean, I'm suspicious, but I think I'm barking at shadows by this point," she admitted. "She really doesn't fit in down here. She doesn't seem conditioned for it. But..." Valeska shrugged her shoulders as she went back to the vehicle. "Maybe she just acts a little too much like me."

At that remark, Videl froze for a moment. Valeska raised her brow, but Videl broke out of it, and they both got back into the vehicle, preparing for their next investigation.

Valeska stared at him as he drove.

"You have something on your mind," Valeska said with a frown, scrutinizing him with her ruby gaze. The rows of fields and hydroponics farms passed them by, glittering glass reflecting the sun brightly as it broke through the clouds.

"It's not like it's weird to fuck me by proxy. I just didn't think that people were raised like that down here. Figured they'd want the kids more obedient or less lippy or something."

He was clearly surprised by what she said, but he slowly relaxed.

"Yeah, she did remind me a bit of you in how she acted. And..."

He hesitated again, glancing into the rear-view mirror, then to her. Then ahead. There was something he wanted to say, but he was clearly worried about upsetting her as they got back onto the main road.

"Come on, Videl," Valeska sighed. "Just spit it out. It'll be less awkward for both of us."

He cleared his throat. It was very uncharacteristic of him. She wasn't used to seeing him squirm. Ever. He even glanced nervously towards the recording Eye.

"Her hair and makeup were all wrong, obviously," he said firmly. "Too much blow keeping her a bit sickly thin, and her eyes..." He was meandering to the point, but he got to it before she could nudge him again.

"You're right. She reminded me of you. How she looked. Reminded me a lot, if I'm being honest."

Valeska made a bit of a face, looking out the window as they drove.

"What, like, you think she's my sister or something?"

He glanced at her out of the corner of his eyes, seemingly gauging her mood.

"It hadn't occurred to me at the time, but... now that you say it. That would make some sense," he said. "Her files did say she's been here all her life. And there aren't a whole lot of you like that."

"Yea," Valeska muttered, her brow furrowed as she

turned that over in her head. "Well, not like I know who my parents are. So, I guess..."

Why was she selected for House Void Star while Valerie was tossed to the grind? She would have only been a baby when her training started, so was it just pure luck? She didn't have any answers, and she shook it off.

Something to worry about later.

"So, you have the hots for me, huh?" she teased, trying to lighten the mood, but it caused him to stiffen in his seat, his shoulders tense.

"If it bothers you, I'll make sure it never comes up again. Even in passing. My duty, to the service, to you, will come first. Always," he said, trying to sound his usual, formal self. The old all-business, loyal Videl. Under-Lieutenant. Her second in command.

But he wasn't quite pulling it off perfectly.

"It doesn't bother me," she admitted. It actually made her stomach twist in an unfamiliar way. It didn't feel bad, really. "I actually think it's kind of flattering. First girl we see that reminds you of me and you can't help but jump her. But you knew better than to be a dog with me."

He seemed to ponder her words for a moment as they wound their way up the coast, the looming mountain at the centre of the island casting its shadow upon them now.

"As much like you as she might've looked and seemed on the outside, she was not you. I would never treat you like some kind of... omega bitch, to use and discard. You're the Alpha Wolf of our pack," he said, carefully tackling a topic that was clearly on his mind for a long time, but had been kept tightly concealed.

Valeska laughed at that, a genuine, pleased sound.

"A man's allowed his fantasies," she teased, her red eyes upon him, a smile tugging her lips. "You always just seemed so... focused."

"Don't mistake my reluctance as weakness, Over-Lieutenant," he said casually. "Were you any lesser than you are, I would have made a move long ago. But I know who you are. You embody the heart and soul of this island. You are going far. And I want to be there with you as you rise to the top," he explained. "If I let on that I was drawn to you, well..." he wet his lips, as they drove past a patch of dark, wilted looking trees on both sides, the cliffs out of view. "You might take that as a sign of weakness in me. To exploit or use. Or simply to discard. A woman like you deserves a real man, not a simpering pussy."

She let out a huff of amusement.

"I'm glad you're playing the game and doing it well. You've shown me who you are, and today only..." she paused, gathering her thoughts. "I enjoyed the show," she finally settled upon. It was strange; she'd worked with Videl for so long, and only now caught a glimpse at what motivated him. Beyond his ambitions to rise through the ranks, that is. It suddenly made sense why he was so disinterested in most of the pleasures and joys of the job; they were just pathetic substitutes for what he really wanted.

Her.

There was silence for a while until finally he said, "Thank you, Ma'am."

The tiniest hint of a smile touched his serious, stoic face.

It didn't last long.

The dark forest swallowed them, and the GPS tracking

system beckoned them in deeper, onto a nigh invisible path, hidden from everything. The light of day was snuffed out in the gloom of the dense woods, the clouds overhead having grown thick and foreboding.

They ditched the hummer, the forest too thick to drive through, and slung their guns over their shoulders. The unnatural gloom was like walking into Satan's embrace, and for the first time since Aran gave her the intel, she believed that they were on the right trail.

This forest was sacred.

Somehow.

CHAPTER 13

SACRILEGIOUS SECRETS

All the stars of heaven will be dissolved. The skies will be rolled up like a scroll, and all their stars will fall like withered leaves from the vine, like foliage from the fig tree.

— ISAIAH 34:4

"Strange fucking place for an infiltrator to get to though."

"To find out about it in the first place…" she murmured. It couldn't be a random attack. If there was a safe house in these woods, no outsider could have hoped to know about it.

"You lead, I'll follow where you step. It'll let me keep an eye ahead of us."

"Yes, Ma'am."

The sleek, black build of Videl's AK-470 seemed to

vanish into the shadows as he took the lead.

They trekked in silence, and after some time, she caught sight of an old building through the thick copse of trees. It was built in the original 'futuristic' style of the first Satanists to arrive on the island, and now had a sort of strange ominousness to it. The dark colour, the sharp angles. It was worn, but still beautiful in its own, sinister kind of way.

Valeska pointed it out, and they found their way towards it until they stood before an old gate, overgrown. The roots had taken hold, and the sliding gate doors had rusted in place, open. It stood like an ominous invitation as darkness competed in the sky with the orange and purple flares of sunset.

Their destination was just a short jaunt up the tiered walkway, perhaps another sixty yards or so. But the house itself was lost in the dark gloom of the mountain behind it, the orange light glaring round that ominous peak.

She didn't risk talking, or making any noise. The darkness would make it harder to communicate with Videl, but they had worked together long enough that she was able to draw his attention, motioning towards a small shed or garage that stood separate from the main house.

Videl nodded in silence.

They had lights, but using them would give them away to anyone on guard. The night vision in their contacts were useless; the sunset glaring around the mountain would only blind them both.

So on into the twilight they went, with Videl going to the garage first. He came to its door and pressed his back against the wall. He looked to Valeska, then did a three second countdown with his fingers before opening the door.

They both had their guns up, but it was just pitch-black inside. Videl turned on his night vision, leading the way inside with careful, silent footsteps.

A chill ran down her spine as she followed Videl in. There was no doubt in her mind. She was trespassing on unholy ground.

Excitement filled her. She'd not found a place like this in... ever. A relic of the original settlers! She knew so much about them, including how paranoid they were, and how much they loved their secret tunnels. She hoped that there was a hidden way into the main building, and she could get the drop on this mysterious spy.

The pitch-black darkness came to life in a red haze as she turned on her night vision, and she began to take in her surroundings.

A car was still sitting in the garage, abandoned for who knows how long. On the walls there were many shelves, containers, and some large drums that must contained a liquid of some sort. An old deep freeze. A fridge. So many strange oddities fit for a garage.

The floor was littered with crunchy refuse, likely drawn in by wildlife over the years since it was abandoned.

Videl checked around the place, circling the car, before giving her an all-clear sign.

She had been taught patience in excruciating trials and tests while she was training to become what she was. But still, that fiery temper did burn bright in her, and she let out a silent huff of displeasure.

She wanted to succeed. To find the enemy that had

thrown off her entire day, and return to the estate triumphant, with a few more secrets lingering in the back of her mind.

So, she bottled up the annoyance, and began to look around more thoroughly.

The night vision helped a lot, but it made it difficult to discern subtle differences in the dark garage. As she walked around for her closer inspection, she felt the floor being a bit... off at one point. When she tapped her foot there again, she realized it was a trap door of some kind.

Getting down, she brushed away some of the detritus, and found a hidden little handle. She tried to lift it, but it was once automated, and the metal was too heavy on her own.

She ushered over Videl, and the taller man helped her lift the hatch up, letting out the strange, stale scent that had been trapped there for a decade.

Together they gazed down into black stairway that led into the dark earth below.

She motioned that she'd go first, and that he'd follow behind her once she was down. There was a risk that someone might come behind them and lock them in, but then, there were always going to be risks, and she felt safer with him close by. Especially if there were any more heavy doors that she couldn't manage on her own.

Down the stairs she went, and as she got into that tunnel, she saw it headed towards the house. But it was quite long, and night vision only let her see so far.

On she went, and soon after Videl came after her, keeping an eye behind them.

Deeper and deeper she went, until she felt like she

must've passed the house off.

She looked behind her, considering if they should turn back, but she forged on ahead. She needed to know where the tunnel ended.

Finally, their way was blocked by an automated metal door that looked like it slid to the side. But without electricity, it was stuck in place.

At least, too stuck for her strength alone.

She shifted to the side, letting Videl pass her off as she readied her gun, just in case. The coolness of the tunnel was making her pale skin prickle beneath her fishnets, and she was starting to wish she'd dressed in something a bit less revealing. Above ground was one thing, even at night, given the volcanic warmth, but under the dirt was a bit chilly.

Videl put his gun at his back, and braced himself against the door. He gave it a couple tries, unsure of which way the door usually slid. But finally, after pushing on that metal a while, he found an emergency manual release lever embedded next to it, pulled that and the door hissed open, and a flood of old, warm, stale air flooded out, to chase away the chills.

But it brought with it an upsetting feeling.

Like they were opening a forgotten tomb.

Videl took his gun back out and they entered into a room unlike any she'd ever seen before.

It was like an underground bunker and shrine in one.

Valeska smiled with excitement upon entering the holy room, but as her dark vision scanned over the carved stones, her blood turned to ice.

It wasn't Satan staring down at her; not the Devil, or any of his Demons Fallen Angels.

It was dark, and otherworldly. It overlooked the room, with its many kneeling pads and adornments, the countless other smaller statues and paintings on the wall, as if it were a grand King or Preacher overseeing its subjects.

"What the fuck?" Videl silently mouthed at her, and she had to admit she was having the same thought.

It didn't feel right.

A small part of her wanted to call it in, let someone else deal with it while she ran back to the comfort of her home. It was the sliver of youthful fear they'd never quite been able to beat out of her.

She moved a little closer to Videl without realizing it, and only when her arm brushed against his did, she seem to realize her weakness.

Her back stiffened, and she nodded towards one of the four doors that led out of the room. It was an arbitrary choice, just something to try to regain her sense of control.

He looked to that door ahead, then nodded to her. Silently he led the way for her, without hesitation.

This door was more of a traditional sort, and it opened much easier. Within she found what appeared to be living quarters. There was an old screen on one wall, several sofas. A little kitchenette to one side. Then beyond that was a long room, full of bunks. The musty smell of human living, long abandoned and uncleaned, filled their senses.

Was this how the first residents of Satanos lived? Packed in a hidden bunker afraid of mainland retribution? It paled in comparison to how they lived now, with their lavish riches and luxuries. But why had she never been taught of the visages that guided the original settlers?

Videl went up to the dark entrance to that room full of

bunkbeds, gun at the ready, using the tip to nudge a pillow out of the way. As they entered, it became clear that when this place was abandoned, it was abandoned in a hurry.

It didn't make a lot of sense, she thought. Why it was abandoned? What the shrines were for?

Why they weren't to any Satanic figure she knew of?

She took a brief look around, but as much as her curiosity was mounting, she was looking for someone. They returned back to the main chamber, and her gaze was drawn to the two doors that were on either side of the statue. They weren't normal doors, not like the one to the sleeping quarters. And they weren't like the heavy, sliding metal doors that blocked out the outside world.

They were smooth, and felt cold, like polished stone. Strange symbols and signs were carved into them, and she ran her fingertips over them in confusion. She didn't recognize any of them... except for one.

Her blood rushed through her, and her hand began to tremble as she traced along the edge of the Void Star symbol at the centre of the door. It was surrounded by so many other strange etchings of unknown make. It looked at once both out of place, and yet... very much where it belonged.

Videl reached out, and their hands nearly touched before he caught himself.

"Sorry, Over-Lieutenant," he said as he cleared his throat. He turned away, and the back of his hand brushed against a carved portion of the door that looked like a tendril. The lightest of touches, yet that lever was over-excited after standing so long untouched.

The door hissed open.

The ancient seal had been broken.

CHAPTER 14

ROLL FOR SANITY LOSS

Then desire when it has conceived gives birth to sin,
and sin when it is fully grown brings forth death.

— JAMES 1:15

An odious smell of something quite old and wrong assaulted their senses.

Valeska couldn't hide her gaze quick enough. The hideous, amorphous creature that was depicted in the statue beside her was both reminiscent of what she witnessed, and nothing at all enough to prepare her.

All around the room lay the strangely mummified bodies of a whole coven of worshippers, their bodies contorted and twisted in strange, perverse and agonizing poses.

At the very head of the room, their bodies were all entangled together as if they'd all died suddenly in some blood orgy. Trapped in eternal coitus, with twisted expressions on their desiccated faces that spoke of a mix of pleasure and pain.

Valeska stared in abject horror.

She had been born on Satanos, had attended her own coming-of-age orgy, and taken part in blood rites that would sicken most mainlanders. The pain she casually inflicted, the spells she cast, they were like child's play compared to the scene before her.

She couldn't tear her eyes away, and her gaze drifted to the far wall. A lump rose in her throat as she saw, in a rounded, hollowed out nook, the mutilated, mangled amalgamation of many bodies. Human flesh trapped together in the form of a creature that was not simply unholy, but unearthly.

Satan himself in none of his forms could have envisioned such an abomination, with its gaping maw made of human flesh, its teeth formed from jagged bones.

And its eyes… hollow, dead eyes, a hundred of them or more.

And all of them were fashioned from the melted, molded remains of human eyes.

It stopped her dead in her tracks, and the cold chill that entered her bones was that of pure terror.

She was confronted with something more hideous than she could have ever imagined, and even the scream was stolen from her as she stared.

It felt like time stopped, or hours passed all at once, with her frozen in place. She couldn't even contemplate what she was seeing, it struck her as so beyond mortal understanding.

And the longer she stared, the more of its horror became known to her. New, hideous details, like how human entrails had been used to craft some of the tendrils. Like how six women's lower halves were positioned at its base, each spread open, their bodies showing the bloody remains of placenta and umbilical cords, as if they'd given birth while a part of this... monstrosity.

She was so lost to it that it took Videl gripping her shoulder and breaking the silence to stir her from it.

"Valeska?" he said, his voice low.

How long had he been trying to get her attention, that he used her actual name? How many 'ma'am's' or 'Over-Lieutenants' had he uttered?

"Wh... what was this place?" she asked him, and in that moment, she couldn't hide the tremble of her voice. She was barely into her twenties, but she never acted like it. Never gave into the luxury of weakness.

Not until then.

She could see Videl's face contort with surprise.

"I had been hoping you knew," he said, before looking back into the room with a stoic, stony face that only betrayed the slightest of cringes. He shook it off and returned his gaze to hers.

"It's like some... some awful ritual was done here. Or just a bloody murder," he said, as the old, stale stench of death grew and he covered his mouth.

"They're... all..." she muttered, taking a step backwards. "I don't think we're meant to see this."

Videl's hand had not left her shoulder, and he helped guide her away from that door as he nodded to her words.

"Some secrets are too dangerous to possess," he

remarked, his usual self. It was a comfort to her, and she leaned on him for a moment as she fought back the urge to vomit.

"What do we do now? Give up and leave?" he asked her quietly. "It doesn't seem like a coincidence someone would make a landing on the island, and come here of all places..."

"No, it doesn't. To know where this place is... Whoever it was, they're dangerous. More dangerous than I figured," she muttered, still in shock. "We need to find them, Videl. We need to bring them back to the House. This place... it used to belong to us. If someone knows it's here, they must have been of Void Star."

It was something they both knew, but to hear her say it so plainly shocked him.

"Are you sure we won't be punished for uncovering this? Or rather... silenced."

They'd found a secret. A real secret. The kind that her House would kill to protect, and he was removed enough to see the situation more clearly. Her loyalty to Void Star was blinding her.

"You stayed outside to guard me. You were never here. Any repercussion is mine," she said, eagerly turning away from the statue and the horrors within.

She had always been drawn to secrets, to knowledge. It was a source of her power and strength, how she'd risen so readily in the Void Star.

But this secret threatened to unravel her mind if she lingered too long upon it.

"The door on either side of the statue leads into that... that nightmare. So, I guess it just leaves the last one. There," he remarked, gesturing to the other metal sliding door, like the one they took to get in.

"We finish our investigation," Valeska said with more bark than she intended. She was overcompensating for her fear, and though Videl's lips parted as if to argue, he nodded.

"I'll get the door," he said, heading to it, popping that manual override.

As the door groaned open, Videl cursed in surprise, reaching for his gun.

A thud of a body rolling down the stairs made Valeska jump, and she had her gun trained at the body of a man. His head just narrowly avoided hitting the floor, and he braced his gaunt body against the floor. He was alive.

"Who are you?" Valeska's voice was trembling, because she knew the answer before she even asked.

His long hair framed his thin face, his skin wrinkled and weathered. He was dressed in a dark survival suit of military issue. It was a black thing, water sealed, air tight, with pouches and things.

And even though she was seeing him in her night vision, and he looked so unhealthy, she recognized him immediately.

But it wasn't him. Not really. He was an imitation of the closest thing to a father she ever had.

The Magister.

His eyes widened in recognition as he forced his head up to stare at her.

"You..." he said, in a wheezing, older voice.

His body collapsed back to the cold floor at the foot of the stairs, limp.

"Shit. Fuck. Fuck!" cursed Valeska, kneeling down next to the man.

She shifted his body, knowing enough first aid to check for his breathing. But as she did, she talked to Videl, "I don't think this is the guy we're looking for. I doubt he could have outrun anyone, let alone our best. Sweep upstairs, this might be a hideout for rebels."

Videl nodded, and headed on up the tunnel into what she presumed was the manor above.

She was left with the old man, and while he had a pulse, it was not terribly strong. He was alive, just unconscious. She stared at him, her body rocking with uncharacteristic fear.

She had recognized him instantly. His features were emblazoned in her mind even more so than her own. It had taken her so long to piece together how familiar Valerie looked and why, but with him, there was never a doubt that he was the Magister's...

Father, she presumed, given the age. She studied him intently for some time, and when the almost sizzling, crackling sound of the automatic AK-470 rail-gun fired off upstairs, her entire body jolted.

"Calm down," she chided herself, readying her gun towards the stairs. Rushing into a gunfight would be a good way to take some friendly fire, since he wasn't expecting her. She trusted Videl, and his capacity to handle the situation.

The silence that came in the wake of fire was almost as loud, the drumming of her heart a steady rhythm in her head.

Her finger tightened on the trigger as a dark figure began to descend the stairs, and she very nearly squeezed it before identifying who it was. Only then did she realize just how jumpy she was with fear.

"I swept the house up there. One man, he was already suffering from some injury. But I shot him on reflex and ended him," Videl explained, and Valeska's shoulders relaxed. "He's dead now. I imagine he must've helped this old guy get here."

"We need to get him back to the House. I think he fainted but... he looks a lot like..." she trailed off, looking at Videl, not wanting to say the words.

Videl pursed his lips tightly and nodded. He knew what she meant, but didn't want to say it either.

"I can carry him. I'll just search him for any weapons first," he said, kneeling down, patting the man's survival suit down. He took away a ceremonial dagger, and a small, light handgun. There were also a few odd little pouches of smelly herbs or spices that he took as a precaution.

Videl lifted him up, ready to carry him through the tunnel back to their vehicle.

"I'll join you in a moment," Valeska said, and she moved towards the stairs.

If she was going to cover for Videl about what happened here, she needed to know where the man was shot.

It didn't take long to go up into that drafty old house, where the windows had been smashed out and the air and leaves flowed straight through. It took even less time to search its big, open rooms, and to find the slumped, wide-eyed body of the man in an identical survival suit.

He had several holes through him, singed from Videl's AK-470. An older wound was patched up with makeshift bandages that were stained with a great deal of blood from his side. He must've been bleeding out while bringing the old man there.

She searched him, found his rifle – some American thing she was unfamiliar with – just out of reach, as if it'd been propped up against the wall beside him, but then tipped over. On his person, she found nothing remarkable, just some standard tools for fighting and survival. Some ration packs. That was it.

Leaving out the front door this time, cautiously avoiding a tripwire trap there, she caught up to Videl on the path back to the vehicle. Night had fully fallen. Her night vision helped her avoid the branches and rocks on the walk back, and she barely even noticed the cold as it prickled her bare skin.

The hummer was a welcome sight, and they eagerly got inside, sealing the unconscious old man into the rear seat.

It wasn't until they were on the road, that he finally asked what they were both thinking.

"What do we do now?"

CHAPTER 15

DO YOUR WORST

The most merciful thing in the world, I think, is the inability of the human mind to correlate all its contents. We live on a placid island of ignorance in the midst of black seas of the infinity, and it was not meant that we should voyage far.

— H. P. LOVECRAFT; THE CALL OF CTHULHU

Valeska didn't answer right away, her ruby gaze staring ahead at the rough, forest road.

"Over-Lieutenant? Should I head back to the House? Or did you want to wait for him to wake up and question him?"

He was so good at controlling his emotions, but she could tell that he was dreading her answer.

"I don't want to know any more about that place than I

already do. But once we turn him over, that's it," she said softly. "Do you think it's his father? That maybe he helped make this place?"

Videl drove along in thoughtful silence for a moment before answering.

"That would make the most sense. But if it's true, and this is how he comes back... I don't imagine it's gonna be a welcome coming home."

"No. But..." she said, not wanting to say it, but forcing herself to look at Videl. "He seemed to recognize me."

Videl's eyes darted to her, then back to the dark, shrouded road.

"Yeah," Videl said after a long pause. "Yeah, he did."

"Do... I guess he knows my mother? That I look like her? Or, fuck, maybe there's a dozen more Valeries out there, and he got me confused with one of my siblings?"

The possibilities...

"Maybe. There's... I don't know. But that's two weird fucking coincidences in one day. And one too many for me," he remarked, gripping the steering wheel. "You're right, of course. When we hand him over, that's it. You'll never see him again. Never hear of him again. He'll be erased."

Videl was a slave to his duty normally. Today was the first time she'd seen him be anything but by-the-book. And yet...

"It's a big risk taking him captive," Videl cautioned. "Especially if Aran tells anyone that you were there, and you don't hand the old guy over."

"We'll hand him over. But this is my mission, and one that the other commander turned down. I have a right to question the suspect," she said firmly. She respected his opinion, his thoughts about the issue, but she knew the only way to keep his nose clean was to put her foot down. If she was digging a grave, she was only digging her own.

"Do we still have those smelling salts in the back?"

Videl nodded, and sighted a clear spot on the side of the road where he pulled over, the black hummer almost disappearing into the small cluster of trees.

"You want me with you, or to stay watch in case anyone noses in?"

"The less you know, the better," she said, paraphrasing what the Magister had told her the night before. She reached over, patting Videl's thigh, and have him a long look. "I know I owe you for keeping these secrets. You've been a good partner. I won't forget that."

He had been looking gloomily serious since they discovered that gruesome scene in the basement, but her touch and reassurance let some of the tension in his body melt.

"I'll keep your secrets. That is not in doubt," he said to her. "And I won't even expect that much in return," he said with grim seriousness before cracking a slight little grin at her. She squeezed his powerful thigh as she grinned back.

"Asshole," she teased, releasing his leg.

"I'll get up in the turret while you handle things."

She went to the back, opening it up and finding the emergency first aid kit they kept fastened to the side of the vehicle. She brought the kit with her as she entered the backseat, towards the old man's head.

She lifted him up so that she could fit in and close the door, keeping them locked together in the utilitarian, but roomy, back of the hummer. It was designed to hold multiple people, after all.

Opening the first aid kit, she found the smelling salts, and steeled her resolve.

She had to know.

The old man startled awake as she put them beneath his nose. And then his hand went reflexively for where he'd stashed that dagger.

He wasn't as old and harmless as he appeared, she could easily tell by that one moment.

He quickly realized he was disarmed though, and looked to her in that lit back area.

"It *is* you," he said, swallowing. That face, so striking, so familiar. It didn't have the same power and authority that radiated from the Magister, but... that was what age did to a man.

"We've never met before tonight," Valeska said, her pale skin glowing a little in the dim light of the moon. "I'm assuming you knew my mother."

The wry grin that crossed his face erased her last doubts about his helpless, feeble nature. Behind those dark, cunning eyes lurked a mind no different from the Magister's. That was the immediate sense she got from that expression on his old, rictus face.

"Oh. That much is true too," he said as he sat up, regaining his composure. He looked around the back of the vehicle. "So, you still don't know what to do with me, is that it?"

"No, it's not that. It's the fact that before I turn you over, I want to know why I'm turning you over. Why you are here. What that place was. Who was helping you. You get the picture. I want answers, and I doubt you're going to readily give them to me, so I thought we'd take some time to chat."

He laughed at that, a condescending kind of laugh. But he didn't lose his grin.

"No, you don't understand at all then," he mused, wetting his lips as he eyed her. Despite his age and condition, she could tell it wasn't an innocent sort of gesture. "Did you really think I would tell you the answers to those things without something in return? Hm?" he asked her, reaching a hand out to grip her thigh, much as she'd gripped Videl's, and she fought the urge to flinch away from him. It was hardly the first time she had to grin and bear it in the face of an older man, and she'd learned to control her response to not give them what they were after.

"Look. I can tell you those things, and *so* much more. I could tell you who you really are. Why you are here. Who your true family is," he said, his teeth showing in a grin. "But not while you can still take me to your superiors..."

"I know who I am and why I'm here," she said firmly. "I want to know why you came here. Why you came back."

"Why did you come back? To that place, girl," he shot back at her, a glint in his dark eyes. "Just to find me? A shame. I don't imagine your... Magister," he said the word with distaste on his tongue, "ordered you to. No. He wouldn't do that to you. Far too risky," he said with a crooked smile. "Even without my answers, you might learn a dangerous thing or two. Operative word being... might."

"You have me confused for someone else," Valeska said through gritted teeth. "I was never in that place before. I'm trying to play nice but you're really making me rethink that strategy."

He squeezed her thigh, his fingers caressing that fishnet covered flesh of hers as he laughed.

"Oh, are you going to beat me? Cut me?" he scoffed at that. "Have at it. I am so old and used to pain, you will probably kill me before I truly feel it," he said with such conviction. "And then your superiors will know you were torturing me for answers too. My, my, what a pickle," he said, as if playing games with her. "No. Do your worst if you wish, V. I'm not sure which one you are," he mused, sizing her up. "Do you dye your hair black? Never mind. If you decide you want to know who you really are, who made you, then you can take me somewhere... secluded. Some-where Void Star won't find me."

Her ruby eyes narrowed at him, and her scowl deepened.

"How many siblings do I have?" she snarled, already getting used to the fact that he'd answer in riddles, and only bring more questions to the surface.

He stared at her, wetting his lips once more before sealing them. He was clearly not going to talk any further, and he signalled this by giving her a pat on the knee and withdrawing his hand.

"I killed your guy after you fainted," she said, crossing her legs away from him, her arms folded beneath her breasts. "Looks like he took a shot for you, trying to save you, and died anyway, because of you."

Nothing of what she'd just said bothered the man in the slightest. Not the least crack in his facade as he sat there, hands on his knees, staring off. But after a moment, he began to mutter to himself.

"Ah, the V's. Such a lovely accomplishment," he said with a sigh. "Lovely little Veronica, with her orange hair. Sweet Vivian, how I adored her. Valerie and her blonde locks... Such a lovely rainbow of colours you were, oh my... What were the other's named?" he muttered, reaching up to stroke his chin.

She would have accused him of making it all up if it weren't for Valerie.

If it weren't for earlier that day.

The strange woman that reminded her of herself, but different. Changed.

That desperation to know was rampaging within her, and she knew that the information would die with him. No one else would admit to even knowing what he was talking about. The ramblings of a spy. A traitor.

She leaned back in the seat, staring at the driver's head-rest as she mulled it all over.

"What do you want for the solution to your riddles?"

His grin was replaced with a simple smile.

"My dear child," he said, so eerily warm. "I want what any man of my advanced age wants... Some quiet, final moments, surrounded by loved ones," he said with a glint in his eyes. "But, to answer it without a riddle, I want you to hide me for now. Take me somewhere safe. Somewhere the House won't be watching. I need to rest for now. It's been a rough journey getting here for a man of my age, you understand. But, after a couple days to recuperate... I can give you your answers."

"That sounds like a monumental level of bullshit," she

hissed. "And I doubt you came here for a peaceful death. You came here for revenge. Why else would you make the trip at your advanced age?" she asked mockingly, her glare hard upon him. "Why would you need strength to see the Magister other than to preserve yourself from humiliation before your defeat?"

"Oh, V, V..."

His eyes lit up.

"Valeska."

A chill went through her again, and she fought the urge to slug him in the face.

How *dare* he know her name.

"I need a couple days to recuperate, so I can give you your answers. After that, I just hope you'll be feeling... magnanimous enough to not turn me over. You can do that for your dear old..."

She stared at him, waiting for him to continue, until her watch buzzed and flashed, stealing her attention away.

A command level alert came through.

"EMERGENCY ENDED. NORMAL SHIFTS RESUME. YOU ARE OFF DUTY. ASSIGN USUAL DUTY ROLLS."

"Wish I left you knocked out," she hissed, pushing open the door and slamming it shut behind her, making sure the vehicle was locked as she made her way to Videl.

Her head was spinning, and her legs were uncharacteristically trembling as she reached him, her arms folded beneath her chest. A petulant pout twisted her lips, and her black hair shrouded her face as she looked up to her Second.

The recording devices were always active. It had become so second nature; she hadn't even given it much thought.

At least, not until the moment she suddenly wanted to keep a secret for herself.

"The suspect is being uncooperative. I need more time with him, somewhere we won't be interrupted," Valeska said sternly.

Videl released the machine gun, and looked down to her. His red eyes locked with hers, as the understanding went unspoken.

She was choosing to do something very dangerous.

And she was making him an accomplice.

CHAPTER 16

BLACKMAIL, BUT MAKE IT SEXY

Heathen, n. A benighted creature who has the folly to worship something he can see and feel.

— AMBROSE BIERCE; THE UNABRIDGED
DEVIL'S DICTIONARY

"Do you have a place in mind?" he asked after that pregnant pause. "The house we came from seemed pretty abandoned. But... Aran at least knows of it, and his friend. It'd be a risk if they shared it with anyone else."

Valeska had no desire to go back to that unholy place. Whatever faith the founders had, it wasn't the one she knew, and the sight there would forever haunt her.

"The place we found Cole. It wouldn't be strange for us to go back there after our shift. I'm sure I can request the private room for a few days," she said, not giving more information than she needed to.

"Okay," Videl said, going along with her request, before he sunk down into the hummer again, then popped open her passenger seat for her.

"I trust you'll know how to repay me, Ma'am." He was blackmailing her with such casual ease, it was enough to make her proud of his acclimation to the island.

A smirk teased the corner of her lips.

"I have some ideas, Under-Lieutenant."

She slid back into the seat, resting into it and letting out a sigh.

"It's gonna be a long night. Should have taken Valerie up on her offer."

Videl arched a brow at her, then grinned a bit as he pulled them back out onto the road.

"What makes you think I hadn't been planning to before this night took a turn for the perverse?" he asked, smirking a bit.

"I meant about the blow," Valeska said, a grin coming to her lips before quickly being replaced by the puzzled stare into the dark road ahead. It was gonna be a long drive; the location they were headed to was on the exact opposite side of the island. It would give her time to think, which was both a blessing, and a very real curse.

"He said there's others. He knew Valerie's name. My name."

"This isn't just any infiltrator. Not that it wasn't apparent the moment we saw the old crone," he remarked as he took them out of the dark forest, and down a more rural road, away from the city. "There's something else,

Over-Lieutenant. She has the same birthday as you. I checked her file again while you were interrogating the suspect."

A chill ran through her, and her mind seemed to shut down the implication of that.

The implication of the monstrosity she'd witnessed.

The six lower remains of women, splayed in birthing position.

She'd spent her entire life on the Isle of Satanos, a loyal follower of Satan and House Void Star. She'd never contemplated the circumstances of her birth, or who her parents were. It didn't seem to matter, when she was constantly surrounded by adults who all had a hand in raising her, in molding her into the perfect citizen.

"Don't access the other files. Not yet. We don't want to poke around where we're not wanted."

"Smart," he said to her, as they cut through the black of night along that quiet road. The only light was the occasional private home or plantation. Beautiful orchards or hedges now and then were separated by big swathes of open land, rocky crags, or trees. "Are we still on high alert? If not, we should re-order the troops, get them back on a more normal schedule. We can't all be working 24/7."

"Fuck," she cursed. She'd completely forgotten. Their captive had rattled her deeper than she expected, and she quickly made contact with her unit, organizing them into their usual duty routines.

She tapped on her watch some more after that, realizing she now had the drone footage to contend with. She fired up the projection before her, going back to the geostamp of them parking outside the secluded house.

But she noticed a curious thing just as they were getting to the gate. The camera feed didn't shut off, it just... suddenly got blurry, then fuzzy. Nothing could be made out. It was as if there were interference. And it was like that for the entire time they were there.

Using her authority as his commanding officer, she checked Videl's feed, and found the exact same issue. The feed became distorted at the exact same moment.

She studied it more closely, triple checking. And she noticed that there was a blip as their geolocation tracking put them back at the vehicle. The feed came back, but then the moment the old man should've been on camera... a strange, different distortion took over. Though it was only over the old man's form. It wasn't cutting edge, and she was helped by the fact she knew the old man should be there, but... the way the footage looked, it was like some algorithm was trying to automatically wipe him from the image. It wasn't a flawless success, but it might fool someone inspecting the recording without suspicion.

"What the fuck..." Valeska muttered, a pit in her stomach.

She suddenly realized she hadn't eaten all day, and that was probably the only reason she didn't vomit back in that room.

The danger she was getting involved in went deeper than she knew, and she ran her hand through her hair, trying to calm herself down.

She didn't delete the footage, but she wanted to. She wanted to delete the entire day from her memory, in fact.

It wouldn't have been the most damning thing to delete it. Plenty of officers did that and got away with it. Military command only cared if they thought you were fucking with them, or being treasonous. They didn't care if you covered up the occasional bit of House plotting, or some private tryst. The service was allowed to get away with things normal people weren't.

But if they were suspicious of her... this could all come back to bite her. The scrambled version, she reasoned, was safer than an absence.

"I'm almost afraid to ask, but... what now?"

"Nothing you need to worry about, Under-Lieutenant," she said sternly, though she couldn't completely hide the regret in her eyes. She was pulling him into something bad, and she knew that loyalty had its limits.

Even when it came to her.

She owed him more than a one-night-stand, that much was for sure.

Whether he knew that or not, well... that was another matter.

She was giving him some pretty intense blackmail material, at the very least.

"Shit. That bad, huh?" he remarked as he took them down another turn, thoroughly avoiding the city as they began to head north again, this time onto the western side of the island.

"You know, Ma'am, if you just want me to compile a list of my greatest wishes, I can do that much for you," he grinned.

She laughed, her ruby eyes sparkling at him, her fangs glinting between her teeth.

"Ah, fuck, I am glad you were assigned to me. I figured

I'd have had to kill my Second by now, yet here you are, turning into a real Satanosite before my eyes."

He smiled and laughed at that in return, his usually stern face surprisingly looking more relaxed in that tense moment than she was used to seeing it.

"Don't worry. I'll calculate my demands so they're hopefully not so much you want to kill me for it. Because as we've established, getting you killed... or me, does nothing for my fantasies," Videl said.

He'd always been good in a crisis. He could always seem to tell what she needed, whether it was loyalty, advice, a live gun, or... some levity, it seemed.

Whether he could give her an orgasm was something she knew she'd find out before the night was out, because he definitely had an inkling of just how much she owed him.

Especially since she was usually just as by-the-book as he was. She was raised to be loyal, and the evening before, her loyalty had been to their House. That was one thing. A rare detour from the official orders.

But they were still orders. Her orders.

Tonight was different. Tonight, she was breaking all of the rules, and he knew it.

"I appreciate that, Videl."

"I truly hope so."

The rest of the drive was in silence, but soon they came to that sleepy little coastal village. Videl waited with the subject while she went and spoke with the creep from the night before. He was all grins and cocky remarks until he saw her walk in.

"Hey, friend," she smiled with a terrifying glint in her

eyes. The patrons all made way for her. One sight of that insignia and they were turned into mewling cowards. "I need a room. I think you know the one."

He looked around at the bar, not wanting to be cowed in front of his customers.

"Of course! Our rooms are the best," he boasted, trying to regain his confidence.

She put a blade on the counter, and he shrank, his gaze drawn to the stiletto that had almost emasculated him.

"Yes, of course you can treat me to the room. But I need privacy. All of the keys, even that spare you keep next to your cockring in your pocket."

His eyes widened in horror, sweat glistening on his temples.

"Yes, yes, you don't know what I mean," Valeska said, taking the words from his mouth. "Now get the fucking keys, hand them over, and swear in front of everyone here that you'll stay out of the Wolf's den."

He quivered as two electronic keys landed on the counter, and he reached into his pants, grabbing the last one. This one was a manual failsafe, and it landed heavy next to the others.

"Good boy," she purred, "And what do you say?"

"Thank you, Wolf. It's all yours. As long as you need it," he quivered.

She wanted to shank him right then and there. She was having to be so restrained, and her adrenaline was pumping. She lifted the stiletto, gathering the metal key on its tip. She grabbed the two key cards, stuffing them in her pocket as she lingered, staring at him.

The sound of fluid splashing on the floor made her hop

up, and when she peered down, she realized that he was fucking pissing himself.

A cruel laugh escaped her.

"You're not even worth a bar fight," she mocked, turning and leaving him in a puddle of his own urine, surrounded by his patrons as their uncomfortable laughter began to rise up behind her.

When she got back, Videl was standing outside the vehicle, rifle in his hands. He gave her a salute across his chest.

"We're all good?" he asked, moving back to clear the rear door for the old man.

"Yea. You'll need to get us some food, but then we're off duty. Let's get him in quickly. I don't want anyone to fucking see him, even if they are all drunk and coked out of their minds."

Videl nodded then got the door for her. The old man was sitting up, slumped to one side, asleep. He woke up as her Second grasped his arm and took him out.

"Ah, reason prevails," he says as he stepped out on shaky legs, immediately aware that this was no place she'd be taking him for official reasons. "So proud of you Valeska," he remarked, trying to act so in control, even as his aged weakness was quite apparent.

"Show some respect for the Over-Lieutenant," Videl said tersely, gripping the old man's arm tight enough to make him audibly wince in pain.

They went to the secret entrance in that alleyway dumpster, with Videl lifting the old guy up into it. He then looked to Valeska.

"I'll go get some supplies then?" he asked.

"Yea. Grab the first aid from the hummer, too," she

said, calling up an app on her watch and instantly transferring him the cash he'd need. "And grab a bottle of something strong. I have a feeling I'm going to need it dealing with gramps here."

"I'll get enough for a couple days. If we need more, I can handle it then," he said, nodding to her. "Be back shortly, Ma'am," he said with his usual crisp air, keeping up the usual pretences in public at least.

Valeska pushed her captive into the tunnel, her sour mood palpable once Videl was gone. He was the only thing giving her even a moment's reprieve from the gravity of her situation, and of what she intended to learn.

Secrets were her refuge, the thing that kept her strong. The reason she achieved so much in such a short amount of time, with minimal damages.

But what this old man knew threatened to break her, and she hated it as much as she felt like a slave to the impulse to know.

CHAPTER 17

FANTASIES DO COME TRUE

For pure will, unassuaged of purpose, delivered from the lust of result, is every way perfect.

— ALEISTER CROWLEY; THE BOOK OF
THE LAW

He beelined for the first ratty mattress on the floor he could find. He wasn't going to be cooperative until he'd rested, and even then...

He got down onto it and curled up, pulling a filthy rag of a blanket onto himself with a sigh.

"Been so long since I've had to rough it like this," he said, sounding almost amused by it all. "But we'll make up for lost time soon," he said, eyes already shut as he rolled to his side.

The room was narrow and small, more of a hall than anything, and she blocked off the way to the ladder that led up towards the tavern, just in case. She went to the table in the centre of the room, sitting on it, her elbows on her thighs as she leaned forward. She stared at the old man, her anger bubbling beneath the surface, only kept in check by the power of her curiosity.

It was a dull wait for Videl to show. The old man was already snoring by then as her Second brought in the bags of food. He had enough to last three people a couple days or so and he placed them down beside her, then took out a bottle of some expensive vodka.

"Saw you drinking this once before," he remarked with a slight smile, plopping down a couple glasses. "The barkeep was generous when he saw the uniform. Threw in some glasses."

"Good," she said, grabbing the bottle and pouring them up two full glasses. "Well, Videl. To a new beginning," she said in a toast, barely waiting for his glass to touch hers before she was drinking it down like water.

Videl drank his toast with her, downing the glass too, albeit not with the same gusto. He took off his rifle and placed it against the wall before opening up his jacket and sitting back with a sigh.

"At least one of us will have to report for duty tomorrow," he said, some calculations going on in his head. "It'll be an exhausting time, just the two of us keeping watch on him for... how long?"

"A few days. I'm hoping less," she said with a sigh. "You should sleep. Report in tomorrow, tell them I'm taking my vacation days to make up for my celebrations being interrupted last night. Speaking of, who brought Abel back to town?"

"Ericia went to get him. She drew the short straw by being late, and she was already in a vehicle."

"She always draws the short straw when it comes to showing up on time," Valeska chuckled. "That girl loves sleeping in."

"Meanwhile, I'm too wired to sleep. This day has been... something else," he said, pouring them both up more of the vodka.

"Yea, same," she said taking a slower sip this time, still staring ahead at the old man. "They never taught me about him. He has to be one of the original founders, right? He didn't even flinch when I told him that his partner was killed. He's just as ruthless as..."

Videl listened and took a deep breath before sipping some more himself.

"I think you're right. He must've fallen afoul of the others, been exiled," Videl said, glancing at the old man. He then got up, went and locked the hatch there, plucking a key out of the lock before coming back. "Maybe because of that scene down there... perhaps he was responsible, and it got him kicked out," Videl said, speaking softly, he then gestured around the corner. "We can get away from him. I locked the hatch."

"He's not in much condition to do anything here. Doors locked, and not like the room has anything he could even use as a makeshift weapon," Valeska sighed, hopping off the table onto the floor and beginning to gather up her glass, the vodka, and her weapons.

The only other way out was up on the next level, and the two of them went there, more secluded and out of the old man's hearing. Hopefully. The noise from the bar helped. There were also more comforts there, some better seats, with actual padding. Videl turned on a dim light.

They laid a chair overtop the open hatch, keeping the Eyes at bay, stuck bobbing against the wood as they tried to follow the two of them.

"Yeah, this place was definitely used to hold people against their will," he said, inspecting it. "So, it seems an ideal location."

"Yup," she agreed, setting down her things, and starting to make herself more at home. "Tomorrow we'll see whether we have to cuff him, but for now, I think we'll get more out of him faster if we treat him... better."

She took off her watch, her paranoia making her cautious, and put it in her jacket pocket, stripping it off and tucking it into a corner. It was far enough away that she was certain it couldn't record her, but near enough that she'd hear an alert.

Videl's eyes were upon her as she took off her jacket, his red gaze on her pale skin wrapped in skimpy black clothes and fishnets. A reminder of why the man was being more loyal than any other Second she'd heard of.

He took off his jacket in kind, putting his watch into a pocket as well, following her example.

She stretched as she paced the length of the room, her body aching from exhaustion, soothed only by the buzz of alcohol in her system.

"Want me to report the dead guy tomorrow?" he asked.

"I called it in earlier. I sealed off the basement, and I doubt the retrieval team will poke around more than necessary. There's something weird about the place, some strange interference on the recording devices, so there shouldn't be a lot of questions unless someone knows about the place's history," she said, continuing to pace, tugging her hair back into a ponytail.

"So, you got that list started, I imagine?"

His lips crooked back into a wry grin at her question as he loosened his uniform tie.

"I cheated. I've been compiling a mental list for years," he said with a flash of his teeth, and those two silver fangs, as he looked at her from the corner of his view.

"Always were an overachiever," she quipped back, her fingers starting to dig under the bottom of her tank top before she paused. "How specific is your list?"

His grin only grew as he eyed her getting undressed. And it was almost like watching his loyalty to her grow in real time.

"Not specific at all at this moment," he said as he pulled off that tie, and began to unbutton his shirt, showing his lean, muscled chest beneath. "Specificity can wait for later. After all... by my tally, you owe me quite a bit," he said with a saucy grin, tonguing the seam of his lower lip.

"Fuck, I would kill so many men if they said that to me," she snarled, pulling the top off her head and tossing it aside. Her black bra had rubbed its mark against her skin, and when she unclasped it, she let out a genuine sigh of relief, her perky breasts barely moving at all. "Fortunately for you, you're not wrong. And I know you'll temper your greed."

He was staring at her chest, appreciating his first good look at her bare breasts without subterfuge. He tossed his hat to the side, then pulled off his whole shirt to add to the pile he was making. He had a few scars, knife wounds mostly, along his leanly muscled torso.

"So far I'm very pleased with your generosity, Ma'am," he remarked, reaching to his boots, taking them off. "And I'm sure this arrangement will be mutually beneficial."

She closed the distance between them, her black ponytail swishing along her back as she walked. She still wore her shorts, fishnets, and boots, but she knew he'd take care of that in time.

"If you treat me like a delicate doll, I swear to Satan, I will kill you," she said as her hand curled around the back of his head.

His eyes widened as he looked at her up close, and only delayed the slightest hint of a split second before his hands went to her hips. Once his skin connected with hers, the flood dams opened, and his face buried itself into her chest. His mouth immediately began to kiss at her breasts, biting a bit, before licking at her sensitive teat.

"Mmm, I would never dishonour you so, Ma'am," he husked as his hands went to her ass, squeezing it as he teased her teat with his sharp teeth before suckling at it with a ravenous hunger that had built up over the years.

Her stand-in sister or... Whatever, had not successfully quelled his lusts. A pale imitation of his true desires.

It wasn't that superiors weren't supposed to sleep with their charges, or that she didn't find him attractive. Neither of those things had played a role in why she didn't fuck him before. Instead, it was a pragmatic need for secrecy. Letting people into her room, into her bed, revealed things about her. Things she didn't want them to know.

But now Videl knew too much, and the secrets they

knew could end them both. If it was going to be their last moments in a Satanic Paradise, she might as well explore her darkest fantasies of fucking someone she actually liked.

She yelped a little bit as he teased her, his fangs pressed into her tit, not breaking skin but sending a rush of adrenaline through her. Her fingers ran through his hair, encouraging him to suckle harder, until she could really feel it in her core.

He stayed there at her breasts, and seemed like he'd have been content to do that for hours. But his hands curled into her backside, squeezing and kneading, before he began to pull down her shorts, peeling them away from her body. His hungry lips moved to kiss across her taut tummy, before finding her other breast.

"You're more exquisite than I imagined you'd be," he said, breathing heavily with desire, as his trousers bulged with his thick girth rising.

"You should see me when I'm cleaned up," she teased, her body pressing into his, holding his head as he lavished her perky tits with attention.

Her leg shifted forward, between his legs, pressing against his hardness with her upper thigh.

"So, no requests for the evening?"

She had never asked someone that before. She'd never indulged someone else's wishes. She simply told them what they wanted, and that they'd like it.

But he'd taken some of that control from her, and she couldn't help but be... curious at his answer.

"I really wanted to fuck you up against the wall, but..." he said with a grin growing across his face. "If you're so eager to return favours, you could ride me in this chair first."

He looked at her with such hungry eyes, licking his lips, before giving her ass a nice, firm slap. It sent a delicious shock through her, and she inhaled sharply.

She shifted enough to step out of the shorts that had dropped to her ankles, leaving her in just her fishnets and boots, her pussy glistening between her thighs. Her daggers were still strapped to her legs, but they were like a second skin to her, she barely even noticed them as she ground against his cock.

"Yea," she said, her tone a bit darker and deeper than he was used to. "You sit there and relax."

His cock pulsated against her leg, cuing her into just how much he not only admired her authority and strength, but how much it fucking turned him on. That hot, stiff organ throbbing excitedly as he fondled her bare ass, and let his fingers dip between her thighs, to feel her glistening honey.

He had a twinkle in his eyes as he sealed his lips back around a teat of hers, swirling his tongue around it as he enjoyed her body with the kind of reverence and desire that Valerie certainly had not received.

She was beginning to relax; his body became a perfect distraction for her to work her aggression out on. She straddled his leg, not in any rush to get the deed over and done with. It would've been blackmail if it were someone else, but with him, she was actually grateful to have the ice broken.

She wouldn't have been able to handle a full night left alone with her thoughts.

Her body was youthful and pristine, especially considering her upbringing. It was always enforced that a mark shouldn't be left upon her, and he was able to reap the rewards of that policy.

"Don't worry, Ma'am. I'm not selfish," he said against her breast, helping himself to her in a way she'd never allowed Abel to even attempt. "I have every intention of leaving you begging for more."

Videl, strait-laced, by-the-book, loyal. Now a ravenous man, supping at her body like it were a feast and he hadn't eaten in weeks. He was aggressive, but not overly so. He knew a woman's body well enough to know what went beyond aggressive and into the realm of just being an over zealous prick.

"We'll see about that. Cock out, Under-Lieutenant Videl," she commanded.

CHAPTER 18

MA'AM

Beware of her.
> Her beauty's one boast is her dangerous hair.
> When Lilith winds it tight around young men
> She doesn't soon let go of them again.

— DANTE'S INFERNO

is large hands kneaded her ass cheeks, and he began to rock her whole body atop his thigh, forcibly grinding her pussy on him as he devoured her perky tits. She pulled her thigh back just enough to give him the room he needed to do so, her wet pussy staining his pants as she rested on his leg.

Videl had always been militant about keeping his uniform clean and tidy, in parade fashion. But he didn't give a single fuck about the fact that his commander's pussy had stained them.

She hadn't let Abel touch her for so long, torturing him with his desire, but she didn't need to tease Videl like that. She could, of course, but she appreciated that he'd been tortured for years already. She had unknowingly denied him this chance so many times, and she didn't want to play games.

For once, she just needed a thick, hard cock to ride, and a man to want her, without turning it into a power struggle.

She could have. Perhaps she should have. But the day was too fucked up as it was, and she needed release.

"Yes Ma'am," he said breathily, as he unbuckled his belt and hauled his pants down. The thick, veiny dick surged upwards, the tip so prominent and pronounced; such a dark, ruddy purple. It glistened with arousal, and Valeska stared at it with carnal need.

She barely delayed at all, tossing her leg over his lap as she began to press the tip of his bare cock against her entrance.

The look on his face was unmistakable bliss as her slick petals began to swallow his tip. He moaned loudly, unrestrained. And his hands gripped her ass and thigh as she got into position over him.

"F-Fuck," he groaned, leaning in, kissing her breasts again, then up to her shoulder as he panted, before pulling back to watch the lewd sight of their loins meeting. "How could I ever serve anyone else now?"

"You won't, baby. You'll only serve me," she said into his ear as she let her weight bring her down along his shaft, taking his raw cock deep inside of her wet cunt. A shiver went through her, and she let out a sigh of satisfaction, her breasts pressed against his chest.

His head and neck arched back, and the long low moan that escaped him was pure ecstasy. He let his strong arms slide around her, wrapping her up in them as that thick shaft filled her up to her capacity and then some. That veiny girth of his was the biggest thing she'd had inside her for ages. Man or toy.

"My commander," his husky, aroused voice murmured into her ear. "Is it okay if I kiss you?" he asked, remembering that her sister chastised him for the very notion.

She pressed her mouth to his in answer, her tongue teasing along the seam of his lips before delving inside. She tasted like vodka, but she seemed as sober as ever in his arms.

Her platform boots gave her a bit of an advantage, and she pushed herself up a few inches before she let herself descend on his cock again, setting up a slow, languid tempo that seemed to please both of them in near equal measures.

They made out like that for some time. Lips locked, tongues intertwining. While his thick shaft pulsated inside her, stretching her open nice and wide, really making her feel its presence within her, whether it was that aching gape or the way his head so easily jabbed her utmost depths.

Eventually his hands got greedy, and began to grip her hips again, and with his physical strength, he began to lift her body, and pull it back down. Their pace and roughness rising with it.

She was only too willing to ride him harder, and her arms wrapped around his neck for support as their rutting became more unhinged.

She was panting as her pussy slickened his full length, dripping along his sac with the force of their thrusting.

Much like earlier, when she'd watch him take liberties with their suspect, Videl showed no signs of wanting to rush to end things. He savoured her body, kissed her deeply, and worked her pussy up and down his shaft with a ravenously growing hunger that showed no signs of abating.

"Over-Lieutenant," he moaned, as their mouths broke apart for a moment, and he grunted, spurting pre-cum into her.

She wasn't in any hurry either. Even though her body was exhausted from the long day, and she was starving, she was satiating herself on him and his need. It nourished her like little else could, and her tits bounced with each ride up and down his shaft.

His hand went to her hair and he gave it a sharp tug, sending intense waves down into her. She wasn't used to being manhandled, and it pulled a cry from her lips. She was panting hard when the first orgasm struck her, and her eyes rolled back in her head as her pussy clamped down around his shaft.

He grunted and groaned, and she could tell he was holding back in that moment. Desperately so. But he got through it somehow, and after that, she suddenly found herself lifted up.

His pants fell to his knees, but luckily the wall wasn't far. He pressed her back against it, the vibrations of the loud music from the bar humming through her. And he then delivered fully on his promise not to treat her gently.

Videl hammered into her, that thick cock slamming in deep as he bit her lower lip. One hand gripped her thigh and another went to grasp a perky, bouncing tit, pinning her hard into the wall.

She squealed, and her legs wrapped around his ass, trying to keep herself in place for him. He was so much stronger than he looked, though the fact that she was so light certainly helped, and his stamina was impressive.

Her nails dug into his back as she held him, not holding back the moans and cries of her pleasure, despite the captive slumbering below.

Videl was groaning, his gruff, pleasured sounds rising as he ravished her against the wall. The wood shook against her back each time she was slammed into it by his thrusts. It was the kind of rough handling she craved, but never indulged in. She had always been in control, but in his strong grasp, she was under his command. It jarred her whole body to a new level of awareness.

Panting, he bit her neck, then rasped into her ear.

"Fuck... Ma'am... I'm going to cum," he confessed. His balls had stopped slapping against her some time ago, as they tightened up, preparing to unload. "I'm gonna do it in you... No matter what you say," he said, nuzzling to her neck then biting it again.

It didn't bother her at all that he took it without asking. If she wasn't prepared to give him that, she would have kept a tighter rein on things that night.

After all, she knew that was his real desire. She'd seen it in his eyes as he watched her while he fucked Valerie. Knew that in his mind, he was fucking her. Finishing in her.

His bite of her neck, those fangs threatening to pierce her, sent more powerful waves of pleasure down through her. A roar rose out of his throat, and his final thrusts came on wild and erratic, extra hard as he began to fire off his load. Moments after his orgasm peaked, so did hers. She cried out again, her limbs threatening to go lax as they came together.

Their long, tense, alarming day climaxed in that moment. Their two bodies glistened in the dull orange light, his muscles tensed and tightening as he flooded her depths with seed. Her smooth, nubile skin alight as if in the fire's of Hell itself.

They both quaked in the fury of their orgasms, and he gripped her hips tightly, giving her a few final, wall quaking thrusts of extra roughness as he finished. And soon thereafter, his knees trembled, and he leaned in against her, almost crushing her against that wall as he panted for breath.

"Over-Lieutenant..." he groaned into her ear.

The pressure of being trapped between him and the wall was welcome in that moment, and she took the time to regain control of her breathing.

Her fingers loosened from his back, half-moons from her sharp nails imprinted deeply into his skin.

He soon caught his breath too, and then finally released her from that pinning hold against the wall. With his hands on her hips, he lowered her to the floor, his cock slipping from her as the mess of their rutting spilled free.

"Hungry?" he asked, as if everything were back to normal.

"Yea, starved," she agreed, his seed staining the fishnets on her inner thigh. She captured some in her fingers, bringing it to his lips and supping on it before she walked back towards their things. "What'd you get?"

That little act brought a smile to his lips, before he went and retrieved the bags. He opened up a series of packaged items from a corner store, and then a couple takeout containers.

"The bar was serving some wings and sides, so I grabbed some of that. But there's also biscuits, dried meat, sweets, other things there, if you're not in the mood," he explained as he laid it out for her on the unpainted wooden table.

"I haven't eaten in way too long to be picky," she said, grabbing a random takeout container and opening it, finding the wings inside. She plucked one saucy piece out of it, and began to devour it, still mostly naked, without an ounce of shame.

"Fuck, that's good. You want?" she offered the opening of the box to him.

Videl finished topping up their vodka glasses, then putting a bottle of water each to go with it before helping himself and sitting down. His own state of undress largely unchanged too. Except that he'd hauled his pants and underwear up to hang loosely at his hips.

"Yeah, thanks," he said beginning to eat. He was already looking much less tense, sinking into his chair more. "Anything you want me to handle when I head in tomorrow?"

"I could use a change of clothes. And..." she paused, looking thoughtful. "Maybe some fine brandy." It was what the Magister drank, so perhaps there was a shared taste for it. The sooner her captive gave her what she wanted, the better.

Videl finished with one wing, then nodded as he grabbed another.

"I can bring that along after my shift. Or leave early if you want it sooner, and drop back," he stated, a yawn beginning to come from him, despite his resistance against it. "I'll need access to your place to get your clothes though."

"Yea. I'm still in the process of moving in, so most of the shit I wear is in the dressers, luckily," she said, grabbing her keys off her belt and handing them to him. "There's nothing interesting there, so don't get nosy," she added with a grin. "Don't make me have to keep eyes on you now, Under-lieutenant."

Videl laughed at that as he put the keys into a pocket in his jacket.

"What makes you think there's anything interesting to me outside your panty drawer anyway?" he quipped with a raised brow, then laughed again as he finished another wing. "I think I might get going now then. Grab some sleep, handle those matters for you. You want me to get the change of clothes first?" he asked as he cleaned his hands and drained some water from the bottle.

"Naw, I can rough it for a night, and I need you to have your wits about you for the shift tomorrow," she said in her usual commanding tone, with just a hint of casualness to it. "Oh, and grab a pair of cuffs and a gag, just in case."

He nodded to her, as he stood up, beginning to redress at last.

"Very well, Over-Lieutenant. Should I grab those from the armoury or do you have a favourite set at home you want me to bring?" he asked with an amused smirk as he buttoned up his shirt.

She smirked back, licking a drop of sauce from her bottom lip.

"The armoury set is fine for this purpose."

Videl laughed at that, and finished getting back into his uniform before picking up his gun.

"I'll see you come daylight, Over-Lieutenant," he said, and she stared at him as he disappeared down the ladder.

The past few days had been a level of crazy she didn't expect, could barely make sense of. Fucking her Second certainly wasn't in her plan. But as she watched him leave, she couldn't help but admit that he had been her rock, and the sex had been as good for her as it was for him.

His presence was quickly missed as those troubling thoughts tumbled back into the forefront of her mind. It was a long night. Worries of what she'd gotten herself into; what she was risking. The unanswered questions that were troubling her... especially when the answers were oh so near, yet far away.

She nearly nodded off a few times. But come the early hours, she heard a stirring below. The shuffling footsteps of the old man, as he awoke after many hours.

"I trust there is some food for me too, yes?" he called out from below.

She sighed as she pushed to her feet. She had gotten dressed at some point, an excuse to move around and keep herself from passing out, but she looked and felt sloppier than she liked.

"I doubt starving you will help me get what I'm after," she called back, picking up a few biscuits and a bottle of water. She tromped down the ladder, putting them on the table for him.

The old fellow still looked feeble and weak, but he was awake. He sat down, and opened the box, helping himself to some of the biscuit as he smiled.

"Feels like old days again, being with a V. Back on Satanos," he remarked with a sigh, drinking some water. "Though I no longer have the stamina I once did. Certainly not the stamina of that man of yours anymore," he laughed.

She tried a different tactic this time. She wasn't going to press for answers, barrage him with questions he was clearly only going to answer in his own good time.

Instead, she joined him, grabbing a biscuit and nibbling on it as they spoke.

"You seem to have slept well despite his stamina."

"You never sleep well at my age," he said with this old, grandfatherly smile at her. He continued to munch, moving at his old, weary pace. "You really trust your Second, hm? Quite remarkable. Why is that?" he asked, brow raised at her.

"Trust doesn't really come into play here, you know that. But he respects me, and knows I wouldn't put him in a situation like this frivolously."

"Mm," he said, munching in a biscuit, then washing it down. "You're counting on his fondness and lust for you to keep him loyal, no?" he looked her over, without that leering gaze of the night before. "You're probably used to that working out in lower stakes situations."

"I know he'll forever have something over my head and that makes him a risk, if that's what you're asking. These things never go the easy way. But we've worked together for a long time. It's enough for now."

"Surprising for a V. You're not usually known to trust anyone. Least of all someone who has blackmail bait on you. Letting him walk off, take command of your unit..."

Valeska took a drink of water to hide her scowl as he tried to get into her head.

"I suppose you're right, though. If he was out there, turning us in now... he wouldn't get to fuck you again. Presuming he didn't get that out of his system. You know how piggish men are, after all. Once they've gotten what they want."

Chapter 19

I Could Just Kill Him

> You belong to your father, the devil, and you want to carry out your father's desires. He was a murderer from the beginning, not holding to the truth, for there is no truth in him. When he lies, he speaks his native language, for he is a liar and the father of lies.
>
> — John 8:44

She prickled at his attempts to manipulate her and seed doubt in her mind, but she resisted the urge to lash out.

"If he was turning me in right now, what makes you think I don't have a plan for that?"

"I'm glad to hear it," he said with a paternal smile, patting her knee as he stood up. "I don't quite want my day to end. Not yet. And certainly not at *his* hands," he remarked as he shuffled back to his bed.

"Your son's?" she ventured.

He laughed at that question, as he got down on the mattress, and pulled the blanket over himself.

"We'll talk more later. I am exhausted," he said, sounding already half asleep.

"Yea," she said with a sigh. She finished her biscuit, staring at him for a while longer before she trudged back upstairs. She grabbed her jacket, and pulled it on, before strapping her watch onto her wrist.

It was going to be a long day.

Eventually a message came in for her, from Videl. This time via text.

"All's fine. Nothing out of the normal. Still a couple hours left. But wanted to check if you needed anything more."

She gave him the all clear, though try as she might, the old man had pricked at her insecurity.

Even if Videl betrayed her, she could deal with it. If she had to kill him, she could do it. She wouldn't let him control her. He was just a mainlander, an outsider. She was untouchable, the chosen daughter of Satan, the personification of Satanos. The pride of House Void Star, ruled by secrets and control.

But her reassurances rang hollow.

So, just as she had countless times before, she turned to the truth. The code of Satanos, of House Void Star, of Astarte.

She no longer needed the books to ruminate on her purpose. To walk in the places between, to gather secrets from shadows, and to never forget that sex and life, war and death, created the core of human experience.

Keeping herself focused on that got her through the afternoon, until Videl finally dropped by, and she let him in through the hatch. He came with a couple bundles, smiling to her as he entered, and relief washed over her.

"How are you holding up?" he asked as he glanced to the old man.

"Bored out of my mind," she answered. The captive had told her how little privacy they truly had in this place, but still she waited until they were upstairs before speaking more. "How did today go?"

"Fine. Nothing out of the ordinary. Except gripes about lost sleep," he said, as he handed her the bundle of clothes, along with the gag and restraints. "Ericia says that boy of yours went and signed up," he remarked offhandedly. Any jealousy he bore was carefully concealed.

"Huh," she muttered in surprise. "Good for him. He's green, has some shit to unlearn, but he's earnest in his faith. Well, mostly good for me. Bagging a convert without even trying!"

Videl didn't much respond to that but for a light, 'mm' as he took out a bottle of fine brandy, setting it on the table.

"No more rumours about yesterday?"

Videl shook his head and undid his jacket before sitting down.

"Nothing I've been privy to, at least. Most seem to think yesterday's alert was a false alarm. That some joy rider must've gotten shot down due to his stupidity, and we all got worked up over nothing. I thought of asking Aran to check with his contacts in Z Company, since they seemed to be aware of more, but I worried it might create suspicion. Thought I should check with you first."

"When I come back from vacation I might ask around, but for now, we'll blend in. I'm hoping," she said, lowering her voice, "that when all this is done, we can go to the House and turn him in. Do things legit. Well... legit-ish."

Videl nodded to her.

"Good. Hopefully even if they do catch on, they won't be too upset about you indulging in some digging anyhow," Videl remarked in a hushed tone.

His eyes then drifted over her.

"How are you holding up? It's been well over twenty-four hours since you last slept," he remarked.

"I don't know," she admitted. "Some of the things he says... It makes me feel like I'm not actually a first genera-tion... Like the experiment has been going on longer than the island. He talks about me as if he knows me. Not just as a child." She sighed, pushing some dark hair from her face. "Doesn't matter anyways, every time I close my eyes, all I can see is that room."

Videl watched her quite seriously, absorbing what she said. He didn't respond right away, but looked quite thoughtful.

"If you want, I can try and offer a distraction. Again," he remarked with a slight hint of a smirk. "But otherwise, you should probably get some rest," he pulled a pill bottle out of his coat next. "I brought these in case you needed help."

"By Astarte's left tit, Videl, you thought of everything." She took the meds from him, opening it up and grabbing two, and swallowing them with a gulp of vodka from the bottle.

"Just a few hours. If he wakes up, he can have food, but don't get pulled in by him. He's cunning, and he'll try to turn us against one another," she murmured quietly.

Videl watched her, curiously.

"So, he's already tried that on you, huh? And you still took two unmarked pills from me," he remarked with a budding wry grin.

She laughed, the sound earnest.

"You don't strike me as a corpse fucker."

"Maybe it's on the list," he said with a flash of his eyes, looking playfully devious.

"Can't imagine it's almost at the top of it, though," she said.

He sat back in his chair, "You can go lay down if you want now. I'll keep an eye on things for the time being."

She went to the padded seats that lined the wall, and laid on her side, her bicep acting as a pillow, under her Second's watchful gaze.

The old man is right. You have grown too trusting of him, she chided herself before swatting the thought away.

"Oh, and if you need something to help you wake up," he said, tugging out a packet of white powder from his pocket. "I remembered what you said. And thought... just in case."

The pills and liquor had already taken hold of her, pulling her into a deep sleep as she stared at Videl. He stood up, walking over to her, his ruby eyes scanning her face as she fought consciousness, and the image of him slipping away to get the blow from Valerie filled her nightmares.

CHAPTER 20

PISSING BLOOD

Astarte

    The one who is the many

    Perpetually flushed with desire

    Our sacred prostitute

    Bringer of pleasure and pain

    The morning star shines upon you

    As you sit upon your regal throne

    Bathed in the blood of your victory

          — HOUSE VOID STAR PRAYER

She awoke blearily Satan-knows how much later. Her head was still foggy from the pills, but when she looked around that upper level, she saw no signs of Videl. She bolted upright, panic gripping her, and in her haze, she knew Videl had betrayed her.

He could replace her with Valerie, have his own copy of

her, but one that was dependent on him. She could dye her hair, steal her rank, her unit, her House, her future. And Videl could tell her everything she needed to know.

She tried to force herself to alertness, pushing past the haze of the nightmares to find out what reality was. The paranoia from her wandering mind tugged at her consciousness, and she was desperate to see where Videl was.

She got to her feet, and felt the dizziness of a pill-induced sleep, so she had to press her hand to the wall to steady herself. She counted to ten, then pushed herself forward, towards the stairs.

The sound of a groan, like someone in pain filtered to her. She made her way down the ladder, her legs not quite obeying her. Her heart raced as she got down further, peering around the corner to see if she could make out who it was.

Relief flushed through her as she saw Videl in his uniform, and beyond him, the visage of the old man. His back was turned, his body nude and exposed. That frail old form was riddled with bruises. Many of them such bright colours, looking awful. He was braced against the wall with one hand as he pissed into a bucket.

"Fucking hell," Videl cursed, looking back at Valeska. "He's pissing up blood."

"No wonder he said he had a high tolerance for pain," she sighed, a tendril of relief swimming in her words. She swallowed, forcing herself back into her commanding role.

"You get those from the fall?" she asked him, under the presumption that he had parachuted out of the craft that was shot down.

The old man looked over his shoulder, his movements jerky and uneven.

"No. That was a distraction," he said as he finished pissing. "I came ashore by a mini submarine vessel. Quite an expensive thing to get. And it's surely gone now. But I wasn't anticipating leaving anyhow," he said with a groan as he went to his survival suit, sitting down, beginning to get dressed again. "But it wasn't easy going anyhow. We came under fire. I got tossed around a lot."

"Want me to leave you alone with him?" Videl asked in a murmur, offering to give her some privacy.

"The less you know, the better," she said back, not bothering to whisper.

Videl nodded to her, put his hand on her shoulder for a moment, then headed back up the stairs. It wasn't long before she heard the door up there open and shut as he exited the secret room into the tavern.

"Charming fellow that one," the old man said sarcastically as he squeezed his frail body back into that suit with a sigh. "But I guess he hasn't turned you in. Yet. So, he has his appeals."

"Perhaps you should remember that and be grateful to him. He's the reason you're still here, just as much as I am," Valeska said, taking a seat back on top of the table. "Are you feeling chatty yet?"

"I wouldn't quite say 'chatty'," he remarked as he zipped up the suit fully. "You have any painkillers, my dear V? Now that I'm not utterly exhausted, the pain is ruining my ability to get anymore rest."

She shimmied from the table as she went back to the ladder and swiped the brandy from the ledge.

"Do you want a glass? I'm all out of ice so I hope you're not a pussy and can drink it straight," she said as she set it on the table.

The old man looked at the bottle with disinterest at first, but seeing what it was... she detected that quick shift into interest.

"A glass, yes. We are not savages, are we?" he said with a grin, and she returned back a moment later with a pair of glasses.

"I'm surprised you didn't fuck your man again when he got back. You know, to cement his loyalty. And to make sure he hadn't gotten his needs taken care of elsewhere while he was away."

"That'd be a fast way to never getting off my back again," she said, setting up a glass and beginning to pour the amber liquid into it. She repeated the motions, and the memory of the Magister doing this for her just days before came to her mind unbidden.

She offered him the glass as she took a sip from hers.

"Given the right circumstances, sometimes you Vs are into that kind of life," he remarked, taking up the glass and helping himself. He shut his eyes as he savoured the sip. Then took another with a soft, "Mmmm. Thank you. You have excellent taste, my dear."

"We're in our twenties. How do you know what type of life we're into?" she asked, trying to keep the defensiveness out of her tone.

He grinned at her question. Those eyes of his, so dark, just seeming loaded with dark secrets in moments like those.

"Oh, you're just the latest batch of V's. Or at least, the

latest I had a hand in. I have been away a while," he remarked with a sigh of regret, then drank some more.

She didn't care for the answer, even though she had anticipated it. She took a sip of the brandy, hoping that the smooth burn would help soothe her frayed nerves.

"How many have there been? How... how long has this experiment been running?"

"Experiment," he repeated, sounding amused. "Such a choice of words," he chuckled. "You're more than a mere experiment, my lovely V."

The buzz of a high-level alert on her watch startled her.

The screen lit up with a message.

From the Magister.

"You're invited to come join me for a drink. We have your future to discuss, Valeska."

She cursed, staring at it. Days ago, the note would thrill her.

Today...

She couldn't even name all the emotions it brought up in her. Annoyance, however, was at the forefront.

"I need you to tell me why I shouldn't hand you over," Valeska said as she slid off the table, putting the rest of her drink aside.

He watched her move, looking almost surprised. But he interpreted the urgency from the message that buzzed through.

"Because I know why you were created. Like those before you. And only one of you can survive of this batch. Same as before," he said. "The others will become... fodder. In times past we let things... work themselves out. But nowadays, I feel the... Magisters, meddle. Sets them down certain paths, dooming them to a fate. I mean, you do want to be the last V standing, no?"

"Saving you might be the only reason that I won't be," she replied, the truth of her words stinging her. She *had* been chosen. She'd always believed that. She was the special one, the girl that would lead House Void Star to a new dusk.

She began to walk towards the exit hatch before she paused.

"What's your name?"

"Caleb."

"The ruthless spy," Valeska smirked. "How suiting a name for you."

Caleb grinned back just as darkly.

"A piece of advice, my dear. Be careful if you're going to him. You may be his favourite, but he never puts all his eggs in one basket. And he is not the only one playing this game. Every House has an interest in this scheme. He's just the most brazen about altering... the plan," he said with a glint in his eyes.

"And what V survives?" she asked, her voice a bit lower now, as though she shouldn't even be considering it.

He nodded rather grimly to that.

"I have an interest in you surviving now. I have no other eggs in my basket, Valeska. Perhaps you'll keep that in mind, when he tries to manipulate you into his bidding, hmm?" he said, brows raised as he took another sip of brandy.

"Is he your son, then?"

He laughed at that.

"No. Not at all," he said with both his usual cryptic flair and a dry bemusement.

"You're a very obnoxious captive, Caleb," she sighed as she went up the stairs, sending a message to Videl.

"Change of plans. I have business."

She grabbed the bag of clothes he'd brought, looking through them as she considered if she should shower. She doubted Videl brought her something fancy enough for a date with the Magister anyways.

The door slid open and Videl came back through, quickly closing out the thrumming heavy metal of the tavern.

"What's the plan, Ma'am?" he asked. He'd brought a full change of her uniform, but as she suspected, no fancy evening wear. "Just babysit until...?"

"Yes. I'm not sure how long I'll be gone, but if I text you with just a V, you get out of here. You haven't seen me since yesterday after our shift."

Videl absorbed that warning and gave her a nod. He then reached out and touched her shoulder.

"Take care of yourself, Ma'am. I still have favours I wish to cash in on," he added with a hint of a smirk.

"I will. The hummer outside? Or did you bring my Audi?" she asked, even as she went back to her watch, typing out a message on the holographic keyboard.

"Does eight work, Magister?"

That would give her enough time to head back to the estate and get cleaned up.

"I stuck to the hummer. I thought it might keep trouble away more than your Audi. And besides, I didn't want to risk changing things," Videl said.

The response came back quickly from the Magister.

"Yes. Freshen up if you like. But don't be late."

"Good man," she smiled at Videl, pausing just a moment to look at him before she grabbed the keys to her house. The hummer was programmed to their watches so didn't need one, but she still liked being a bit old school.

And just thinking about it...

How her house felt like it was made for her...

She couldn't entertain that right now.

"Thank you, Videl. I hope you know that even if I wanted to betray you in this, I couldn't. Not without making myself look worse," she said, her voice quiet.

He looked down at her, pondering her words.

"You're probably right," he said at last, wetting his lips thoughtfully. "I wish I knew something I could say to reassure you in return. But beyond what you already know about me and my desires... there's nothing else to say. Just make it through, so we can rise together. Me one step behind you to the end," he said, with a hint of a smile.

"The first secret to winning the game is knowing you're playing one," she replied, one of the mottos of the house seeming especially fitting.

"Astarte guide you, Ma'am," Videl said.

"I'll walk in her shadows."

She didn't linger any longer. She went back downstairs, intending on exiting out the dumpster as she had before, so as not to get on anyone's radar unnecessarily.

Before she could slip out of the hatch, Caleb's gravelly voice called after her.

"Don't trust anyone you can't destroy with the flick of a wrist."

Chapter 21

Astarte, Don't Fail Me Now

Their wine is the venom of serpents,
And the deadly poison of cobras.

— Deuteronomy 32:33

"Fucking asshole!"

A tourist swerved into her lane, and instead of slowing down, she gunned it. The massive hummer was a force to be reckoned with, and the tourist who was trying to play chicken with her instantly lost their own, stupid game. They veered back into their lane, and Valeska hoped they were sitting in a puddle of their own piss for getting in her way.

She had enough shit going on, and having to fulfill some tourist's fantasy of being a big-shot was not on her to-do list.

She barely had enough time to shower, dry her hair, and put on some dark lipstick and eyeliner.

She selected her favourite dress – the red one with a V-neck that went to her bellybutton and ended just below her ass – and some fresh fishnet tights. She stepped into a platform pair of mary-janes and dabbed some perfume on her wrists before she dashed downstairs.

Once she was outside, she slowed her pace, casually making her way towards the headquarters.

Void Star's location wasn't far from where she lived, so it was a thankfully brief trip before she arrived before the big columns and banners. The guards stood at attention outside, and as she strode past, they saluted.

She was barely inside before an adjutant came up to her.

"This way, Over-Lieutenant."

He ushered her along, back through the ritzy, marble corridors of the house. She wasn't taken to the Magister's office this time, but back into a private section saved for special rituals and ceremonies.

The ominous statues that lined the big hall she passed through gazed down on her with menacing eyes, as if they knew her secret.

Like the chimera, she carved away the part of herself that felt fear. She would tell no lies tonight, for there were no lies to tell. She excised them from herself, so that when she walked into the beautiful dining room, she was brimming with confidence. A fireplace crackled, and she spot a bottle of wine, the dark liquid beckoning her.

"Stunning. As always," the Magister said as he emerged with a paternal smile. He gestured to a seat at the table for two, pulling it out for her.

"Thank you, Magister."

Start with the breathing, make it natural. Truths and lies serve the same purpose, to preserve your life. Your station. There is no difference. Walk between them and know them as the truth.

He was dressed in a stately suit, perfectly tailored fit to show off his tall, trim form. A glimmering crimson cravat she'd never seen before caught her eye, and she couldn't help but notice how much more vibrant he seemed. More youthful. The mature lines on his face had softened away to nothing, and she couldn't help but stare. It had to have been some impressive makeup to pull that off.

He pushed in the chair for her as she sat down, and she snapped out of her inspection.

"How have your duties been going, Valeska?" he asked, as he filled their glasses with wine, then uncovered the meal before her. Veal and delightful delicacies looked like something from an exquisite restaurant, and her mouth began to water. She hadn't eaten real food in far too long. Even before the crazy few days, she typically grabbed something quick and easy when she was looking for food, often too busy to plan in advance.

A fine meal that she didn't have to pay for was her favourite food.

But with the Magister, there was always some payment due.

She took her glass, swirling the red liquid in it as she watched.

"No one suspected a thing about the man's state of existence, if that's what you're asking."

His ruby eyes met hers, and he cracked a smile before sitting down with her.

"To the Void Star. And to you... and me," he said, in a toast, moving to clink his glass to hers.

She gave him a smile, one that she'd given him a hundred times before, and hoped her eyes didn't betray her.

She sipped the wine, letting out a sigh of satisfaction.

"You always have the best drinks."

"I know. A perk of the position," he said with a fanged grin as he looked at her. "Have you been thinking about your next step? Or is it more of a... leap?" he asked her with a widening grin, as he began to eat. His motions were that of a refined noble lord, and she did her best to follow his lead.

"I can think of nothing else. Especially as it has become clearer to me how many more secrets there are to wield. The machinations of the other houses have always fascinated me, yet ours, the house of secrets... I'm still a child when it comes to unraveling those."

He observed her, his grin fading. Then becoming a smile. He took some time to sip his wine before saying anything more.

"Leave it to you to not ask for something simple like a promotion. More material goods. No, you ask for power in the form of secrets," he said, sounding amused and thoughtful at once. "We are approaching a turning point here, on Satanos. Our efforts over the long years are bearing fruit. And the six houses... well, let me just say, I don't foresee us needing all six forever," he remarked with a smile.

"No, why would you need six, when one will clearly

dominate in the end?" she mused before grinning a little, exposing her fangs. "Except..."

He quirked a brow at her, as he ate. Then slowly smirked.

"Go on," he urged her. "Speak your mind."

"Competition is one of the surest ways of control. Six may be too plentiful, but one is too few. Stagnation is sure to follow, complacency. A lack of risk will bring about apathy. Perhaps six houses aren't needed to promote growth, but one on its own will eventually crumble. But if one house were to move through shadows, manipulating the other five to always be weakening the others..." she trailed off, beginning to cut into her veal, taking a bite of it as her ruby eyes stared into his.

He smirked a bit at her words as he continued to eat. Until finally he washed it down with some wine.

"You're quite right, my dear Valeska. We won't be... erasing them from the isle's perspective. But we will work to remove some pesky leaders behind the scenes. That are in the way of us guiding things more effectively," he said with a smile. "What would you say to the opportunity for a promotion to Colonel? And to off a rival House Magister, leaving the door open for someone more... amenable to our methods, hmm?" he asked, pursing his lips, watching her.

She wasn't expecting that, and paused her chewing.

"I'm sure all the houses are on alert after the warning yesterday, but..."

He shook his head as he put down his wine glass.

"It's been handled," he said to her, sounding quite confident. "To the satisfaction of the house leaders, the infiltrators were taken down. Not just the plane above, but a simultaneous boat landing. And a curious little mini-submarine too," he said, laughing softly. "If anything, they will be eager to get back to normal. Get caught up on lost sleep," he remarked with a devilish smile, his pale skin illuminated in the fire's orange glow.

Her eyes scanned his face, so much more youthful and handsome than she'd seen him. He certainly didn't look like he'd been up all night tossing and turning, that was clear.

"Has it been handled to your satisfaction, Magister?"

There was still that strong resemblance to Caleb. But less so, thanks to whatever it was he did to make himself look younger that evening. He had started to remind her of someone else.

"Why? Was something about it troubling you? Did you have anything more to report?" he asked, reaching over and placing his hand atop hers on the table. His touch was cooler than most, despite the warmth of the room.

"You just spoke of them as outside yourself. I was curious if the man who sees behind the machinations felt that it was nothing of note."

He caressed the backs of her fingers gently, before taking his hand away.

A thoughtful look crossed his face as he peered off.

"It was an old rival, returning to ignite a former feud. But the old fool's body was found floating in the water. A desperate escape attempt from his sub before it blew," he explained. "A shame though. I was looking forward to doing it myself, if he could have been brought in alive," he said with a sigh.

The cogs began to spin, clunking into place.

Six houses. Six V's. Why not six Magisters as well? She

had presumed that Caleb was his father, but what if it was something else? Only one could survive...

She shook her head free of the thoughts, trying to bring a smile back to her lips.

"I'm not sure if you were informed of my role yesterday?"

"Oh?" he asked, brow raised curiously as he began to eat some more, finishing his veal and seemingly done with the plate.

"I received information that one of the other commanders wrote off and ignored, tracking someone reported to have escaped. From the North shore."

"Such initiative," he remarked with a grin. "Well done. So, you were the one who tracked them down to that old place in the woods. Anything interesting about it at all?"

She stared at him, studying him.

He was so fucking calm.

He revealed absolutely nothing, even as he goaded her to reveal all.

He walked between the lies and truth so easily. He had long been a role model to her in that regard, exemplifying the ease of blurring the lines of reality.

"The comms didn't work in the area. I wouldn't be surprised if someone else had noticed that in the past and used it to get away from any eyes."

"Hmm," he said simply, taking up his wine, sipping it. He took his time before saying more.

"That would make sense. The interior of this house works similarly. And that place was once a secret location, used by some of us first generation inhabitants, I believe.

Probably given the same treatment in the computer's code," he said with a smile.

She took another sip of her wine, considering her next words.

She had pieces of the puzzle, things that she was able to put together, but she had no confirmation of her theories. She was still missing information. Like... how six girls could be born at the same time, all looking similar, but a rainbow, as Caleb put it. Placed into different situations, to see who would thrive and who would be destroyed.

And the Magister was even less forthright than Caleb, and he shared a name with a biblical spy.

Revealing what she knew to him could be rewarded for her subterfuge, her exemplification of Astarte's whims.

But despite their religiosity and devout belief, she knew that things on Satanos were often twisted to suit the will of those wielding it. Especially since what was worshipped there would be almost heresy.

The Magister could just as quickly decide that her cunning deception was a threat, something to snuff out before she set her sights too high.

"Has anyone my age reached the rank of Colonel in our history?"

A grin grew once more at that.

"Never," he said. "You would be the first. And I have a sinking suspicion, if you can pull it off... a follow-up to General-Major would follow soon thereafter. And at that point you would be of high enough rank to be worthy of a special role in the halls of our house. One I have been grooming you for so long, Valeska..." he said, his voice an almost delicious, sultry manner.

He put his wine glass down, and took her hand. He stood up beside her, lifting her hand and guiding her to stand with him.

"You can be Magistra within this House. A bride of Satan. Consecrated on His altar."

His ruby eyes were alight as they stared intensely at her, as if boring into her mind.

"By me."

Chapter 22

Murder & Wedding Bells

And their daughters they took to themselves for wives, and their own daughters they gave to their sons, and they served their gods.

— Judges 3:6

She felt so small compared to him, even in those platform shoes. He'd always seemed like a giant when she was a child, but as she grew in skill and confidence, she'd become less intimidated by him.

But in that moment, she felt like a bug between his fingers once more.

He was offering her the thing of dreams and nightmares, of something beyond most Satanosite's grasp, and the honour of it was paralleled only by the fear of not attaining it. Knowing it could have been hers, if only.

"Magister," she murmured, staring at his hand before forcing her gaze up.

What he was proposing was marriage, as true as it could come on Satanos. An alliance of the young power with the old, for the sake of more power. Consecrated in the eyes of their Dark Lord, through sex or a blood sacrifice.

Or both.

He'd never hinted, in all of her years, that he wanted her in a carnal way. He was always stiffly paternal, but his words about grooming her for that moment...

Such a long wait it must've been.

He reached his free hand up to caress her cheek.

"You and I will be one step down from the very top. If you accept, that is," he remarked, touching her softly, until it became more controlling. "Does it bother you? To think of wedding me atop His altar? It's okay if that's so child. I know I have been the closest thing to a father you've had. If the thought turns your stomach, you can admit it. I will even enjoy knowing it, if we proceed. It will add to the moment," he said with a twisted grin.

She kept her eyes on him, studying his expression, the curve of his lips, as she tried to keep her breathing under control. Her heart was racing, and her mind seemed hazy, unable to anticipate his reactions, his next move.

She instead focused on how she would have reacted, if she'd not known about the other V's. About Caleb.

"I won't disappoint, then," she quipped, bringing a smirk to her lips.

He bent down, tilting his head to kiss her darkly coloured lips. And he put a hand upon her hip, around to the small of her back as he let his tongue pierce betwixt those morsels, into her mouth.

"Mmm. You have never disappointed before now, sweet Valeska," he said, after breaking their lips apart. "You are still so very young, but you have such potential. Such skill and cunning. And most importantly... you are mine. Shaped in the image I set forth for you," he said, his dark red eyes alight with a twinkle.

She knew she couldn't trust him. It wasn't just Caleb's words that told her that. She knew, instinctively, that those with the power are those that determine the future.

Out on the Island, she was a Wolf.

But with the Magister, she was just as much a lamb as Valerie. She had always wanted his affection, and to be able to please him. She could never have anticipated that this was his end goal.

She yielded to his manipulations, his kiss, even as it sent twin shivers of disgust and delight down her spine.

"I have looked forward to the day you met your full potential... for so long."

"Who do you want me to kill?"

He smiled at that question, and his hand went to her ass rather blatantly, squeezing it. His fingers curled, slowly inching up her red gown as he kissed her lips again and spoke to her as if they were intimate lovers.

"The Magistra of House Abaddon," he said, speaking of the brutish house of destroyers. They were the house tasked with executing traitors to the faith. "I have found she will be alone. Or nearly so. At an isolated spot on the island. It would be the perfect time to erase her. And put into place my puppet," he said, as her dress reached her waist, and his hand felt the bare skin of her ass.

No amount of careful breathing could control the pace of her heart as it rushed to escape her chest.

His desire for her to assassinate a Magistra paled in comparison to the shock of his actions, and she squirmed beneath his grasp, placing a hand on his chest.

"When?" she asked, not quite pushing him away, but putting a bit of pressure there, to keep him in place.

"Tonight. Once we are done here," he said, as his strong, cool hand squeezed and fondled her backside. Those fingertips found the absence of panties along her hips, and he smiled with approval.

"So eager to cut this short, child of Astarte?" he asked, brow raised.

"You're the one that likes my discomfort," she pointed out, grinning and showing the glint of her fangs. "You can't be shocked that this all comes as a surprise."

He laughed at that remark, his fingertips lightly prodding at her vulva, as his other hand went to her chest, to fondle her breast. She hadn't worn a bra, given the cut of her dress. She hadn't anticipated the turn the evening had taken, and her nipple was coaxed to stiffness beneath his palm. She always was an oversensitive type.

She was spinning out of control, and all she wanted to do was to bolt. Yet there was something so deeply ingrained in her, and his approval, his desire for her, it twisted her up inside.

For years she had done everything she could to please him, and she hated how excited his possessive grasp on her was.

"We both know I could force you into whatever I wanted," he said, kissing her lips again. So softly, so sweetly, in contrast to his words. "But I could give you a choice this evening."

"What would be my reward for consenting, and my punishment for leaving?"

"What makes you think leaving was one of the options?" he said with a grin and a chuckle. He fondled her perky breast and backside, then finally released her from his hold. "There will be plenty of time for us in the future," he said, pulling her hand up, kissing the back of it as his eyes remained locked on hers. "It's taken a lot to not play with you for so long, Valeska."

She was just as startled by the release as she was by the embrace, and she stared up at him in surprise.

"I wish I knew half of what was going on in that mind of yours," she breathed out. Her ass was still exposed, but she didn't rush to tug her dress down or pull away from him. That would be like baiting a trap with her own flesh.

"Oh? You can't guess what is going on now? I would have thought it was a simple calculation," he said, looking down over her body, trailing a finger between her breasts, across her taut tummy. "I am still a man with desires, after all. But... I also don't wish to begin this new phase of our relationship on the wrong foot," he said simply, before taking her wrist, guiding it to his groin to feel his hardness throbbing there, as he kissed her lips. "Long term plans and all, hm?"

Her fingers flexed atop his masculinity, not quite grasping, not quite recoiling, but almost a mixture of the two. A rush of excitement and fear snaked through her, and she gasped at the intrusion of it all.

For him, it had been calculated, years in the planning.

For her, it was far more sudden.

She had been his protege, the woman who longed to follow in his footsteps. He had laid the path for her, and she walked it alone, never seeing where it would take her. As much as anyone could, she trusted him. Trusted that, as long as she didn't disappoint him, he would meet her at her destination.

It felt almost crass to realize just how base his plans for her were.

"I..." she sputtered, trying to blink the haze from her mind. "Magister, you've always just been... very official with me. You'll pardon a girl for not seeing it coming."

"Ah, I know. Blame me for feeling a little more vigorous of late," he said as he kissed her again, then pulled back, going to his wine glass. "I will make all things clear to you in time. But it will take time for you to understand. It will be a lot to wrap your mind around," he said, draining what was left of his glass before going over and taking an ornamental box from atop the fireplace.

"When you kill her, it has to be done with a blade weapon. Not a gun. That could cause problems," he said, as he came over to her, offering her that rectangular shaped box. It was about the length of her forearm.

Her gaze went from him to it, nodding as his words made their way through her befuddled mind.

"I will see it's done properly, Magister. I know what it is you're offering me, and I will not return to your disappointment," she managed.

"Good," he said, smiling lightly. "And we'll find time to readjust our relationship. To both our likings, hm?" he remarked, before opening the box, showing a very peculiar – and all too familiar – ornamental looking dagger.

So intensely familiar in fact, it quite shocked her.

It looked just like the one she'd taken off the old man, Caleb.

"What... wow. It's beautiful." The words tumbled off her lips, and she hoped it would hide the recognition in her gaze. "It has meaning?"

"Oh yes," he said, patting her pale cheek again. "And you'll understand that once you use it. I'll explain things to you, things you could not have guessed. But only after you take this first, real step," he said, smiling to her again, as if they had not just had the most alarming encounter of her life together.

"The details of where to go will be on your wrist by the time you get home and change," he said, looking at her with that hint of longing still.

"A shame we never had some fun all the same."

He was coaxing her along. He knew her so intimately, better than she knew herself at times, and even in her confusion, she hated leaving him like that. He had a way of making her want things, even when she didn't.

"I wouldn't want to sully you if I prove to not be up to this task, Magister."

The air turned chilly, a frown tugging his lips.

"Such a silly thing to say."

He didn't spare her a glance as he left her alone in that room, the weight of his disappointment suffocating her in his absence.

CHAPTER 23

FAMILY REUNION

Behold, I am sending you out as sheep in the midst of wolves, so be wise as serpents and innocent as doves.

— MATTHEW 10:16

The island contained secret pockets of time and space that she'd never considered. She'd always taken for granted that the devices and maps were mostly accurate, with tiny blips that could potentially be exploited.

She had been too trusting of her environment, that much was becoming abundantly clear.

She was to make her way to the North-West side of the island, to an empty place on the map. Even the satellite view showed an empty ridge. A second set of coordinates came, informing her of where to ditch her vehicle. It left what looked to be at least a good half hour walk in between.

It was going to be a challenging evening, and she was grateful that she'd taken the opportunity to sleep when she had it.

She decided to travel light. Her regular platform boots would help protect her from the brush, and the leather jacket would keep her concealed. She decided to wear her only pair of pants. They were black, skin-tight, and had a good amount of stretch, so they'd better allow her to flit through the darkness without worry.

In her pockets she brought a few painkillers and a tourniquet, just in case things turned dark. Other than her watch, she left behind anything else that might link her to the scene, as a precaution.

It was a long drive. A long, lonely drive, past the tavern that held the only one she'd come to trust. As she bypassed the turnoff onto that little community, a communication came through her wrist. Over the voice link, she saw it was from Abel.

She ignored it, continuing on into the night.

She really didn't have time for a booty-call.

When finally she got to the northern shores of the island, she turned off onto a dirt road, which then became little more than a path. By the time she reached the location to abandon the vehicle marked on her GPS, already knew there was no other option. The path ahead was too narrow.

From there, it was night vision or no sight at all. The night was so black, and the trees were clustered at the base of the mountain.

Up and up she went, as the path became rocky, and its

incline grew steeper. Until finally she saw it. There, up nestled into the sides of the mountain was another strange, oddly old-fashioned idea of a futuristic building.

Much like the one where she'd captured Caleb.

Identical in almost all regards.

A shiver went through her.

The horrors she'd seen were still vibrant in her memory, try as she might to forget them.

She strengthened her resolve, taking in a breath as she took the ceremonial dagger in her right hand, getting used to its weight.

It wasn't built for pure utility, like the daggers she was used to. But it looked almost beautiful in its macabre elegance. The jagged hooks on the blade would make it an excruciating thing to plunge into someone. And then rip back out.

It would certainly get the job done.

Though as she continued on towards the building, one thing immediately stood out to her: This place didn't look abandoned. Didn't look run down at all, in fact. It looked quite well kept. And when she reached the fence, same as around the other one, she found the gate sealed shut.

It took her some time to search around the edge of the gate, to find a place she might get over. But eventually, a big old tree, with a thick branch that extended over the fence was located, and she was able to risk climbing up it.

Her slender frame crawled up along it, using some spiked tips protruding from her boots – on the push of a button – to keep her lodged in it. Soon she was precariously out over the spiked metal fence, the branch crackling beneath her.

It was a terrifying moment, as she dangled down, the branch creaking even more. Until she let herself drop and she hit the ground, crouching immediately to lessen the impact on her knees.

Once in, though, things did not get easier. There were guards at the gate. But she knew how the other place had worked. And she bypassed it, heading for the garage.

Things were easier from there, because the hatch here was powered. The air from the tunnel was crisp and fresh, but it mingled with the memory of the other house, and bile rose in her throat. She swallowed it back, forcing herself down the faintly lit hallway, towards the looming, metal door ahead.

It was so similar, like an apparition that was haunting her, and she forced herself to look away and focus on her mission.

No secrets or deception would matter if she wasn't able to pull this off. She was trained how to be single minded, but the lure of that horrible scene was putting that all to the test.

After that moment's hesitation of her hand hovering over the door's switch... she pressed it, and it hissed open.

The sight that greeted her was far different than the one from the other house. This didn't look like some old cult bunker. Immediately the view of a sterile laboratory greeted her. So many bubbly tubes and canisters. Strange, fleshy things growing inside them.

And over where the statue had been was instead a glass wall, looking into another chamber. In which some scientist in a lab coat, worked on the body of...

Cole?

No sound came through, but the young Cole screamed as the scientist cut into him, then turned to a specimen jar at his side.

Valeska's eyes widened in horror.

She had tried not to think about Cole's fate, done so much to distract her from it, but to see him like that...

She had been raised a proud daughter of Satan, able to take joy in suffering so long as it wasn't hers. Pity was just another word for weakness, and she was brought up to feed upon it. She'd never been exposed to someone who was worthy of something else. Something more.

But Cole...

He was the only one who had brought that feeling up in her in so long. There was something about him that made her want to protect him, and she had no idea why.

She wanted to rush in there. Stab the scientist. Free Cole and tell him to run far from this place.

Her pity would get her killed, just as it would get him killed.

She had to find her target. Once the Magistra was dealt with, then perhaps she could indulge her pity.

Valeska focused back on her target, and assumed that a Magistra would not be hanging around in the laboratory area. So she accessed that door to the house, and it opened with a hiss.

The sound of angry music greeted her, growing louder the higher up she went. Once she was peeking her head up through that stairway, she saw a well-appointed home. A manor of sorts, with strange, eclectic art of Satan, the many visages of his angels. Whether paintings or busts, all manner of things.

The lights were dim, but there was a staircase that went up. A quick look around showed nobody. A dining room, kitchen, living area, all lavishly appointed, but quite empty. So there was only up.

As she got up there, she found herself looking at the back of someone, standing in front of the window. Her long, white hair draped down her back, as she stood there in a black dress.

It had to be her target, right? This strange, pale woman amid the curious office space. The blaring metal music, so angry and intense.

Her grip shifted on the ceremonial blade, not too firm, not too loose.

The Magisters and Magistra had security that Valeska couldn't even fathom, and she didn't want to give this woman a chance to activate any failsafe. It had to be quick. Efficient. Stealthy.

As she moved in to make the kill, the blaring angry music drowning out and sound she could make, the woman began to turn.

Valeska was so close. So very close! And that sheet of pale hair swept away, until she found herself looking into a face that was so upsettingly familiar.

Valerie. Her. It was like looking into a mirror that aged her before her eyes. An albino version of herself, only maybe... sixty years old.

And in her shock of the moment, she still tried to do the deed. Only to find between her and the woman, a clear, transparent wall barred her way.

The smirk on the woman's face was so fucking familiar it made her skin crawl.

Valeska didn't give her the satisfaction of cursing, or acting surprised.

She just stared, her ruby eyes boring into her near-double.

"Don't make this a bigger thing than it needs to be."

The other woman never lost her smirk. But she softened a little.

"Sorry it had to be this way, little V," she remarked, as if a mother to her child. "You did a remarkable job making it this far. Surviving the game as long as you did. But I've played it a lot longer than you. I had an advantage," she said, that pale, albino image of herself stepping closer to the invisible barrier, her naturally red eyes scanning over Valeska.

Valeska could only grin.

She had no plan, and was at a disadvantage. But this was a test that the Magister clearly didn't intend for her to fail, and somehow, that gave her enough confidence to at least *act* like she had the upper hand.

"You might have been the queen of your crop, but each time, we come back a little bit better, don't we," she said, as if she were certain.

The other woman's smirk vanished, replaced with a look of amusement.

"It's such a shame, how we must work. I always admire you other little V's. So spunky. So fiery. And the lower you get – the lower we get – the bitchier we become. I can't help but admire it and be amused each time," she said, a little wistful. "I sometimes miss what it was like to be like you. Up and coming, so full of fire. Having everything under your control is not as appealing as it might seem," she said, pacing a bit, back and forth, never keeping her eyes off Valeska for long.

"Then how about I allow you a death wish. You can tell me what you'd have done differently, and I'll consider honouring it once you're gone."

Valeska began to pace with her, discreetly trying to find a way past that barrier.

The other V stopped, and looked at her, as if she were a mother, touched by something sweet her child said.

"Fiery to the bitter end," her older doppelgänger said, touching her dainty hand to the glass. That size and shape... so alike Valeska's own. The proportions identical. Her nails even polished black. Fuck, even the taste in music suited her so infuriatingly well! "Okay. I'll do you a favour," she said, licking her lips, "I'll tell you. Because the key to every V's downfall so far has been one special thing. And, if I'm being honest... I was no more immune to it at your age, than you are. We are the same after all."

Valeska knew that, no matter the answer, she wasn't going to like it. But her damnable need for information, for secrets. Her curiosity was a torture she could never find a salve for.

So, she stood, staring at the other woman.

"I met Valerie. The blonde. She drew the short straw this time," Valeska said, trying to deny that burning desire for this older V to tell her what her downfall would be.

"Oh yes. I never liked that. It never felt sporting to give some of us a head's up. And others..." The older V shrugged, acknowledging the truth of the matter for Valerie. "But the C's... they just have to control everything. Have to have backups, in easy access," she said with a sigh.

"But yes, that brings me back to your weakness. Men," she said, a hint of distaste to her tongue.

"Always men. Trusting the wrong ones, over and over, in the hopes that we get to the point we realize they're all the wrong ones. The moment you trust a man is the moment you die, sometimes it just takes a while to realize it."

Valeska stopped in her tracks at her words, a foggy memory suddenly becoming so clear.

The Magister had said something like that to her before.

The day she tried to save that sweet, soft faced boy from drowning.

Suddenly she realized why Cole was so familiar to her. That beguiling face, the innocent, wide eyes. His hair was darker, but she couldn't deny the truth any longer.

It was in that moment of clarity that Valeska was struck in the side with a blow, the silence of the music being cut deafening.

Before she could recover, two big, strong guards grabbed her by her arms. She tried to slash up at them with the dagger, but they anticipated it, knocking it out of her hand.

Their damned approach had been utterly masked by the noise, the dim lighting, and the distracting talk with the older V, who was no longer smirking. She let her guard down, just as the Magistra warned her. As the Magister warned her.

"Perhaps I was the only one of us to realize there is no such thing as a trustworthy man," the albino said. "And that is why I will go on. Regain my youth. And you... Well, I'll try not to make it too bad for you. But knowing us, you'll just hate me even more for the sympathy," she laughed.

"Is Cole one of the C's?" Valeska managed to croak out, not that it mattered. None of it mattered.

But she still had to know. Always.

"Of course," the albino said, as the guards began to haul Valeska away. The invisible wall must have retracted, because she casually stepped forward and picked up that dagger of hers. "But I guess you are still so young. It must be hard to imagine how such a sweet seeming thing can grow into such a..." she paused, pondering her words as she followed after, to the top of the stairs, as Valeska was hauled down lower. "Conniving dick."

She let herself be dragged, to feign defeat, but she knew that this V would see right through it.

Apparently, girls like her don't go down without a fight.

She glanced up at the guards, her tiny form easily dragged by the much brawnier men. But if there was one thing she learned, the bigger the man, the harder they fall. She just had to wait for the right moment.

And as she did, she glared back at V.

"So, I guess you castrated these two to keep them leashed?"

The albino V laughed at that as the stairs spiralled around, and Valeska soon came out of view of her.

"I can't believe you never asked which one it was that turned you in. They usually ask that," said the albino, her voice echoing down the stairwell. "Maybe you learned the lesson I imparted after all. And just intend to hate them all," she mused.

Valeska prepared to make her move, trying to catch the

momentum she needed, she felt the strength drain from her. Her arms and legs were no longer working as reality bled away.

It wasn't until that moment she realized that the hit to her side had not been a mere punch. The fucking brutes must've jabbed her with some drug and *knocked... her... out.*

CHAPTER 24

Why are you incensed,
  and why is your face fallen?
  For whether you offer well,
  or whether you do not,
  at the tent flap sin crouches
  and for you is its longing,
  but you will rule over it.

— GENESIS 4:7

Cold air greeted her naked skin as her back was pressed into a metal bed. She tried to move, quickly realizing her wrists and ankles were strapped to the table, and she was utterly prone. The sterile scent of laboratory equipment wafted towards her, the bubbles in the vats and beakers periodically breaking the surface.

237

She yanked her head up to look around and found Cole beside her, strapped down, his incision sealed back up.

"Hey," he said, looking at her with those handsome, innocent looking eyes. "You're awake."

"Hi, Cole," Valeska sighed, still groggy as she began to look around. She should have just done the stupid thing and tried to save him. Maybe then she wouldn't be next up on the slab.

She should have seen it coming. It was almost like a warning sign, him being here. Why would the Magister give his enemy a captive that she'd had to go behind the upper brass to save if this wasn't all a set up?

But then she turned to Cole, thoughtfully.

"Have we met?"

The look on his face answered the question right away. He looked at her confused, brow furrowed.

"No... at least I don't think so. My name's not Cole, for starters," he remarked, stretched out nude beside her. "I'm Cain. How'd you end up here?"

"Oh. Well... nice to meet you, I guess," she said, her ruby eyes scanning him. At least they didn't take her contacts. Not that night vision was going to help her here. "And I guess I was betrayed, that's how I ended up here. Too stupid to see it coming. You?"

"Oh, they just grabbed me out of my bunk one night. I don't know why," he said, sounding so sweet and innocent. It was truly hard to imagine the young C's and the older C's – like Caleb and her Magister – being the same men. The young ones looked so sweet and innocent, like they'd never hurt a fly, let alone a lamb. But she knew how cold and calculating they were. How Caleb felt nothing about the death of the man who saved his ass.

"I wish we could've actually met another time," he said. "You're very beautiful," he said, with a twitch in his groin that went unhidden thanks to their nudity.

She couldn't help but let out a small laugh.

It was the perfect encapsulation of the Isle. Tied up in a lab, waiting to feel pain beyond their darkest imaginations, and still flirting.

"Thanks, Cain. I saw them working on you earlier. I wanted to save you, but I had to take care of something first. Then they ended up taking care of me instead. How long have you been here?"

"I have no idea," he said, looking around the room curiously. "They drug me every so often and I black out."

As if on cue, a door slid open. This one leading from a room she did not expect to be there, as she'd seen no parallel in the other bunker. But out of it came a man in a shiny smock and lab coat, a gas mask and goggles on.

"Oh no, not again," Cain said with a sigh, as the man came and injected him with something.

Valeska watched, her eyes scanning the butcher. She didn't have any intention on giving up and having her body cut into and reassembled, but her opportunities for escape would be... narrow, to say the least.

Maybe non-existent.

She refused to believe that.

Abaddon was the House of destroyers and executioners. But they were apparently proficient torturers, and if she could find a way to turn the tables...

As she studied the butcher, she caught sight of the

many medical implements that were tucked in the many pockets of his smock.

He bent over Cain, and one of the metal tools was tantalizingly close to her hands. She reached out for it, just as he shifted position, inspecting Cain's eyes as if she weren't even in the room. She waited, biding her time, until he moved towards her again, leaning down to open Cain's mouth.

She stretched her slender fingers as much as she could, trying to grasp that thing.

In a miraculous win for style over substance, it was her long, black nails that saved the day. They tilted it towards her, and just before it clattered to the ground, she wrapped her hand around it.

Immediately the butcher began to turn, and she had only a split second to try and tuck that scalpel in under her wrist to hide it. After all, she had nowhere near the movement needed to wield it as a weapon.

He turned and looked down at her, red eyes staring through his goggles as he inspected her.

She furrowed her brows, blinking her eyes groggily, as if she were still trying to wake up from whatever drug it was that they gave her.

He then went around her, to the other side, as Cain looked at her. His eyes were heavy with weariness.

"Damn, guess it's lights out again... in case we don't meet a second time, it was nice meeting y-..."

He was out, and then she felt the butcher jab her with another needle.

Soon her own consciousness bled away, once again...

She had no idea when it was the next time she awoke.

But she was laid there, with Cain still beside her, though he looked quite out of it still.

She instantly remembered her little scalpel like tool that she had swiped, and a quick inspection of the room told her that she was alone. And so, she took that limited time to begin to get the blade in place, and start to cut through her bindings. They were thick, perhaps some kind of nylon.

The scalpel was not going to make short work of them. It would take time, operating it at that angle. There was a thinner strap that would be easier to cut through, she wagered, but it was on top, and she couldn't line it up appropriately.

As the moments of silent tension went by, finally she was making progress, cutting through it in such a way that it would hopefully go unnoticed if she was caught partway.

But that was put to the test sooner than she'd like as the door hissed open, and that albino V entered into the room. The butcher was at her side, and Valeska had to hide her work.

"Awake, are we?" said the Albino version of her as two of her brawny men came in behind. Four of them, all together. Even if Valeska could get out, she had no hope of taking on that many. Nude, and still mostly strapped down.

"Awake and refreshed," Valeska quipped, trying to play things casual. "I could go for breakfast now. I imagine it's around that time?"

The albino smiled at her, looking amused as the butcher of a scientist went about his work.

"You didn't have much on you. Just your watch really," the albino remarked as one of the brutes went and put that watch into a box. "But do you want me to send it to anyone? Any..." she hesitated, "Any message for anyone special to you?"

"I actually had some pain killers on me too. Wouldn't mind having those back. And you can send the watch to the one who betrayed me. Who did you say that was again?"

The albino smiled wryly, seemingly endlessly amused with the younger version of herself.

"Holy shit... your mom is the one who put you in here?!" Cain piped up, apparently having just awoken. He sounded horrified and in disbelief.

Sweet lamb.

The albino only laughed.

"Get her ready for the ritual," the albino said as the butcher injected Valeska with another syringe. "Then take her into the room, anoint her in the oils. I have something to tend to, but tomorrow I should be ready," she said as the men all nodded and began carrying on their grisly tasks.

"Sorry it has to be this way. I survived the last generation. And as tepid as things can be, I don't really care not to keep surviving these rounds," she said, as reality began to bleed away for Valeska again.

The last thing she heard was the albino's voice, sounding distant. Faint.

"We'll arrange for the transfer of this other one once I'm done. Things are moving quickly now."

Silence.

Blackness.

What happened after death was always somewhat of a riddle to her. They were taught that death is the end, the finale, and that avoiding it at all costs was the most desirable thing. That pain could be welcomed, as a reminder of being alive.

Yet there was always a question mark at the end of it all. A strange lilt to the voice that beckoned your mind to wander, and ask, *what if there's more.*

What if there was something following all this?

Not a heaven, not a hell, but for her... reincarnation. Of a sorts. A continuation of her story that was to be cut short.

It wouldn't be her, but what was she anyway? The other V saw through her so easily, with that soft recognition of something that bound them together, and then... pity.

Pity it had to be like this.

Pity only one of us could survive.

Her stomach churned as she began to prod at the edges of consciousness, the snake within her coiling up in warning. She would not be a mouse to be pitied.

THE RED LIGHTS shone up through the floor of the corridor, casting eerie shadows on the walls. Valeska rose her head slightly, but when she saw *that* door, her heart stopped.

She cut off her screams as the door pulled open and she was surrounded by the eldritch carvings, the bizarrely wrong creatures.

A great statue of some monstrous thing that conformed to no angel of Satan loomed over her as she was brought into the shrine to darker things than the Dark Lord himself.

She was still strapped to the same gurney, but it was tilted upright. Panic nearly made her drop the scalpel as she wondered if she still had it. She rebounded in time, clinging to it as the two big brutes pushed her into position. They detached the metal plank she was strapped to from the gurney, sliding her onto the altar.

If she had been seeing it all for the first time, she would have lost her cool.

Seeing it for the second time was...

Not much better, honestly.

Especially since she'd seen the remnants of the last ritual.

She remembered what V had said. Take her to the room. Anoint her in oils. Tomorrow she'd be ready. Perhaps that was today, now. It was difficult to tell.

"You guys aren't that chatty, huh?" she asked, her voice still a bit groggy. She couldn't let terror in. Chop, chop, chop it all away. The chimera would be proud.

The men were wearing grim looks as they gathered up some old, ceremonial looking pots. They appeared as if they were downright ancient in fact. They didn't reply to her, instead taking heaping handfuls of some kind of oil, splattering it onto her nude body, then drizzling more onto her.

The way they were rubbing it into her flesh, coating her all over, would have been downright hot, if she didn't know her end was coming.

But she had the scalpel.

She had her chance.

And she had almost gotten through the binding last time.

"Fuck, I wish I had your guy's jobs," she said, watching them work the oil into her pale, unblemished flesh. She just had to keep them distracted as she started to squirm, hopefully shielding her more frantic cutting motions from them. "I hardly ever get to give anyone a hot rub down where I work."

That managed to get a smirk from one of the men, who then got a little too generous with the oil along her thighs. Especially the inner thighs.

"She's got a point, mate," said the smirking fool as he slathered his thick, oily fingers along her slit. "What if we took some liberties with this one before the ritual?"

"You nuts? She'd kill us," said the second oaf.

"How? There ain't no cameras in here, or anywhere near here. And she won't be by for a while. And this one is gonna be dead before long anyhow. What's it matter if we give her a final send off, huh?" said the smirker as he leered at Valeska, fondling a breast with one hand as he tried to finger her a little.

The oil helped disguise any hesitancy Valeska felt in that moment.

And honestly... it wouldn't be the worst thing to happen to her today.

They were big and rough looking, and though it never came up in the bedroom, she was fully capable of playing submissive when she had to.

Valeska grinned at the one fingering her, rocking her hips forward a little.

"Wow, she really did basically castrate you guys if you're only just realizing the perks of your position now."

The oaf snorted at that, while the smirker with the

accent only took the encouragement bait. Letting a finger probe into her slit deeper as he fondled her perky tits.

"I'm gonna put the dagger on the altar, before we forget. You know how she likes everything perfect," said the oaf.

"Miss out on this if you want, but I ain't passin' her up," said the smirker as he helped himself to her more and more. Those big, beefy hands groping, fondling. Valeska cut off the part of herself that felt disgust at their disrespect, setting it along side the pity and fear on her altar of emotions that would get her killed.

"I never said that! I just want this done first. It's not like we get these opportunities a lot. She hasn't claimed one of these younger Vs in all the time I've been here. Not gonna get many chances to help ourselves to one out in the middle of nowhere."

Luckily for Valeska the room was dark, and with how distracted the guy fingering her was, she was able to dare cutting into the bindings a bit more.

"Fuck you're greedy," Valeska moaned, her sensitive body responding obediently to the attention. "She's playing with fire, letting you get so pent-up. Not really following in Satan's hoof-prints on that one."

Her head pressed back, her eyes fluttering shut as she let the man help himself to her body, a brief tendril of pleasure making the skin on her arms prickle pleasantly.

"She's really into it. Fuck, she's a fiery one, mate," said the smirker as he continued to finger her as he began to unbuckle his own belt.

Valeska was in a moment of decision then. This was her chance.

Two of them.

One of her.

She was strapped down, but she felt the scalpel cut through the last of that one binding. She wouldn't be able to free herself from the others quickly, but she could stab one with the blade at least. The other though, was the big issue...

She nearly cried out for joy when the more 'reluctant' oaf came back, unbuckling his own pants. Right near her face.

"Might as well go out stuffed nice and full, eh sweetie?" said the oaf as he whipped out his hard cock near her face.

And Valeska could see it play out in her mind. This was how she'd win.

"That's what I'm saying," she said, eyeing that dick with a hunger that wasn't purely carnal.

"I'm Satan's daughter, and if there's one thing I was taught, it was that there's never a bad time to indulge in the pleasures of the flesh."

CHAPTER 25

CHEKOV'S TEETH

A strange girl, all phosphorous and cantharides, burning with every desire! And burning with every vice!

— JEAN LORRAIN

Her tongue ran along the point of her teeth. They were the last line of defence from someone taking too much. A weapon not easily removed.

They should have yanked them out when they had the chance.

She watched as that big guy plucked his finger from her pussy, and then got up between her legs on the altar. That thick, meaty shaft slid over her lips, as if teasing her.

She knew then that she had them. She could do this. The dumb shit was too stupid to even think about those silver fangs in her mouth as she wrapped her lips around his shaft, then plunged them in.

The look on his face as his blood flowed into her mouth was something to remember.

It was a shame she couldn't savour it. Before he could cry out, her arm was swinging for that smirking bastard atop her.

The scalpel found his neck, then found it again, and again, as he was too busy lining up his dick for her pussy to defend himself in time. As he slumped over to the side, the other man began to scream as his cock was gripped by her.

He was trying to pry her head off his junk, but she just brought the scalpel into his arm, severed his muscles, then began to stab into his neck and face too.

When all was done, the two brutes were slumped down, and her pale flesh was spattered in crimson. It was like being born anew upon that altar, and she began to cut her other bindings away.

It was easier once she had full motion of that hand, and she freed the other. Her two ankles followed.

She slipped off the altar, springing to her feet with just a moment's dizziness.

Fuck, how long was she out?

There wasn't time to consider.

Her gaze landed on the dark, ceremonial dagger – identical to the one the Magister gave her, identical to Caleb's – sitting there before the ominous statue.

Fuck it, it would make a better weapon than the scalpel at least, and she grabbed it up, before heading to the door.

Nude and spattered in blood, Valeska went down that hallway, dagger in one hand, scalpel in the other. The red lights that lined the floor made her look like one of Satan's fallen angels herself.

As she opened the door into the next room, she saw that fucking butcher, in his scientist garb. The look of shock on his face was obvious, even with the gas mask and goggles.

She didn't hesitate. She was running on adrenaline and rage, the snake that was constantly rattling within her lashing out with a fury she hadn't felt in too long. She'd become detached from her work, disinterested in even taking advantage of her position. Of rising up and becoming something more. It had all just become a cold calculation, divorced from her own ravenous desires.

In cutting off all the emotions the Magister required, she had become a shell of the fiery bitch she was meant to be.

She lunged at him, the scalpel swiping low in a feign as she brought the ceremonial blade to his gut.

He was no match. Though he swung a motorized saw at her, she was the far better, more agile fighter.

She impaled his gut on that blade, then stuck the scalpel up into his arm, forcing him to drop the surgical saw onto the floor. His eyes were wide behind his goggles as he slumped back against the wall, coughing blood into his mask.

The spray of red mist shot out of its exhaust, showering her naked body with his gore.

"Fuck you," she cried out as she brought the dagger down into him again and again, his twitching body finally falling limp as blood pooled around them. She was panting as she pushed herself up, slipping in the blood before she grabbed the empty table where Cain had been.

Cain was gone. The 'transfer' the albino had spoken of was handled.

She went for the box they'd put her watch in, and as she reclaimed it. It immediately lit up with dozens of messages, almost all of them from Videl.

"Where are you? Should I pick you up?"

"Reporting for duty, Ma'am. What are your orders?"

"The unit is on routine duty. I hope you're enjoying your vacation. If you need anything, I remain at your command."

"Over-Lieutenant?"

They became more frantic after that, without the coded concern.

Valeska heard the taunt of V echoing in her head, so similar to the warning that Caleb had given her. Trust no one. Count on no one. Trust will get you killed.

And then the Magister's voice, from so long ago. The words that heralded her decimation, the vivisection of her being.

"He was sent here to kill you, Valeska. There are no friends for you in this world. The moment you trust someone is the moment you find a blade between your shoulders."coords

Videl could have turned her into the Magister, and set all this up. Let her walk into a trap, reaped the rewards from the House. That level of intrigue was rare from an outsider, it would make him standout, and rise up higher than he could, even under her.

And still, Valeska queued a message to Videl.

"Had some business to take care of, got in over my head. If you get this, hopefully it means I'm still alive. Will send coords when I can."

There was no signal in the bunker, so it wouldn't go out until she got back in range, or out of the jamming area, but...

She really did trust him.

She began to play the message from Abel that he had left the night she got captured as she searched the body of the butcher.

"Hey, it's me. Remember that one-night stand?" came Abel's voice, a bit shaky and hesitant. "Not making a bootie call, I swear. Wish that was the case. So anyhow... I signed up. Still in training... obviously. Not like I could graduate in so little time."

Valeska sighed in annoyance at his rambling. If she were on the phone with him, she'd tell him to spit it out.

This is why she hated voice mails.

"But something's been bothering me. I wasn't sure how to bring it up. Or if I should. But that morning, when you ran off... fuck," he swore, sounding so uncomfortable. "Hard to say this. Especially as a message. But there was a guy, and he threatened me not to ever tell you. Said he'd ruin me, my hopes of staying on the island. Just... gimme a call back, okay?"

"Fucking chosen son," Valeska hissed in annoyance. Why were mainlanders always so meek?

The butcher's wrist device lit up, a message from 'Valeda' coming through, an image of the albino on the screen.

So that was the Magistra's name.

"What's going on there? Getting alerts from the facility, and no response from those two buffoons."

She was running out of time. She grabbed the watch off the dead man's wrist, and when she looked up, she saw the klaxon light blinking outside in the viewing area of the laboratory. The sirens must have been screaming, but the soundproofing of the room was impressive.

"Shit!"

She stood up, glancing around the room for a weapon, when the flashing lights drew her eye to the edge of the room. There was a shadow where there shouldn't be one, and she went to the wall, her fingers tracing the straight seam of a hidden door. In the blindingly antiseptic light of the lab, it was invisible, but as the red warning went off, it revealed a precious secret.

She pushed in, and found a small storage room, and there in the corner was her officer's sword and belt.

Her heart leapt out of her chest.

"Thank you, Lilith," she swore, her fingers tracing the sign of the eternal mother on her bloody torso. The pattern of a snake wrapped around her in a protective, possessive hold. She grabbed the belt and strapped it on her hips, sheathing the ceremonial dagger as she took the scalpel and her favourite stiletto in her hands.

She was naked, covered in blood, and burning with rage.

She had no illusions about her way out being anything but a gory flurry of anguish.

It wasn't going to be hers.

She exited the secret room just as a man burst through

the lab door. She met him a sharp stiletto dagger to the gut as she sliced him open in the gizzard, before he could even spot her.

She ducked, avoiding his swinging assault with a cudgel, her scalpel slicing through the skin and muscle of his calf. He toppled back, knocking into the next guard that was rushing into the room.

He didn't stumble as he raised a handgun towards her, but she threw the scalpel with an expert precision. His eye was punctured as the sickening scream melded with the klaxon siren. She took advantage of the moment, plunging the stiletto into the throat of the man on the ground, ending him with a clean maneuver.

But more were coming.

Two of them had electrified cattle prods, and they tried to flank her as she stepped into that big room.

Out came Valeska's sword, and she parried one of their assaults with an electrical spark as her blade met that electrical weapon. The grip on her hilt was shielded from transmitting the flow of current, and she quickly rebounded.

She laughed as her sword flashed through the air, finding his jugular as a gurgling scream struggled from his dying body.

Her nude form was a canvas for the messy spray of blood all around her.

He collapsed to the floor, grasping for her legs, but the blood let her slip easily from his weak attempt at restraint.

"Stop!" shouted another in the doorway, pointing a taser at her.

She ignored it. The other cattle prod was coming for her, and she gnashed her teeth in a growl as their weapons brought them to a standstill. She pressed forward and up, towards the taller man, as she let him think he was pushing her down to the ground. She waited for the right time, and when he pushed his arm forward, her stiletto pierced the crook of his armpit, expertly slipping between the ribs into his lung.

The taser hit her just as her stiletto pierced flesh again, this time impaling his heart.

Pain exploded through her and she screamed out, falling to her knees.

Or rather one knee.

One more. She had to kill one more.

Gunshots rang out in the distance, and the ground shook with the impact of an explosion. More were coming for her.

But for now, it was just him and her.

She stubbornly, resiliently got up and began to walk at that man.

The taser was still embedded in her, and the man sent another jolt through her, but she didn't let it do more than just destabilize her for a moment. She was blinded by the fury, and protected by the primordial she-demon. Lilith.

Whatever experiments had been done to bring her into existence, whatever dark rituals and prayers had been offered, she knew: She was chosen for glory.

She was not a mere human.

He stared in shock, unable to parry as her bloody sword swung down and his hand slid to the ground, the taser clattering on the laboratory floor.

She wasn't even able to gloat as two more men rushed into the hall, AK-470s in hand.

They stormed into the room, lining up along that wall, pointing their guns at her as she backed away.

"Freeze! Or we shoot!" they bellowed.

She was too far away. Even if she tossed the stiletto, it would be too slow to stop their bullets. She panted for breath, and for a second, she thought it was over. There was no dark miracle that could protect her from a spray of bullets.

But a smile teased at the corner of her lips.

Valeda didn't go through all this trouble to let some goons kill her.

She had to be sacrificed on that altar.

They wouldn't pull the trigger.

They wouldn't fucking *dare*.

"Stop! Don't fucking move, bitch!"

Her bloody footsteps were wet on the floor as she prowled closer, a Wolf ready to devour its prey. She would enjoy this one.

But she didn't have a chance to call their bluff.

A dozen shots travelled through first the one near the door leading out through the garage, then passing through each of them. Valeska's eyes widened in surprise as their heads exploded in a spray of red mist. She squeezed her eyes shut just in time as their bodies were eviscerated, showering her in more gore until she was covered, head to toe.

When she wiped the blood from her eyes, all she could see was a gun pointed right at her chest.

CHAPTER 26

LILITH WOULD BE PROUD

At evening, the radiant star, the Venus star, the great light which fills the holy heavens,

the lady of the evening, ascends above like a warrior, the people in all the lands lift their gaze to her...

As the lady, admired by the Land, the lone star,

the Venus star, the lady elevated as high as the heaven,

ascends above like a warrior, all the lands tremble before her...

— ANCIENT SUMERIAN TEXT

Her eyes were blurry from blood, and she didn't move, her weapons still in hand, as her gaze rose up from the tricked-out AK-470's muzzle. A tall man in full military armour towered over her, a full gas mask and helmet concealing his identity, a red visor covering his eyes.

"Fucking party pooper," she said, panting for breath from the exertion. Her black hair was matted to her head, her body stained crimson, and all five-feet-nothing of her stood as tall and as proud as she could muster. "You just stole my kills."

The gun fell, no longer pointed at her as the figure's shoulders slumped. He reached up and pulled his gasp mask down, and Videl's relieved face stared down at her.

"Shit. Why'd I even bother organizing this?" he said, smiling proudly at her. "You look like Lilith Herself," he said, before lunging down to hug her in his powerful arms.

And she wrapped her arms around his neck as well, letting out a mixed sound of laughing sobs.

"That's what I was going for," she laughed in surprise. "Holy shit, I can't believe it's you. What the fuck?"

The relief she felt in that moment was potent, and she didn't even fight to get control of herself. Maybe it was the adrenaline still flowing in her veins, or maybe the anointing oils that had primed her for the blood-spray painting made everything feel a bit more real.

Hardly mattered.

She'd managed to find the one person on this hedonistic island that she could actually trust, and that felt pretty fucking awesome.

But their joyous reunion had to be short lived.

Gunfire continued to ring out above ground and he pulled back from her, eyes actually a bit watery. He got that under control fast.

"We have to go," he said, as she picked up one of those

unused AKs off the floor. "It's a long story. The Magister had me organize a rescue effort, but he refused to let me take them into action. I couldn't wait any more. I was only able to muster one other to back me up. And well, he's not the greatest..." he said, just as she saw another of Valeda's guards coming from above.

She very smoothly brought her AK up and opened fire, mowing down the latest reinforcements as Videl jerked his head around in time to see them slump down.

"I'm sure we'll do fine," she said, her grin turning feral as she was able to fling herself back into the fight.

But this time, it was knowing that she had help.

Someone on her side, without question.

Men can't be trusted my ass, Valeda.

Videl pointed his AK up the hall into the building, then fired another grenade round. The eruption collapsed the path before he turned and ushered her through the garage.

"We have to get down to the hummer," he said as they went up through. Emerging from the garage, she watched as some hovering gun drones fired at the manor.

"Backup?"

"Only the best for you," he grinned, his arm in front of her chest to keep her back. He did a three second countdown on his fingers, then together they charged out.

The scream of metal and gunfire filled their ears as they fired into the manor, running towards the blown open gate. Parts of brick and stone showered down on them before she hopped over the gate, spinning around just in time to pick off a man that was about to open fire.

Videl pumped the grenade launcher a couple more times, then lobbed two more blasts at the front before he ushered her down the path. The two of them ran through the woods as the gun drones still fired behind them, but with how many explosions she counted, they weren't going to last much longer.

She was barefoot, but the rush of battle, and the fear of the spectre of death, it all made the discomfort of her soles pale in comparison.

Luckily the grass along the sides of the path made for a soft journey. And the two of them raced along, heading down that path she'd trod that one night. Only now it was under the burning light of day.

"How'd you get the drone guns to fire on that place? I figured their programming would prevent that."

"Yeah, they did. They wouldn't even fly in there. Not at first," Videl explained as they rushed ahead. "But my backup knew a little trick to solve that."

She was going to ask more, but they were both breathless with the chase. And soon, they were coming up on the hummer, the turret's AI pointing at them, but then, thankfully, not opening fire.

"Hop in. I brought a change of clothes for you too," he said as she opened the door and got inside.

"About time," Caleb said, putting aside the remote-control device for the drones. "There goes the last of my pretty little drones," he sighed. "I don't suppose I'll get to play like that again any time soon."

Videl pulled the vehicle out onto the road as Valeska whipped around, looking at Caleb's pouting face.

"Shit. Not who I expected," she said, her bloody body sticking to the leather of the seat as it began to dry. "Is the cleaning kit back there, Caleb?"

The old man looked around, then handed her a kit through the slot. It was full of wet toilettes, used to clean wounds in a battle situation. She'd probably have to use nearly the whole thing to manage her current mess though.

"Nice to see you too," Caleb said.

Videl rolled his eyes as he drove them on down to the road, veering off to the left in a speedy rush that made her slide across the seat a bit.

"I kept trying to find out what had happened to you. Eventually," Videl said, dropping his mask and helmet into the storage bin between them. "Eventually the Magister relented, said he'd found out where you were being held. And we'd do a rescue mission. We were on alert around this area the past couple days, but he refused to give us the final coordinates and the go-ahead," Videl said, frustration in his voice.

"That was where I came in," Caleb chimed in, sounding both smug and amused.

"Yeah, it is," said Videl, shooting him a look in the rear-view mirror. "I took a gamble. Went to him at the hideaway. When I told him where we were camped, he knew right away where you must be held. I knew I shouldn't trust the old bugger, but..."

"Who else do I have but you two, hmm?" Caleb said dryly, folding his hands in his lap.

"Yeah. He explained some to me, and it fits with what I knew. I don't think he has a chance without us. He needs to off one of the other C's. Like the Magister. But he's too far gone to manage that without help. And who the fuck else on this island is crazy enough to offer it?" Videl said.

It panged her.

Even with the Magister's shift in temperament, even with his refusal to actually rescue her, she couldn't bring herself to want him dead.

In her mind, it was just a test, to see if she could escape from a much more experienced and prepared V.

A V who knew she was coming.

Because someone had betrayed her.

With Videl and Caleb having risked themselves to save her, it was hard to reason it was one of them.

There was always a chance that someone had been spying on her. Valeda had said that some of them knew about the others when Valeska had mentioned Valerie, so maybe she'd decided to take out the competition. But Valeda had wanted her to believe it was a man, and there was only one man who knew where she'd be that night.

A sharp ache stabbed her heart.

She tossed dirty wipe after dirty wipe down to her feet until finally she was mostly blood free, shimmering with the remains of the luxurious oils they'd been polishing her up with.

"What happens if you kill another C? You're pissing blood. Internal bleeding is pretty serious," Valeska said, once more asking a question she didn't want the answer to.

"Life renewed," said Caleb, with the tenor of a preacher to his voice. "Gone my aches and pains. Away goes my world-weary self," he said as Videl drove off and up onto some private, sheltered property. It was nothing lavish; a simple house in the 'country' of the island.

"It's like taking a step back in time, oh... twenty years or so," he said wistfully, as if he'd just recited a poem.

Valeska's guts wrenched.

So that was what happened to Cole. That was why the Magister looked so vibrant. It wasn't just good makeup or high spirits. He'd taken the youth from the man she thought she'd been saving.

But she couldn't plead ignorance. She knew that life was worse than death for some sheep.

Maybe that was how the Cs became such control freaks. Such heartless assholes. The pain they suffered had pressed their sweet, soft souls into jagged diamonds that could cut through anything.

Videl pulled open the door and got out. He activated something on his watch, and a hidden gate–disguised as trees and bushes–closed off the way in, before he rounded about to open Valeska's door.

"You gonna send me those coordinates any time soon?" Videl asked with a wry smile, as he tapped his watch. The message she'd queued up earlier had just arrived.

"When I get a chance," she said, slipping out of her seat, her pale skin glowing in the midday sun. "I gotta make a call, then I'll get dressed. I'm sure you two don't mind my nudity a while longer."

"Never, Ma'am," said Videl with a grin on his face, as if he was just so glad to have her back and in charge. He picked up the bundle that likely contained her clothes before following after her.

"Little help?" Caleb called.

"You can stay there for a while. The AC's on," Videl remarked as they went up into the house together. It was a nice enough place, not ostentatious like Valeska's, but new and clean, with all they'd need. "The old guy had purchased this place ahead of his little infiltration. Was going to use it as a base of operations," he explained.

"I guess when you're staring death in the face, you'll do pretty much anything to avoid it," Valeska said, stepping inside and glancing around. But there was something she had to know.

"Videl, did you threaten Abel?"

CHAPTER 27

I'VE HAD A HARD WEEK

Stab your demoniac smile to my brain,
Soak me in cognac, love, and cocaine

— ALEISTER CROWLEY; DIARY OF A
DRUG FIEND

"I wouldn't waste my time. I'd just put him in his place if I thought he was a threat," he said, taking off his heavy body armour, dropping it by the door then putting her things down on a coffee table near the sofas. "What the hell could he have to do with anything? He's just some mainlander lamb."

"It's probably nothing. I ignored the call, figured it was just him being needy, but he left a voicemail. There's information he has that I need," she said as her watch started dialling Abel's number. She leaned against the wall, her skin leaving a slick imprint of her backside as she casually rested in the entryway.

Videl got out of all that excess armour, just down to his usual uniform, as she waited for the call to go through. And just as her Second began to prepare her some food and drink, she heard Abel pick up.

"Valeska," he said, sounding surprised to hear her. "I didn't think you were gonna call me back after all this time."

"I was tied up. You left a super awkward voicemail, though, which added some levity to the mayhem I was involved in. Didn't quite make it to the point, though," she said as casually as she could manage.

"Oh. Yeah," he said awkwardly. "Listen, they threatened me not to tell you, but that day when you left, you trusted me to lock up behind you. And I was going out to wait for that ride you promised. Just as I was coming out the door, this guy in a uniform, I don't know who he was..." he said, sounding hesitant. "He said if he could just peek around inside your place for a minute, that he'd make my dreams come true."

"Honey, listen. I have had a really hard... when was it that we saw each other last? How long ago?"

"Oh, it's, uh been over a week. But listen, he looked intimidating. And I was afraid to say no, but I wasn't going to piss you off. I'd already decided I wanted to join, so I pretended like the door just slipped my hand and shut on its own. He didn't fall for it though. And told me if I told you or anyone else that he was there I'd pay. In various ways he'd outlined. I didn't tell you sooner because, well... he never got in there to do anything anyhow. So why risk my

ass over nothing? But the more I thought about it, well...
the knowledge that someone was even trying to get into
your place and do Hell-knows-what? He could have put a
tracker in your clothes, rob you, I don't know; that
might've been useful to you. And maybe I'm still a bit of a
sucker."

"You're allowed to be a sucker with me. Now. Are you
somewhere private?"

"Not really, no," he said, as she watched Videl check
some of the building's security, activating some armoured
shutters that blocked out the windows but kept them extra
safe. "Why?"

"Text me a detailed description of what the guy looked
like. And if anyone asks, you haven't heard from me in a
week. I've ghosted you, isn't that what you tourists
call it?"

"Yeah, got'cha. I'll do that ASAP. Kinda getting glares
from my teammates at the moment though so it might take
a bit," Abel said.

"I'll owe you one if you make me top priority," she
teased, and without waiting for a reply, she ended the call.
She shifted her attention to the other watch on her wrist,
and the deluge of messages meant for the butcher.

It was a lot. Including a lot of "*Fuck offs*" and "*stop
messaging me*" from women the guy was annoying the hell
out of. But among them she found and deciphered some
official messages. The ones that grabbed her interest
pertained to the business in the bunker lab.

And poor Cain's delivery.

It was still afternoon, the sun was still bright, but the
messages detailed a location to deliver Cain for a 'trade'. It

wouldn't happen until three in the morning, so that gave her about twelve hours to kill between then.

And kill them she'd have to, if she wanted to intervene, since the instructions were that the area would be swept for interlopers up until right before the meeting, at which point all armed forces had to vacate.

That was protocol for a high-level summit between house leaders. Magisters and Magistras.

Valeska started to get dressed again as she mulled it all over, pulling on her fishnet tights and a strategically ripped t-shirt that let her black bra peek through. She tugged up her shorts and stepped into a pair of platform boots, then made her way into the kitchen.

"Do you have a cigarette?"

"Yeah," Videl said, as he fished one out of his breast pocket, handing it to her. And as she put it to her lips, he took out a silver, engraved lighter, to light it up for her. "What's on your mind, Over-Lieutenant?" he asked.

She took a long drag of the smoke, fidgeting with it in her fingers as they spoke.

"Someone is out for me, and I don't know who," she admitted. "Did you get the coke from Valerie?" She could tell he was jacked on something. Probably to compensate for lost sleep. Or just because he took her rescue mission extremely seriously.

It wasn't usual for Videl, either way, and that lucid dream of seeing him meet her still nagged at the back of her mind.

"No, I grabbed it from one of the men's lockers. They confiscated it from someone else. Saved me a trip," he explained simply and immediately. Valeska scanned his face, but there was no trace of deceit in his gaze.

"Valerie could have bugged the hummer. Or maybe Aran wasn't happy with the speed of his reward..." Valeska muttered. "I mean, I've probably pissed off a lot of V's and C's and who the fuck knows what else with my promotion. The Magister's favourite, right? That's what they say."

The mention of the Magister made something light up in Videl's head.

"Valerie didn't strike me as someone with her life together enough to plot something like that with you. As for Aran... definitely possible. But..." he wet his lips, narrowing his eyes thoughtfully.

He didn't want to be the one to say it, and she didn't want to think about it.

She stared at him, wetting her lips before she took another long drag of her smoke.

"Speak your mind, Second," she commanded, and he grinned despite himself.

"The Magister kept putting me off. The last thing he told me was that the rescue team would move out tomorrow morning. He said we couldn't move too soon, or else risk a deal the House had going on. I know it was foolish of me, but at that moment I didn't give a fuck about his deal. I knew you were held hostage for over a week, and I wasn't gonna wait a moment more if I could find a way to pull it off."

To hear her strait-laced Second in Command talking about breaking ranks and disobeying direct orders – from the House, if not military command – was something else.

"Tomorrow. Because I was the trade for Cain," she said

as if a knife were going through her heart. "But..." she paused, flicking her cigarette. "No, I don't think it's as simple as all that. He doesn't want Valeda to live. Or at least, he's indifferent to it. I still don't believe he intended me to die, though I'm sure he knew the possibility, especially since the fucking dick didn't give me any kind of head's up. He said I'd understand, once I used that dagger on her."

Valeska began pacing back and forth, smoking occasionally as she tried to step inside the Magister's grand design.

"A sweet, soft boy, hardened by life. A fiery woman who doesn't watch her tongue. Adam and Lilith. Made of the same clay, they were equals, but he hated her for that. He wanted someone smaller, more easily manipulated, so he banished her, replacing her with a part of himself. And then he had to pay the price for his weakness, because Eve was just what he wanted. Weak."

Valeska paused her mutterings, looking up at Videl.

"He had everything, and then nothing. Worse than nothing. He's cursed to die and rot in the ground, having once tasted paradise. The price of knowledge. The C's start out as innocent, but that pain is revisited upon them, to mold them into what they need to be, but they'll always be at war with themselves. Longing for an equal, while wanting them to be subservient. The amalgamation of Lilith and Eve, the perfect paradox."

Videl listened attentively to her ramblings. But if there was anyone who could draw out understanding from it all, it was him. He'd been privy to almost as much of this as she had, after all. And he had a quick mind, and a helping of wisdom.

His brows furrowed as he tried to make sense of it with her.

"Something the old man told me," he said of Caleb. "The Cs and Vs can't wipe each other out. There has to be one of each left in the end. He wouldn't explain why exactly, not without riddles at least. But it's necessary. There must be one of each, at least, or the whole island falls apart. Or so he said," Videl remarked, taking a breath. "So, if he sent you against this older V... maybe it was in the hopes you'd triumph. But... if you didn't, he still had her," he wet his lips and ran a hand through his sleek, swept-back hair.

"If he gave you too much warning, this older V would know he betrayed her. Egregiously. And that would bite him in the ass should she triumph anyhow. Because according to the old man, they're not above sabotaging and torturing one another, even if death is off limits. So, it seems like he might've been playing the safe game, covering all his exits, but his top priority is getting that other C to fuel his... Immortality or whatever. Either way, he wins."

"And she doesn't know that he already recently had a C. The Magister... when I saw him, he looked less than forty. I know... we gave him an edge that the Magistra won't realize until they're face to face. I guess he wants us to be the same age, as if that word has any meaning," she mused. "Covering all his exits. That sounds like him. It's not the first time he's tested me, but I think this was the big one. And I still haven't succeeded."

Videl looked troubled by her line of thinking. But he didn't object.

"You should know. To get the old man to agree to help rescue you... I had to promise to help him knife the

Magister and regain some youth, or whatever," he said, scratching the back of his neck. "Now, hear me out... I will follow whatever you say, of course. But I think it might actually be in your – and our – best interest to do that. Think about it," he said, reaching out and touching her shoulder. "He's helpless now. Needs us. And even if he can replace the old Magister, he'll still be unaware of recent going's on in the house. The island. Everything. He'll still need us. And we'll have the goods on him. You'll effectively be the puppet master then. Magistra and sole leader of the whole house, in all but name," he said, looking into her eyes quite seriously.

Her gaze held his before she dipped her head down, and for the first time, he saw her look deflated.

"We don't have any good options here. But you didn't ask for this. I mean, fuck, I didn't either, but like... Videl, tomorrow is going to greet us, and no matter what we do, it's going to be a new fucking dawn. I have to do this. But is this the *real life* that you're looking for? How you want to belong? Because there are at least five more V's, and then six more after that, and after that, and you and I both know how real shit is going to get on this path."

He heard her out, stared down at her. He had over a foot of height on her, but still he saw her as the authority. But in that moment, he answered by lunging down and pressing his lips to hers.

The kiss was not chaste, not gentle. Not even passionate.

It was beyond that.

It was desperate, relieved, it was frenzied. And his tongue delved inside her mouth as he held her face in his two hands while they made out. And only after that had gone on a long while, did he break away.

"You're what I want," he said breathily, his crimson eyes alight. "And all the pretences around that went away when you were in captivity. I know it's a dirty word here, and I don't expect you to return it, but..."

His mouth froze open, and she knew what he was going to say. What he wanted to say.

She stared at him, her brows raised in panic.

"I love you."

CHAPTER 28

YOU'RE TOO KINKY

As the worst of the venom left my lips,
    I thought, 'If, despite this lie, he strips
    The mask from my soul with a kiss—I crawl
    His slave,—soul, body, and all!

— ADAM, LILITH AND EVE; R.
BROWNING

"I will walk in your shadow to the end of my days. An old frail man, seeing you remain young and powerful. Knowing you can't return that emotion. And it won't matter. I'll still keep loving and serving you. In whatever capacity I can, until the bitter end. That is my pledge. That is my desire, Ma'am."

She shook her head, her raven locks brushing against her pale cheeks.

"Fuck, Videl, what in Satan's name did I do to get assigned

you?" she asked, her hand going up to his cheek, her thumb tracing along the scar. "This is probably the kinkiest thing that's happening on the island right now. I knew there must be a freak under that stuffy exterior, but this is a bit much."

Her lips quirked into a teasing grin, and she pressed her mouth to his, giving him a brief, but rough, kiss.

His long arms wrapped around her, and in that moment, he lifted her up off the ground. Her much smaller form supported by his, held against him as they kissed. She was lifted up to his level then, in fact a bit above.

"Abuse that knowledge all you like, Over-Lieutenant. Because after a week of not knowing if you were alive or dead... I am still high on seeing your blood-spattered body emerge triumphant," he professed.

For so long, he'd been her rock. Steady, predictable, loyal.

But it took the stress of the last couple of weeks to show her who he really was.

Who he could be.

Trust was a word even more deadly than love.

She had enemies working in the shadows to take her out, and she should know better than to have faith in anyone but herself. Abel could write her back, describing Videl to a t, but in that moment, she just wanted to revel in the sensation.

Her legs wrapped around him as he held her, the cigarette butt falling from her fingertips as she hugged his neck.

"I did look really fucking hot back there. I caught a glimpse in the metal door."

He grinned at her. Not in amusement, but in hungry agreement. He leaned in and bit her lower lip.

"You looked hotter than even I could've imagined, Ma'am. I will not let a night pass without visualizing it again. Because I fear none of the cameras were working," he said before kissing her once more, making out as he held her up. One hand on her back caressed her, the other grabbed her ass.

She had been so keyed up for so long, and while the massacre helped work out some of her aggression, it didn't take it all.

Especially since she was still reeling from the Magister's pass at her.

Feeling Videl's body against hers, grinding her hips against his uniform and having her shorts tease her clit was a perfect reclamation of her sexual power.

He was rock hard inside his uniform trousers, and he kept her aloft, pressing into her tightly in return as she ground against him. He groaned and pinned her against the wall, as they kissed ravenously at one another.

But finally, their passions rose so much that grinding was not enough. He carried her to the kitchen island, laying her ass down upon it as he pulled back, enough to begin stripping off his uniform, peeling away his jacket and shirt without delay or kindness to the fabrics.

And though she'd just gotten redressed, she was quickly following suit, tossing off the t-shirt and bra. She squirmed from around him just enough that she was able to slide her shorts down one leg, leaving them dangling on the top of her platform boot on the other calf.

Her pussy was drenched between her thighs, the ripped crotch of her fishnets framing it beautifully.

Videl certainly thought so, because he stared at it with such intensity as he unsheathed his cock. That thick, long, veiny dick practically a violent red with hardness. The man was ragingly erect for her, and lunged back in, kissing her again as that thick tip nudged at her slick slit.

The first time they'd fucked, she had been tracking her cycle, knew when she could take a man raw without risk. Now a week had passed, maybe more, and she had no idea. It was the type of thing she'd usually shut down, but in that moment, she didn't care.

That night they were going to try to kill the closest thing she had to a father, along with a nearly identical copy of herself, and who knows how many others, all so that an old man could steal someone else's life force to become younger.

Things were fucked enough, and if she was going to die, she was going to die knowing that she didn't spend her last moments on Earth fretting about getting knocked up by a man who professed his love for her.

Her legs wrapped around his hips, and she angled herself perfectly for her nether lips to kiss his crown, drawing him into her valley.

And Videl took that offer without a split second's hesitation. It was like their bodies were one in how perfectly they moved together. In unison, he re-sheathed himself up inside her with a firm, hard thrust, and the two of them began to fuck on that kitchen island. The hard marble made for a steady base as he gripped her hips, using them to truly pound into her.

He groaned and moaned in between kisses of their lips, the wet slaps of his shaft and balls impacting her groin resounding through the hideaway home.

Their first time had been good and hard. But this? This was something else. So much longing and pent-up emotions, yes, just like last time. Only now the fire was fuelled by the death they'd dealt and defied. The hunger for release that only they could give one another in that moment.

She almost regretted that they hadn't been fucking all along, but she knew it wouldn't have been the same. She'd have treated him as expendable, pushed him away, kept him at arm's length.

To feel the intensity of the tumultuous emotions they shared, it needed to happen just as it did.

Her lithe body bent back, taking more of that thick masculinity inside of her, the cries of pleasure already surrounding them.

Videl knew just how to serve her. And there was no doubt of that in the moment, as he leaned over her, pounding his cock with such rapid intensity. Her much smaller, petite body was being hit with enough force to send her sliding off over the other side of the island, if he wasn't holding her in a tight grip.

"Valeska," he groaned out, as his dick pulsated within her, stretching her narrow slit wide as he hammered away. His own nicely muscled form glistening from the day's exertion and now the rabid rutting. Her name on his lips was like an oath, and she cried out.

She was lost to a haze of bliss, and she didn't hold back. She wasn't playing games with him, toying with him, stringing him along. She had no goals or desires beyond that moment, and it made her reckless. The orgasm that struck her was earth shattering, and she screamed as she clung to his body.

"Fuck!" he shouted aloud, as her climaxing pussy clenched around his shaft so exquisitely tight. It was a challenge for him and his stamina to hold on through that. A challenge too big it seemed, because he lost control. Perhaps it was the week of longing he had for her while she was in captivity. Perhaps it was just the fire of the moment. But Videl came inside her, his whole body quaking.

But he never slowed, never stopped. He was trembling and sweating, but he kept rutting into her with that wild need. The two of them reunited again, and he did not wish it to end.

Older than her by ten years, he still proved himself with a younger man's vitality and lust. But then, he'd attribute that purely to her kindling it in him. And he kept thrusting, pounding her puffy red pussy, making her feel each hammer blow of his dick as her depths were stuffed so full of cock and cum alike.

Her sensitive body was no match for it, and long before he met his second end, she was awash on the rivers of the abyss. Each orgasm seemed to crash into the next like a wave, the current building up to such a strength that it threatened to drown her. She lost herself in another person in a way that she'd never allowed herself to before, and her spritely form was a quivering mess against his.

She had half a day to kill before that meeting between Magister and Magistra. And yet somehow, Videl and Valeska managed to fill many of those hours with ease.

It was pitch black outside when at last, he was quaking with orgasm, and flooding her with a second load. Somehow they ended up on the floor, having migrated places throughout the long, ravenous ordeal.

"Valeska," he gasped, as he shuddered and quaked, his body trembling atop her as their sweaty, gasping forms clung to one another's.

Despite them surviving a bloody, explosive escape from that complex, it was their passionate sex that had left them most sore and weary that day.

"Fuck," she gulped, holding him in her arms, her fingers trailing up and down his back, memorizing every muscle, every mole, every bone. She wanted to know him perfectly, completely, but she knew that the preparations needed to be made.

She hoped Caleb had decided to sleep so at least one of them would be well rested before the meeting. She'd forgotten all about him in those blissful hours of unending ecstasy.

Checking her watch, she saw they still had plenty of time.

And there awaited her the message from Abel.

"Here you go, my best description. He was a tall, thin man. In full uniform. Pale, with a scar on his face."

Videl's pale, scarred face smiled down at her, his body still locked with hers.

CHAPTER 29

ASHTRAY OF PISS

If I sharpen My flashing sword,
    And My hand takes hold on justice,
    I will render vengeance on My adversaries,
    And I will repay those who hate Me.
    'I will make My arrows drunk with blood,
    And My sword will devour flesh,
    With the blood of the slain and the captives,
    From the long-haired leaders of the enemy.'

        — DEUTERONOMY 32:41-42

I ce began to crackle through her veins, and her vision momentarily blurred. She blinked, trying to clear her eyes to continue reading, but it felt as though time were standing still.

She'd asked Videl. She knew him, better than she knew

anyone. She would have been able to tell if he was lying to her.

She couldn't let the fear creep in. Valeda's warning threatened the one good thing in her life right now.

Valeska closed her eyes, inhaling a deep, calming breath, letting it out slowly, and when she opened her eyes once more, her vision returned.

"The biggest scar was across his neck and mouth."

Scars... on his neck and mouth.

Her body was flushed with heat in the wake of the ice receding.

Not Videl.

There was no way Abel could confuse a gorgeous, powerful scar across a man's eye for one on his neck and mouth.

"So what's the plan, Ma'am?" Videl asked, having caught his breath enough to rise up, and slowly slide from her. A smile was on his face for her as he reached for the paper towels nearby. They'd been knocked from the kitchen island in their passion, and he tore some off to help them both tidy up.

She pushed herself up slightly, grabbing the offered paper towel and looking at him, seeing him in a new light.

Her feelings for him were a weakness, something that others could exploit. How quickly had she feared that Abel was describing him, upending everything she thought she knew? She was jumping at shadows, when he had always been a source of light for her.

Trust didn't come easy, not to anyone on the island, least of all her.

But somehow, she'd have to learn to steel herself against

the prickling reminders that vulnerability, and trusting someone else, was a poison that would one day kill her.

"We need to get Caleb in here. I still don't know what the Magister meant about the sacrificial blade. And if Caleb has to be the one to..."

A lump formed in her throat, and she swallowed it down.

She knew what she had to do. There was no future for her with her Magister. Not the way she wanted it. All her life, she'd tried to please him, to be his favourite, and perhaps she was. But he also wanted to possess her, have her as a wife.

He might forgive her for the massacre, for fouling up his plans, for concealing Caleb from him. But he'd never forgive Videl disobeying his orders. He might not kill him outright and risk Valeska's loyalty wavering, but the tiny cuts that would bleed him dry over time would be worse.

It would be in the Magister's interest to cut her off from a loyal follower like Videl anyhow. He'd never allow another to undermine his control over her.

"Caleb will be able to tell us more about what to expect," she said, clearing her throat.

"I'll bring him in. You should eat in the meantime," he told her, reaching out, taking her hand and hauling her up to her feet. "He's a wealth of information. Once given incentive to talk," he remarked with a bit of a grimace.

Videl left her to her own devices, the meal he'd set out for her a few hours earlier still waiting for her at the table nearby.

She was still in a state of undress, but she devoured what food she could. She was a small woman, but after being drugged for so long, followed by the fight for her life, she was ravenous. It was only the knowledge that was imparted on her as a child – gorging oneself after a famine could kill – that gave her any restraint.

She swallowed back some water as she began pacing the room once more.

It wasn't long after that, when Videl and Caleb came into the house. The old man was not looking terribly impressed with his long period in the vehicle.

"I had to piss in the ashtray," he said irritably.

"He really did," Videl said, making a face.

"And why?" Caleb sniffed the air. "So you two could fornicate?" he said with a sigh, as he went and sat down, and Videl brought him some food too.

Valeska rolled her eyes.

"Because Videl had to fill me in on your plan," she said, as if it were obvious. "I'm sure that's not the most humiliating thing you've had to endure, given what you've risked to get back onto the Isle. I guess the rest of the world is as shitty as they say?"

"I'm not here to discuss the rest of the world. What interests me is here. The power to go on," he said, his eyes wide and excited. And it was clear he was getting over the upset quickly. "Your man let me in on a few of the details. Let me see that watch you took," he remarked, making grabby hands towards her.

Videl helped himself to some food too, though at a much more relaxed pace than either of them, resting his back against the kitchen island.

She handed over the watch to Caleb, her heart leaden in her chest.

She couldn't believe she was really entertaining this idea.

Patricide.

Funny how that never really featured in her lessons on Satanism and the Bible of the old faith.

Caleb inspected it for a while, read over the pertinent messages.

"Ahh," he said, his eyes lighting up. "I know this location... yes, it's a spot we Magisters and Magistras set up for our exchanges and meetings. Long ago. It is quite hidden," Caleb said.

"Can you help us win there? I assume they won't be undefended after all," Videl remarked.

"None of your guns or gizmos will work there. And this time, even I can't override that," Caleb said quite firmly. "This place was intended to stop Magisters like me from doing exactly that, after all."

"Fuck," Videl said, running a hand back through his hair.

"Don't even try bringing any of your weapons. Other than the swords and daggers. You'll suffer if you do," Caleb said with an ominous ring to his voice.

Valeska licked her lips, leaning against the counter before she looked at Videl.

"I need another smoke. Caleb, how many people are we expecting?"

Videl went right to his jacket pocket, taking out a cigarette for her, then lighting it in her fingers as the old man pondered.

"The rules were... back in my day, no more than six guards or assistants per Magister. So... if it's a meeting between just the two, you can expect a dozen. Plus them, of course," Caleb said, wetting his lips and thinking hard.

"Well, hopefully she's down a couple after today. We have to presume they've figured out that Videl broke rank and saved me against the House's orders. But..." she said, taking a long drag on her cigarette. A plan was forming in her mind, and she grinned at the two of them.

"I could turn myself into the Magister. Tell him that I knew he sent Videl to free me, but he died in the shootout, and thank him for his mercy. Tell him I won't fail again. Then he could take me to the meeting place so that they can make their little trade..." Valeska mused, looking between Videl and Caleb.

It was strange for her not to simply give the command. It would have been simple to tell them what to do and stay in control of the situation.

But she'd come to appreciate the fact that they had special insight that she didn't, and their advice could be the thing that stands between annihilation and success.

"I don't like it. That's very risky," Videl said, immediately bristling at the idea of her putting herself in such danger.

But Caleb looked far more intrigued.

"No. It may be the only way. After all, it's highly likely that the Magistra knows of the breakout by now. If she does, she likely won't show at all, and our whole plan will be a bust. We'll have missed our chance to get them both," he said, looking to Valeska and ignoring Videl's glower.

"But she'll undoubtedly be bound. Without any weapons. And I doubt you'll be of any use in a fight," Videl said, standing up straight, gesturing aggressively at the old man. "As much as I'm committed to seeing this through whatever it takes, I'm not super confident in my ability to hack down a dozen armed men with a sword, while getting to the Over-Lieutenant, freeing her and handing her a sword to fight with."

Videl's ruby eyes were wide, his emotions high. His nostrils flared, and Valeska grinned at him excitedly.

"There's another option. A way to prove to the Magister that I have the cunning and skills to be his bride, while still giving Valeda what she wants."

A grin twisted her lips.

"I can offer him Valerie. It'll show him that I understand the game, and I'm ruthless enough to win it."

Videl softened in his near rage at that suggestion and he began to nod.

"Yeah. Yeah, that might work. I mean, she's not gonna like it, but... She's a lamb, not like you. She won't have much of a choice," he said, rubbing his chin as he thought it over.

"So glad we could figure this all out together," Caleb remarked, eating some more.

"The Magister will still want to see me succeed. And to do that, he'll bring me with him. Caleb, you said that the C's and the V's can't end each other, only torture, yes?"

"More or less, yes. I mean, we certainly could, but... the impact that would have on the Grand Design would be disastrous for all of us. No C or V in their right mind would seek to end another directly. We would certainly set them up to be ended by another of their own, however. Happens all the time," Caleb said.

"Yea, well, it at least means he won't fucking kill me for

failing him," she groaned. "The Magister said if I stabbed the Magistra with that dagger, I'd understand. I suppose that's how things get... passed on? And without it, they'd just be dead?"

"More or less," Caleb remarked as he continued to eat and drink periodically. "The daggers are a spiritual conduit to eldritch forces. They channel the life-force of your... clone, for want of a better word, into you," he said.

"So, killing a 60-year-old V would make me, what, a child again? Because fuck that," she frowned. "Do you... remember things after? Would I remember if I'd done this before?"

"It's not like that," Caleb said with a sigh, sitting back in his seat, with a groan, touching his back. "You cannot be reduced in age beyond adulthood. For you... the benefits would be purely..." he gestured vaguely, trying to find the words. "It would be more like a rush of power. It would keep you from aging a while, keeping you roughly where you are longer than natural. And you'll get occasional bursts of memory from the other V," he explained. "It is not time travel. You do not forget anything."

"Oh," she said, letting out a sigh of understanding. "I guess when the Magister offered me another 'pretty plaything', he really was offering me another C. Him," she said with a snort, seeing a dark humour in it all. "So, do we all understand the plan?"

"Hold on," Videl said, speaking up after a period of thoughtful silence. "I don't like the idea of you going to the Magister." There was a hint of pained concern in his eyes, and she opened her mouth to protest, but he interrupted.

"Hear me out. He will expect you to be cautious and

clever. This won't interfere with the plan," he said, holding up his hands. "We have someone you can trust deliver Valerie to him. With a video note from you. He'll understand that you didn't want to be there yourself, in case he tried to offer you to her as well."

"Hm," she frowned, nodding along. "Videl, you are a clever fucker, have I told you that? Brilliant. We could ask Abel. I found him cute, Valerie probably will as well. And it'll help him get started off on the right foot serving the House."

Videl cracked a slight smile at her words then nodded.

"I'll have someone arm Abel, dress him up as a real Wolf for the task," he said, tapping on his holographic keypad.

"And you're both lucky I know the real location of this site. It won't be easy assaulting it, but... once the Magister and Magistra are in there, it'll be a communication lockdown inside. No interference. You can shoot the guards at the lift, then ditch your guns to head inside," Caleb said.

"Wait, Videl," she said, interrupting him before he could put out the message. "First... Who do you know with a scar on his mouth? And neck. Tall, pale, uniformed?" She could almost picture someone fitting that description, but the House had so many guards, they had all blurred together in her mind over the years.

Videl paused and pondered that, before shaking his head.

"Nobody," he said simply.

"Fuck, okay. Well... don't trust anyone with a scar on his mouth and neck."

She then looked at Caleb.

"Do you know who my Magister is? Which... C?"

Caleb's eyes narrowed, and he hissed the name, "Caspian."

He didn't have to say more than that to hint at the history between them both.

"Were you the same... batch? Is that what we're called? Or maybe a cluster of C's, and a vat of V's?"

"No," he said with a tone of finality. He did not seem to want to discuss it in real detail.

"Alright, I've informed one of our subordinates. They'll see the task through. Outfit Abel from head to toe. There should be enough time to track her down and bring her in before we lose our window," Videl said.

"Caleb, what needs to be done for your role in all of this?"

Caleb grinned and patted his thigh, where he was presumably storing the dagger.

"Clear the way. Save Caspian for me," he remarked. "I will probably need one of you to restrain him. I won't come up until the fighting is well underway. I trust you'll understand why," he said simply, though rankling a bit at his inability to contribute more. Or more accurately, at his weakness.

"You told me to never trust someone you couldn't destroy, but once this is over, you'll know the score between us, yes? We all have something to gain from this, but I'm the one with everything to lose."

"This is my last chance. If I fail now, do you really think I will get another shot, hmm? No. We both have everything to lose. But... we have a world to win."

CHAPTER 30

SYNCHRONIZED SNIPING

Her gates are gates of death, and from the entrance
of the house
    She sets out towards Sheol.
    None of those who enter there will ever return,
    And all who possess her will descend to the Pit.

       — THE DEAD SEA SCROLLS; 4Q184

*"*M*agister,*
Your mercy is undying, and I will not fail you again. I thank you for sending my Under-Lieutenant to save me. He died in the shootout, but I was able to escape on my own, and now I understand what I need to do to be your bride. I have procured you a gift. I believe the lamb's name is Valerie, and I trust she will suit your needs for tonight.

When dawn breaks, I look forward to reaping the rewards as your Magistra.
May Astarte's Shadow shroud you,
Valeska."

Abel knew how important it was the deliver the message – and the bound package – but still every moment felt like anguish. When her watch finally buzzed with the Magister's reply, she let out a long-held breath.

"I knew you would find a way. Once this is done, we'll be better able to work together, my sweet little Valeska. I can tell you everything."

"I see the vehicles coming in," Videl said, peering through a scope on his rifle from their hiding spot in the forest. They had been prepared for the last hour, and the wait was far worse than the bloody slaughter she committed earlier that day. "It's a regular motorcade. Has to be one of their groups."

"Every house has its own approach," Caleb said, the old man leaning against a tree. "The Magistra of House Abaddon will come from another side. It's to prevent needless friction between their retinue of guards."

Valeska was strapped with her daggers and sword, dressed all in heavy leather to keep her protected from any blades. Her long, black hair was pulled up into two twin buns on the top of her head so that no one could grab her as easily.

She hoped she had thought of everything, but she knew, even if they planned perfectly, they were outnumbered. All it would take was one misstep, one miscalculation, for her house of cards to crash down.

And she was having to betray the closest thing she had to a father. The man who raised her. She loved him, in her own twisted way. He'd tried to beat it out of her, cut her soul down to its quick so that she'd learn, but there was still that seedling in the shell of her heart that panged at the thought of his death.

A hesitation like that would get her killed, and she tried to cut that tenderness out, like the lessons of the Chimera demanded. Just as the Magister had taught her.

"We'll wait for the initial sweep to be complete before moving in."

"Sounds good," Videl said.

"Yes, they'll do their final sweep, then fall back. I'd expect only one guard at the elevator, leading up to the meeting place. Just remember, you can shoot the ones at the base of the elevator. But don't take the guns with you up there. It won't be pretty if you do," he said, suggesting special horrors with his tone of voice.

Valeska brought her own scope up, and saw the centre vehicle come to a halt. There, a white-haired man stepped out. And it could only be Caspian. Her Magister. Someone else was brought behind him, and a series of soldiers went into a door into the mountain.

After a while, she picked up through the distance that the remaining soldiers finished their sweep, and fell back to their vehicles. The secondary retinue departed, leaving the solo guard at the entrance of the mountain.

She waited until the vehicles were completely gone before her finger began to tighten on the trigger. It had been a while since she had the opportunity to snipe someone, but her training was embedded deep into the sinews of her body. Her heart rate slowed, her breathing became shallow, and she got used to the subtle sway of her hands.

The area was sheltered from the wind, with the mountain and trees, so the calculations of velocity were uncomplicated.

But as she lined up her shot with the remaining guard at the base of the elevator, another stepped out from just out of view. The two of them flanked the entrance into the mountainside door.

"Shit. There's two," Valeska said.

Videl immediately raised his rifle.

"You go left, I'll go right. Sound good?" Videl asked.

"Hell yeah," she said, as they lined up their two shots. "On my count... three, two, one..."

Simultaneously their shots split through the night with nothing but a soft hiss of air. The two guards went down in perfect unison together, not even twitching.

"Good shooting, Ma'am," Videl said with a wry smile at her.

"You too, Second," she grinned back. His smile caused a flutter in her chest that she'd never felt before, and she didn't fight against the warmth it filled her with. "Don't get distracted once we're in there. We both have to make it through, and worrying about each other..."

She'd never had to say that before. The words felt so... strange. Stranger that it was as much for him as it was for her.

"Yes Ma'am. I won't let you down," he said, as he lowered his rifle into a casual position at his hip. He had two swords, criss-crossed at his back, and he was in his full suit of body armour again. He looked ready to assault Hell itself.

"If you two are done licking each other's taints, can we get going?" Caleb asked.

"I really hope you're more pleasant once this is done," Valeska bit back, but he was right. It was time.

"Oh, if you'd spent as long inside a rotting husk as I have, you'd be cranky too," Caleb said.

The three of them headed out, with Videl and her leading the way.

They had their night vision activated as they closed in on the entrance, guns sweeping the area ahead as they got nearer, but there were no other guards waiting them. They got to the doors, and stepped over the bodies, as Videl hit the button to call back the elevator. Videl took out his handgun, and deposited it to the ground, then stacked his rifle against a wall just out of view. Valeska laid hers next to his, until both were down to just their melee weapons.

"I will wait down here. I'll give you ten minutes to clean up the refuse there, then I'll head up. There are no calls that can come in or out of there, after all," he said. "And if you failed, my life is over anyhow."

He wiped his brow, clearly winded just from the journey from their sniping spot.

"I won't fail," Valeska said, her words filled with utter conviction.

This time, she'd be the one getting the drop on Valeda, and she wasn't going to fuck it up.

The elevator finally came to their level, and the black doors slid open, inviting them into that coffin like interior, lit up red.

"Show no quarter. No hesitation. And definitely no mercy. You fight for your lives. And mine. No two V's or C's have ever come out of there alive before," Caleb cautioned them, coughing into his hand thereafter.

Valeska flexed her hand, pulling on a gauntlet she kept in the hummer for interrogations. It was chainmail, light and adaptive, but along the knuckles were dense rings, and each finger was capped with a dagger sharp claw.

"Thank you, Caleb," she said, looking at him earnestly. "You'll remember you said that once this is over. We're fighting for *your* life."

"Oh, girl. A C always needs his V. And now you'll be mine, hmm? Works better for me this way. The old always has something to offer to the young," he remarked as the doors slid shut.

It was just her and Videl then, the quiet of the elevator traveling up along the towering side of the mountain, which housed a dormant volcano.

"About him, Ma'am," Videl said, looking to her quite seriously as he took out his two long blades. "The other C. I didn't want to say it where he could hear, not before it was necessary, but..." Videl licked his lips. "I don't think we should give him both. We can hold the younger one some-where safe. That's more leverage we have over him, once he's in the Magister's seat."

"I know this is the cycle, but Cain and Valerie..." Valeska sighed. "It doesn't feel right to just... Fuck, maybe I am soft. Whatever. We won't be killing captives tonight."

Videl looked at her for that split second, then leaned in and kissed her lips.

"You are not soft. You are my Alpha. My commander.

And if I die here tonight, I'll go to Hell knowing I died for a worthy cause. You," he said, his eyes upon hers so intensely.

She reached up, the claws of the gauntlet dragging lightly along his skin, not enough to break the flesh, just barely a tickle, and she smiled at him.

"Once this is over, you can teach me about the strange things you learned back on the mainland. Like this whole love business you mentioned. I think you've piqued my curiosity."

He grinned at her, then kissed her again.

"Yes Ma'am," he said. "I'll teach you everything I know."

The elevator began to slow, and they got ready as it came to a halt.

The doors slid open, and the pair emerged from the elevator to see two surprised guards at the sides of them.

They didn't even have a chance to call out before they were met with a flurry of their blades, killed without remorse.

Blood dripped from their bodies as Valeska looked into the massive chamber that they'd entered. Heated smoke wafted up from the dormant volcano below, casting strange shadows on six great statues that loomed above them. Valeska's skin crawled as she took in the ominous depictions of hideous things, each unique from the other.

It felt like they were part of the lips of the volcano edge surrounding the fuming pit, more than carven statues. As if they had always been there, since time immemorial when an object struck the earth, and all the manmade edifice around it was added much more recently.

Valeska stepped forward on the ledge, overlooking a

great, hexagonal shaped platform. The volcano was so massive that their entrance hadn't yet been noticed, and it gave her time to get familiar with the surroundings.

Down below them were the Magister and Magistra in a private conversation, with four guards ringing the area.

In the centre there were two people strapped to up-right gurneys.

Valeska gestured for Videl to go fan out, towards the other side that still had the Magistra's guards at the elevator. She began to make her way towards the outer edge of the platform, her dark uniform camouflaging her against the obsidian rock.

Nobody had expected assault to come from anyone but the other side. Even on the Isle of Satanos, a coup was unheard of.

It was only as Videl got near those guards, and they charged at him, that the presence of intruders became known.

She didn't need the advantage a moment longer.

In a twirl of metal, her two blades struck out, the fine point rending through the weak points on the armour of two unsuspecting soldiers.

The Magister's soldiers.

Valeska hadn't yet broken a sweat. She moved as fluid in the heavy leather as she did in her usual clothes, and the years of harsh discipline focused her mind on what needed to be done.

She was to become death, reborn in the ashes of her progenitors.

CHAPTER 31

EMBRACE THE CHAOS

Chaos is Peace... Blackness, blackness intolerable,
before the beginning of the light. This is the first
verse of Genesis. Holy art thou, Chaos, Chaos,
Eternity, all contradictions in terms!

— ALEISTER CROWLEY; THE VISION
AND THE VOICE

The Magister and Magistra twisted to look at her
and Videl from the central dais, just as Videl
swung his two blades, taking out the guards
behind the Magistra.

"You impetuous little tart!" Valeda said, before breaking
into a laugh at that. The older version of her was dressed in
an elaborate bodice, with a thick semi-circle dress ring
behind her, while in front she wore tall leather boots and

pants. Her older 'clone' looked intensely amused by her, as usual.

"Valeska?! What are you doing?!" demanded Caspian.

Valeska had been completely composed until she heard the chiding in the Magister's voice. Even knowing the depths of his betrayal, the idea of betraying him made her stomach churn. Suddenly she felt like she was a child again, looking up at him with tears in her eyes as he sneered down at her when she'd saved that boy.

She had tried to prepare for that moment, knowing any hesitation would get her killed, but the power he had over her went deeper than she knew.

It created an opening for the Magistra's guards. She had been readying herself for the pair of guards in front of her, but two more swept down from above, along zip cords.

"Behind you!" Videl shouted.

Valeska just barely managed to duck and an attack with their electric prods. She swept up and sliced off one of their arms with a pained cry, but the remaining three of them circled her, as the albino V took out her own blade.

"A two for one meal tonight then, I guess. I really do admire your spunk, little one," Valeda said, as she watched Valeska do battle.

Three against one in that moment, with a fourth waiting in the wings, and yet her petite form moved and dodged with such elegant fury.

The other two had come at her in her momentary distraction, and she'd been put on edge. She was forced to keep backpedaling as they jabbed and slashed.

She was the more skilled fighter, the nimbler V, and she took a daring risk in that moment.

She charged at one, but then ducked down and slid along the smooth marble flooring. She avoided their slash, and came in low at two of them. With a stiletto in one hand, her sword in another, she severed one's Achilles tendon, and just chopped the leg off beneath the knee on another.

Blood sprayed from their severed limbs as she spun around and sprang up, just in time to deflect a blow from the last remaining guard.

The other V refused her that triumph.

"I hate these moments, little Valeska," Valeda said.

Though she was older, she was not lacking in skill, and Valeska felt her blade slash through her leathers, so that open air touched her flesh. She was two against one, and she was forced into a defensive stance.

"I truly don't like having to end us. But... this is more exciting than anything I've done in years," Valeda said with a grin as she closed in on her younger double. The clang of blades echoed through the platform from the other side of the hall as Videl kept up his part. She couldn't tell how he was doing; there was no time for that.

"Pathetic. This is just another Tuesday night to me," Valeska hissed at her, fangs flashing.

The adrenaline was pumping through her, and Valeska welcomed her clone's distraction. It pulled her mind from the Magister, and that was what she needed more than anything.

"You have everything that Satan could ever give you, and still your fires grow dim, and your lust for worldly pleasures fades. You should thank me for your death, after taking the Earth's bounty for granted."

The two continued to circle about her, and Valeska finally found herself in a tight spot. After all, this wasn't just another guard she was facing. This was herself. With decades more experience and expertise to pull from. And she showed it off in her every movement too. The way she slashed, how expertly her blades glided through the air itself, feinting, parrying, thrusting.

It was all Valeska could do to keep up with her and her mook.

"Just you wait, little girl. Suppose you beat me now, huh? You really think that your life will turn out so much better than mine? You think you have learned anything in your short life that I haven't learned and digested a life time ago?" Valeda asked, before thrusting her blade at Valeska, then twisting her wrist and slashing.

Valeska's initial attempt to dodge was used against her, and she felt her skin slice open along her thigh. A deadly place to get a wound, as she felt blood begin to flow immediately, in great amounts.

"You haven't learned half of what I have," Valeska bit back, trying to mask her pain. "You have become what you loathe. You said the Cs seek to control everything, and in your vengeance, you became just like them. I embrace the chaos!"

That remark seemed to piss Valeda off. The woman growled and brandished her blade as if she was coming in for an aggressive charge. But it was another trick. Something to distract her from the mook that managed to graze her with his stun baton, and a charge of horrifyingly painful electricity coursed through her.

That look of anger on Valeda's face turned to a grin.

Was this it? The end?

She could see Videl beyond her, fighting the last remaining guard on his side.

But that love-struck fool saw her predicament, and she watched as he sank a blade into the one guard's gut, then abandoned it to pull a throwing knife from his hip. The Magister darted in with a rapier, but Videl ignored the deadly threat. In that precious moment, instead of saving himself, he threw the dagger towards the guard that was attacking her.

Valeska knew it would strike home, and end the charge that was coursing through her, but the price...

She saw it as if in slow motion as Caspian stuck his thin blade through Videl's torso. The look of surprised pain was etched on Videl's face, just as she felt the electrical charge end.

There was nothing left now but to go at Valeda, the lone figure between her and the Magister. The rage boiled over within her, striking the older woman by surprise. Their blades clanged together faster than the eye could see.

But in this brute force competition of endurance and speed, the younger had the upper hand. Even as Valeda managed to parry and knock the sword from Valeska's hand, her free one had grabbed the ceremonial dagger from her thigh.

It was on its way straight for Valeda's heart before she could slash back and cut Valeska down.

In that moment, time seemed to freeze. Everything but the two of them came to a stand still as she felt the life-force of this older woman drain and pull from her, into Valeska. It was a rush like no drug could offer. It was like she felt the pulse of the universe, felt her own flesh begin to knit back together, the deadly wound in her thigh closing off.

She watched the light dim in Valeda's eyes.

"Thank... you..." the older woman choked out hoarsely, as her life-force withered on the vine.

Valeska stared into the face of the woman that she, one day, would become.

Could become.

This was the cycle of life, for one of her kind.

"You won't die in vain," Valeska promised, but her words sounded so distant, so disconnected. As if the world were expanding out around her before being violently tugged back into her orbit.

By the time Valeska pulled her dagger free of the woman, she was naught but a shrivelled, alien husk. She looked inhuman. Bizarre. Her bones jutting through the leathery remnants of her skin not looking human or natural at all. It reminded her of the hideous scene in that abandoned facility.

It reminded her of the indescribable statues that loomed over head.

But there was no more time for feeling disgusted or horrified. Valeska swished her sword through the air in a flurry that sent the remaining blood splattering to the marble floor. She felt ten times stronger in that moment. Like she'd been pumped up and grown ten feet tall, even though she knew that wasn't the case.

"Glorious," said Caspian, watching her with his red eyes wide, a smile on his face as he held a dagger to Videl's throat. Her Second was on his knees, a sword sticking out of his gullet.

"I knew you were the best. Because you were mine. From the very beginning," he said, tightening that blade to Videl's throat until blood ran from it, down into his black uniform.

"That's fucking right," Valeska said, fury in her tone, her ruby eyes blazing with hurt and rage. "You made me what I am. What you needed me to be."

She took a step forward, and she swore the ground trembled beneath her platform heel.

"Did I make you proud?"

"You did," he said with that toothy grin on his face, as he wrenched back Videl's head. It showed off Videl's neck, strained, veins bulging. That dagger was ready to sever them all and end him. "Now we can be together. Forever. You and me. And we will find a way to control all the other houses, and lead them into the final era," he said, his eyes alight with manic ecstasy.

"Drop your sword, Valeska," he said as she approached. "And kneel. Then we can begin again," Caspian promised.

"You can't kill me, but even in my triumph, you try to control me," she said, taking another step closer to him. "But you forget. The daughters of Lilith and Satan cannot be tamed, dear father. And oh, how we resent the cage that fearful men try to place around us."

She raised her dagger, licking what little of Valeda's blood still clung to it.

"You broke my heart so many years ago. Still, I thought I loved you. I wished that you could love me. But now I know the truth. You're too *weak* to love a woman like me."

CHAPTER 32

THE CHIMERA'S PATH

All the kings of the nations lie in glory,
 each in his own tomb;
 But you are cast forth without burial,
 like loathsome carrion,
 Covered with the slain, with those struck by the
sword,
 a trampled corpse,
 Going down to the very stones of the pit.

— ISAIAH 14:18-19

A flurry of emotions passed across his usually stoic, unreadable face.

 He thought he understood her, looked giddy and grinning at first as she took that step towards him, making him think she cared not for Videl's life.

A lesson learned, he assumed. But then to hear her further words...

His expression contorted into one of shock. Confusion. Then anger.

And in that moment, as if he could read the smouldering air itself around them, Videl – brave Videl, stuck through, battered, with a knife at his throat – lurched himself back and thrust his fist in an uppercut. He punched Caspian in the fucking balls, and though that blade was a split second from slicing his throat open, a split second was all that Valeska needed.

Imbued with the raw, fresh power of her elder self, she closed that gap in the blink of an eye.

The only question wasn't: could she do it?

It was: could she restrain herself from killing him entirely?

Valeska's red eyes flared as she pounced upon Caspian, knees battering into his chest and sending him spinning away from her and Videl onto the marble floor. His own dagger went flying, skittering across the marble to the very edge that loomed over the volcano below.

And good, loyal Videl slumped to the side, clutching his throat where it bled.

The power surged within her, and the serpent within her lashed out. She lost sight of everything except the Magister, and hot tears burned in her eyes.

She dived atop him, her pale skin a furious red, her face twisted with pain.

"You think that Satan was the one that beat the love from you, that love is God's domain, but I know better," she said, her knees pinning him to the ground. She was half his size, yet in that moment, she was as powerful as a giant cobra.

"If you had loved me, we would have been unstoppable!"

The Magister looked up at her in shock, startled by her raw power. And in desperation, his one free arm let loose a blade, to try and cut her. But she was too fast, and struck like a viper, pushing his arm with a bloody crunch from the spiked tips, ruining that wrist and sending the cracked blade sprawling to the marble floor.

"My ch-child – " he sputtered as she grabbed his neck and squeezed it. She felt like she could make his eyes pop out of his skull and his head burst in that moment, if she just put more strength into it.

"Nobody controls me anymore," she hissed at him, raising a fist in the fury of the moment, ready to cave his skull in as she gripped his neck with just one hand, choking him to death.

"Wait!" came a wheezing voice, breaking her rage-filled reverie. "Don't! You'll damn us all if you finish him," Caleb pleaded as he shuffled up, panting and wheezing breathlessly from the hurried journey.

She was broken from her trance of revenge, but she couldn't even delight in the reveal of the extent of her betrayal. Instead, she pressed her lips to Caspian's forehead, leaving a trace of blood upon it.

"I took those lessons of the Chimera to heart, father. That I must always be deceitful, and never trust anyone, for they will deceive me. Especially the man who taught me that lesson. I walked the Chimera's path in the shadows, waiting until it was time to strike."

Caspian, choking, gasping for air as she'd left his larynx damaged, couldn't say another word. He just watched in wide-eyed horror as she got up, and the feeble old Caleb got down upon him.

Caleb didn't waste time; he plunged the dagger into Caspian and grinned.

"You played the game well, boy. But in the end, the real deal has won again," Caleb gloated in that moment, as he stole the life from the Magister.

Valeska took a step back, then another, before she rushed to Videl's side.

He was fumbling with a med kit at his thigh, trying to bandage his neck. He'd already yanked the sword from his midsection, and sealed both ends of his punctured body.

She got down and helped him, taking out the self-adhering wrap, and placed it to his neck. That wound sealed up tight, the miracle of modern invention that was that bandage already beginning to knit his skin back together.

"You are glorious in your victory, my commander," Videl wheezed out, as she helped him up to his feet.

She couldn't bring herself to look at the Magister, see his mummified remains, though they were burned into her mind regardless.

"Thank you, Under-Lieutenant. You were perfect. And I think your new scars will be badass."

Videl grinned at her, gripped her shoulder and looked ready to kiss her.

Until he saw the visage of Caleb going for Cain next.

Only now he wasn't shuffling so poorly.

He still looked about the same age, no changes noticed

there. But he was invigorated. And thirsty to end another of his duplicates.

"Hey stop," Videl tried to intervene, but the old man shoved him back and he toppled over onto his rear, staring up in shock at the sudden surge of strength from the old man.

But Valeska was younger, faster, and still surging with the power of her duplicate.

She leapt forward, grabbing Caleb and tugging him back.

"You said no two V's or C's have left this place, but tonight, that's going to change," she said in a tone that brooked no dissent.

Caleb's eyes were wild. A raging inferno of power beneath that gaze. But though he looked ready to hit her too at first, power respected power in the end.

"Are you mad? Now's the time for us to reap the spoils! You and me both," he said, no longer sounding weak and wheezing. His elderly voice rejuvenated, even if his outward looks were slow to follow behind. "Don't you feel that power? Don't you want more?!"

Valeska's smile twisted, hand still holding onto his shirt.

"There's a reason you don't all kill us when we're children. When we're small, we only have an iota of what we can offer. But now we have two copies, that we can keep. And our patience will be rewarded."

She could see rage bubbling inside him. This old man – so long feeling his weak, powerless form deteriorate – was drunk on the idea of reclaiming so much youth all at once.

So much power!

But she was the true victor that night, and he had no choice but to back down, reluctantly. Petulantly.

"I will need him before long," he said, pointing to Cain. Then the old man began to head off towards the elevator, defeated. "I'll wait for you both at the hummer."

She watched for just a moment before her gaze returned to Cain and Valerie.

"You get him, and I'll carry her," Valeska said to Videl, heading over to her sister. They were both still out from whatever drugs the Magister and Magistra had used, but carrying one-hundred pounds of dead weight wouldn't be an issue for her.

Not that night.

"Hope you weren't planning on a victory celebration," Videl said as he began to wheel Cain out on the mobile upright gurney. "Because despite the bandages, I gotta hit up a hospital after this," he said, his voice still rough and raw.

"I think I'd break you if I fucked you right now," she laughed, squatting down and grabbing Valerie. She brought the other woman over her shoulders, and easily stood back up with the added weight. She chanced another glance around the room, over the statues that stared down at them, and she couldn't resist the pull. She turned towards the Magister, and found that when the fury subsided, sorrow was left in its wake.

So many secrets died with him, so many futures she could have had. She put Valerie back down, and walked towards his corpse, each step leadened.

"I hope you're walking with Him down his halls," she mumbled in prayer, crouched down at his side, bringing herself to caress the leathery carcass that resembled nothing human.

The pain was sharp and dull all at once, a rusted blade twisted through her heart, and she knew that she had failed him. He had never managed to beat the love out of her, not fully.

"The next Caspian... I'll see that he'll be stronger."

She lingered there a moment longer and heard the elevator doors begin to open.

Amid the crusty remains of his flesh on his chest, she saw something. It was like it was embedded into his torso, but she wasn't sure if that had been the case before his death, or just a curious result of his withering end. But she brushed some of that dried refuse away, and found a curious amulet. It contained a diamond shaped stone, embedded in a pentagram etching, all set in a hexagonal piece of silver or maybe platinum.

"Hate to be that guy, Over-Lieutenant, but..." Videl said, as she tugged the amulet from the Magister's neck, shoving it in her jacket pocket and zipping it up.

"I know," she said as she went back to Valerie who was beginning to stir. Still, Valeska hauled her up, tossing her over her shoulders as she jogged to the elevator. "Hospital time, I get it."

CHAPTER 33

WORSHIP YOUR GODDESS

O irresistible Astarte, you who impose pain
　　Or else deliver in joy, listen to me,
　　Take me, possess me, wrest bleeding libations
　　From my contented body!

— PIERRE LOUŸS; HYMN TO ASTARTE

The throne room of Void Star House was big and opulent. Thick, black and crimson drapery lined the walls, with statuary and art positioned between each. Lush red carpet lined the walkway from the door to the gilded, ornate throne. And Valeska felt... really damn good on that thing.

It was big beneath her, a little oversized, but that was okay. Gave her plenty of room to stretch her legs open, as she felt her pleasure rise.

Her long nails tapped on the armrest as she leaned back,

taking in her new surroundings. Her eyes lingered on each beautifully twisted object, and then fluttered closed. Her nostrils flared as her lips curled into a wicked grin, the ecstasy within her rising.

She still felt Valeda's power pulsing in her veins, quickening with each beat of her heart, knowing that she was really at her peak.

"Yes, right there," she commanded, her ruby eyes dipping down to the man who knelt before her in subservience.

She was not yet fully promoted, and definitely not officially Magistra. But with the 'new' Magister under her thumb, she was as good as it. And with Videl down on his knees, face buried between her thighs for the past hour or more, she certainly felt like Magistra.

The attentive way his tongue bathed and caressed her vulva, teasing her clit. It was exquisite. The man knew how to worship at the altar of her pussy. And more than that, he craved to. And that dedication shone through more than anything else. It truly was an act of worship by her dutiful Second.

She'd come out on top, but she knew that on the Isle of Satanos, nothing lasted forever. She was living proof of that. Unlike her forebears, she was able to embrace the chaos, and enjoy the full spectrum of human emotions. She knew that hatred was just as much of a weakness as love, but that love could be an even stronger weapon. Videl had shown her that without her even realizing.

She purred as the wave of pleasure lapped at her clit, the power building as he kept up those diligent motions. She watched him with such tender affection, his head pressed between her pale thighs, still unblemished, despite the scarring slash she'd taken along one. The rejuvenating effects of taking Valeda's essence had solved that.

"Right... there," she moaned, and in another second, the tsunami crashed atop her and she screamed, the opulent hall ringing with her blissful pleasure.

It hadn't been her first orgasm on the throne, not even in that one sitting. But it was the most exquisite. And Videl dutifully kept up his work, pushing her through that climax with such vigorous motions of his tongue, so insistently driving her wild. He groaned into her mound, sending pleasing vibrations through her body as her thighs seemed to be trying to crush his skull.

But it wasn't enough to deter him as he knelt there in full uniform, pleasuring her.

Her skirt was hiked up around her waist, the red v-cut dress clinging to her body. At first, she'd thought of burning it, the reminder of the 'date' with the Magister still so raw.

Instead, she reclaimed it, and now all it would remind her of would be Videl.

The throne had a puddle of her sweetness on it, and she squirmed upon it, grinding the scent of her exquisite lust into it. And when finally her barefoot was on his shoulder, gently pushing him back, a hazy smile spread across her entire body.

"You've gotten almost too good at that."

Videl pulled back, almost reluctantly. Even though his jaw ached and his knees hurt. But he only grinned up at her, a sparkle in his eyes as he stared at her with adoration as he licked and wiped away the copious honey from his face.

J.M. Keep

"There is no such thing as too good, when it comes to you, Mistress," he said with a seductive husk to his voice. His throat had healed nicely, but his speaking seemed like it would be permanently a bit rougher thanks to the cut. It certainly didn't diminish his attractiveness though. Especially not when he ate pussy like that, then showered her inner thighs and mound with soft kisses.

"I do love it when you call me that," she said easily, her finger stroking over the older scar along his eye with fondness. "I never asked how you got this one. A welcome gift to the island?"

"No," he said, gently leaning into her touch. "A gift from before I got here. It was a prize from my youth. When I tried to stop my father from hurting my mother," he explained so calmly, despite the tinge of pain beneath it all. It didn't stop him from kissing her thigh again.

And Valeska stroked it affectionately, looking down on him with such respect.

They were both forged in the fires of hell, in their own way, and still...

"Did you get him, in the end?"

He looked thought for a moment, his hands on her flesh, letting her touch him freely. But finally he met her eyes again and answered.

"In the end he got himself," he said simply.

"Good," she said, leaning in and placing a kiss upon his lips, tasting herself there. "I still feel... grateful to the Magister. The maelstrom hasn't calmed within me, but I know that it was only through his death I could become a full person. Not just a woman made of a man's rib."

Videl kissed her back with such tender devotedness. It

328

was something she'd never experienced before. Never even really imagined.

"You could never be so little as that, Mistress," he said with such conviction. "You were made for greatness. True greatness. And someday the whole world will feel it. The Magister and Magistra were just stepping stones. Soon to be forgotten, but for the lessons you learned along the way."

"Like that sometimes the mainland can give us precious treasures like yourself?" she grinned.

He didn't react as she expected.

Oh, yes, he smiled. But it was such a touching, emotional gaze. That hardened but handsome face looking vulnerable. Happy. A look nobody but her had ever seen on Satanos.

"Thank you, Mistress," he said sincerely, leaning in to kiss her lips again softly.

"I haven't forgotten what you said," she whispered against his mouth, a tremble going through her body. "And I have learned the lesson you taught me as well."

His eyes opened again, staring right into hers. Their ruby pairs locked.

"What lesson was that, Mistress?" he asked, genuinely curious as his hands caressed her milky thighs.

He never needed her to say it.

She never expected to want to.

But in that moment, in the afterglow of her multiple orgasms, sat atop the throne of lies, she told the truth.

"I do love you."

He knew it. And yet to hear it was such a shock. She could see it in his face. That intense surprise.

Then the heartwarming melt as he leaned in and kissed

her once more, slowly this time. Passionately. Their bodies, so disproportionate, yet melding together so perfectly.

They had set in motion far bigger things, and she still only had an inkling of the secrets that the Isle of Satanos had to offer her. Yet in that moment, the tender embrace of the two lovers made the rest of the world go quiet.

ALSO BY J.M. KEEP

Series:

Possessed by the Vampire:

Claimed

Hunted

Caught

The Warlord:

The Warlord's Concubine

The Warlord's Queen

Her Master

Her Master's Madness

Her Master's Corruption

Novels:

War-Torn

Her Descent

When Dreamers Wake

Chanting the Ancient Lay

Corrupted Hearts

Magic Academy

Unleashed

Vile

Outcast 1 & 2

Novellas:

In Her Dreams

Brutal Passions

The Enforcer: 1

The Enforcer: 2

The Fembot

Bound as the World Burns

Shorts:

The Seductive Nymph

The Curious Nymph

Wherever in the White House: Saved from the Lizard Lady

The Angel and the Demon

Packing' It In

Packing' It In: Not All At Once

The Virility Elixir

The Elven Babe: Stuffed

The Elven Babe: Dragon

The Elven Babe: Demonic

Shifters in Heat

Dancing for the Vampire

The Queen's Secret Lover

The Fertile Elf

Beast and Beauty

Bundles:

Darknest: A Dark Fantasy Anthology

Erotic Dragons Boxset

The Elven Babe: Trilogy

Wicked Monsters Boxset

About the Author

J.M. Keep is the pen-name of a husband and wife who are already living their happily-ever-after.

Maybe because their real life is so sunny, they love to write dark and twisted tales with morally challenged characters. Most of their stories are dark fantasies where horror and romance are intertwined.

Make sure to sign up for the newsletter for exclusive content, information on new releases, and free books!

facebook.com/jmkeep

instagram.com/jmkeep

bookbub.com/authors/j-e-keep

amazon.com/J.M.-Keep/e/B00DFW3QTM

www.ingramcontent.com/pod-product-compliance
Lightning Source LLC
Chambersburg PA
CBHW050924220726
48290CB00018B/1526